WHAT THEY TELL YOU TO FORGET

Pay attention to what they tell you to forget

pay attention to what they tell you to forget

pay attention to what they tell you to forget

—Muriel Rukeyser, "Double Ode"

What They Tell You to Forget

A NOVELLA AND STORIES

WINNER OF THE EDITORS' BOOK AWARD

PUSHCART

FRED PFEIL

Winner of the 1996 Editors' Book Award

ISBN 0–916366–49–9
LC—95-072083

Nominating Editor: Christopher Howell

Sponsoring Editors: Simon Michael Bessie, James Charlton, Peter Davison,
Jonathan Galassi, David Godine, Daniel Halpern, James Laughlin, Seymour
Lawrence, Starling Lawrence, Robie Macauley, Joyce Carol Oates, Nan A.
Talese, Faith Sale, Ted Solotaroff, Pat Strachan, Thomas Wallace. Bill
Henderson, Publisher.

Grateful acknowledgement is given for permission to reprint the following
stories, some of which appear here in slightly revised form:

"A Buffalo, New York Story," from *Fiction International;*
"Dirty Pieces," from *Mississippi Mud;*
"The Angel of Dad," from *Witness;*
"Plus You," from *Triquarterly;*
"Freeway Bypass (detail from map)," from *Witness* and Bill Henderson
      et al., eds., *The Pushcart Prize XVII: Best of the Small Presses*
      (Pushcart and W. W. Norton, 1993).

CONTENTS

WHAT THEY TELL YOU TO FORGET

A BUFFALO, NEW YORK STORY

Basically, though, this story is set not just in Buffalo but in the U.S.A., center of the free capitalist world, during the years 1957–58 when the chemise was here to stay, Sputnik was first in space, there was a crisis in American education, and rebels up in the Sierra spread terror all over Cuba against Batista, jaunty dictator, not such a nice guy himself. Most people around at the time must have known more about this than I did, even in the small town I grew up in, up there in the hills. But it was around, in the air, even for kids like me, eight or nine, in those days when the taste was for wide long stories which picked themselves up and over great arcs of Destiny rising towards the triumphant yet quietly satisfied goal of justice for all, happiness for the good, and an end to historical time while we were ahead. You

3

will know this if you have ever seen either of two movies I recall seeing with my grandfather on our family's semi-annual trips to the city, Buffalo, New York, *The Big Country* or *The Vikings*.

Or here is another view of the same thing, using my father instead. He owned a store in this small town, and worked there all the time, from eight in the morning until nine at night, six days of the week and a good part of Sunday, trying to give us a good safe life, I suppose. There was no time off for him to come to Buffalo, not even on a one-day trip. Even when he was home from work on Sunday afternoons he was generally sacked out on the couch, so far gone my sister and I could walk up and touch him, press our fingers into the flesh of his forearms and hands, watch the white spot form under pressure then go back to pink when you took your finger away. But he would wake up by five or six so that he could eat supper with us, then go back to the couch and sit up to watch *Maverick* and *Bonanza* with his son, i.e. me. His arm—that same arm whose flesh I had pressed— would be wrapped around my shoulders, filling me with a sense of its strength and ease, while off in the kitchen my mother and sister had to do the dishes without me lifting a finger to help. Watching TV with my dad was therefore a moment of official happiness, and so for the most part I remember nothing more real about it than I could recall of most Christmases past, or any Fourth of July. But my point is this: one night I asked a question about something that had just happened on whichever show it was, where yet another rustler/killer/bad guy of some kind had just left behind at the scene of his outrageous crime yet another piece of evidence like a knife with his initials on it or something else equally dumb; and so—less from any desire to investigate or find anything out than to enlarge this officially happy moment by having the son, i.e., me, ask a question and the father, i.e. Dad, answer it—I asked why bad guys were always so stupid; and my father laughed, lightly, easily, and explained, Because they were bad.

Long arcs, certain outcomes—see what I mean? It was the style of the times, my father was not an ignorant man. Failure and wrong were interchangeable, either one meant bad, you had it or you didn't and if not there was nothing you could do and you had only yourself to blame. Whether you are a person or a country, this kind of attitude works just fine as long as the odds are stacked in your favor so you can get or do just about whatever you damn well please. But as soon as you make a mistake, or get beat, or just start sliding downhill, you feel helpless, you don't know what to do because from this same point of view the only conclusion you can reach is that there must be something fatally wrong with, essentially bad about, you. Like when I went out for Little League baseball around this same time of my life (as you pretty much had to do, *want* to do, even, if you were a boy) and found out that I was terrible at it, batting, throwing and catching alike, I knew it had nothing to do with Practice Makes Perfect, there was something wrong with me and that was that. Or like when at this same time the Russians beat us out and put up Sputnik first, and *Life* magazine did a survey and found out—this was March 3, 1958—*that the American people are far less prone to blame President Eisenhower or his administration for the U.S. lag in science than the commentators, editorial writers and columnists seem to think. . . . Far from blaming the Eisenhower administration for the nation's science problem, many people feel a curious sort of personal guilt . . .* Which is why the announcement, made by my mother, that I could now come to Buffalo too filled me not just with excitement but with a certain amount of dread. There was no telling what tests Buffalo, New York had in store for me as part of my great or wretched but in any case well-deserved destiny, no sense in preparing or training even if those tests could have been foretold. The night before we left I lay in bed staring straight up into the dark, released from the need to peer down at the rag rug on the floor in the dim light from under the door until the faces swam out of its twisty shapes, or to see Reds busting through the windows and/or hiding in the closet in their brown uniforms with their guns, or to fight them all together under the blankets until they were dead. This was the real thing, real test, adventure; I could feel it foreshadowed already like the whiff of a balmy breeze on my cheeks, or the harsher lick of a draught: Tomorrow will be in Buffalo.

Next morning I did not even make it to the car; in the first moments of my first trip, standing in between my grandparents and my sister, I puked in the grass at the edge of the driveway as my mother backed the Plymouth out of our garage. There it was, on the ground, watery white with soppy brown flecks, mainly composed of the milk and Frosted Flakes I had spooned into myself such a short time ago: it had fallen out of my still-

6

trembling body like a shout. While I stared down at it in hopeless amazement, Grandma, my mother's mother, murmured sympathetic surprise; the weathered face of my tall grandfather assumed an expression of incredulity and contempt; and my sister Cathy, three years older than I and ecstatic, wrinkled up her pug face over a fiendish grin and started in on me right away.

The Russians could be exaggerating, of course, but I am plenty worried, Mrs. Mayme Bay, widow of Minneapolis, said to *Life* magazine back then. *They are ready to send men up into space. I think we'd win if we had a war—we always have. But I hope our leaders are able to keep us out of it.*

Cri-min-*ee*, David, said my sister. What's the *matter* with you?

And etcetera, the rest of the way. My mother, who always turned the wheel over to Grandpa in the drive, would make a few feeble attempts from the front seat to shut off the flow of abuse, suggesting some dumb car games like license-hunting and something else called car poker which I have since forgotten, except you got so many points for things like cemeteries on your side of the road. Eventually, if Cathy went on long enough about what a dumbo and baby I was, how she couldn't stand to ride on the same car seat with such a stinky pukeface much less be seen in the city with him, etc., and if I started hurling insults back, e.g. you snotnose, you pig-face, she would offer us a dime apiece to keep our mouths shut for at least an hour, then if we kept on finally would yell at us to just shut up. How far the whole process played itself out, though, depended on how long

I held out: and as early as the second trip I managed to contain myself all the way through and beyond our town's streets down to the factory by the river, over the ribbon of state road rolling through the huddle of hills, almost to the flat plain with its four-lane highway stretching north from small grey towns like Franklinville in whose Dairy Bar I finally lost it, there at the shiny yellow booth watching the grownups sipping their midmorning coffee, squashed in between my grandmother and sister, sensing the rise of the hot disgrace in my throat a second too late. A year later, and I could pretty much count on making it to the giant switching yard on the southwest outskirts of the city itself, where under a strange yellow sky more sets of tracks and boxcars than I could count flashed by the windows of our Plymouth until I had to mumble Stop the car, and hope somebody heard it in time; another six months and with luck it was all the way in.

Luck I say, but it was a skill. How I did it was like this: learning to wait, watch, listen, until you can feel the first hint of it growing inside, that panicked excitement, that particular fear. You have to be on your guard as you move towards any new trial or challenge we are all supposed to like, especially men. Take for example in *The Vikings* when the Vikings led by Prince Einar (Kirk Douglas) approach the English king's castle at the end of the dunes. What you are supposed to feel is a simple, rising excitement, just as easy as if you were watching yourself on the screen, leading up to the moment when Kirk Douglas gives the call and waves his broadsword, after which all the Vikings run ahead throwing their axes and the attack is on. But if you have any reason to think in your own specific case that excitement is maybe a little different, if the mere thought of Buffalo the city or the castle rushing at you makes you so excited that you puke, then the only way not to look bad is to shut things out, don't look, pretend you are not even there.

There are a great many worried people in the U.S. today. But it is an abstract sort of worry: almost nobody thinks we are going to be blown up by a Russian ICBM next week or next year. Millions of people remain more alarmed by the nation's domestic problems, including juvenile delinquency and the economic situation, than by Russian scientific triumphs. Incredible as it may seem, a blissful minority of four million Americans has neither seen nor heard of the Sputniks and a great many more entertain some very curious ideas about them. Better to let your eyes fuzz the line of smokestacks at the sky's edge, smear the grainier, dirtier light, let Prince Einar raise the sword not me. I don't even know what's going on, what I'm doing, couldn't bear to find out, I'd puke. I'll just follow along behind.

Here again is *Life* magazine, that same article, March 3, 1958:

Q: Do you think we should work hardest at keeping out of war or at having the strength to win a war when it comes?

A: Keep out of war 34%   Win war when it comes 60%   No opinion 6%

My grandfather was a careful driver, and overall a silent, capable man. The kind of Gregory Peck-type guy like *The Big Country*'s Jim McKay who would do both the things in the question above, work hard at keeping out of war *and* have the strength to win when it comes. When we came in to Buffalo through the residential sections to the south, for example, and the neighborhoods turned all black just before we reached downtown he would tell us to roll up our windows and lock the doors, though we knew full well we were safe given how he glared around at everybody standing on the sidewalk, each and every car beside ours at the lights, demonstrating the strength to win.

My grandfather had a high barrel chest, and long almost apelike arms that seemed to reach almost to his knees. He had worked construction all his life, from Erie to Buffalo and all stops between, he had a working-class boozer's red veiny bulb nose in the center of his long horse face and always wore the same red plaid flannel shirt with a brown string tie and shiny suitcoat whenever we went up to Buffalo. You would never mistake him for Gregory Peck, and it may seem funny to compare him to this other character Jim McKay, who after all in the movie *The Big Country* is from an old East Coast ruling-class family of sea captains you are led to believe goes way back, maybe all the way to slaveships or before. But my Grandpa had something like that same reserve and set of rules; and he knew a real coward when he saw one; and he saw one in me. His disapproval of me was distinct in a principled way that goes back to the Jim McKay way of dealing with the world, which I would have liked to but cannot share to this day. In *The Big Country* Jim McKay (Gregory Peck) comes out West to marry his fiancée (Carol Baker) and meet his future father-in-law, peppery Major Terrill (Charles Bickford), owner of the biggest spread in those parts. The initial hitch comes when he declines the offer to mount a wild, bucking horse the Terrill ranch hands have invited him to ride, then refuses to fight the head cowboy and foreman Steve Leach (Charlton Heston) when the latter casts aspersions on his manhood in front of his increasingly shocked fiancée. Ultimately, of course, McKay will prove what you in the audience know all along from his being Gregory Peck, that he has as much guts as the next man if not more but deplores senseless shows of prowess and/or violence for their own sake; like after this big long terrific fight he finally does have with Charlton Heston/Steve Leach when no one but the audience is around he says What did we prove, Leach? What did we prove?

The origins of my own cowardice on the other hand go back to another story of my hard-working father and TV. One night when my father came home from the store, somewhere shortly before this same time, he found me still in front of the TV where my mother had let me stay up to watch a program called *Alas Babylon* not knowing what it was about, which was without going into a lot of detail the aftermath of a nuclear war and how all the characters ultimately died. When my father walked in the door my mother was still doing something else upstairs or someplace, and the program was ending, the last couple huddled dying on some dingy steps, and I was seven years old, up late, tired and scared. You have to remember how rarely in those days downward plot trajectories like this one were offered to anyone, let alone little boys, to imagine what happened next, when I stood up and followed my at least equally weary father over to the coat closet and asked him, Daddy what is an atom bomb?

I still remember where and how I was, what I felt. By the corner of the maple desk where my father sat to pay the bills, three fingers of my left hand resting on the cool smooth familiar surface of the desktop, coming to its rounded edge; standing very still, totally still, feeling somewhere down at the base of my gut the cold sick heave of that ending, irreparable loss. My face was downturned, looking off at nothing. He was there no more than a foot away, shrugging off his coat.

Daddy what's an atom bomb?

My father sighed—he was tired, I don't blame him—gave his coat a little shake, reached up into the closet's darkness, brought a hanger back out.

Oh, he said, lower and quiet, drained-out: it's a kind of bomb we have, and the Russians have, which if it ever goes off will blow up everything in the world.

I doubt my grandfather ever was acquainted with what followed, much less this part I have just told you, which to my knowledge not even my mother ever found out for sure. All she knew was that for a good while afterwards if the fire siren down the street blew more than two or three blasts or the grade school had an air raid drill and we were ushered into the halls with their dry reek of wood/dust/paper/chalk and made to huddle against the walls with our heads jammed between our knees, arms wrapped on our heads, the flutter in my chest would swell to an unbearable machine flapping of pressure until I started screaming and exploded and they had to call my mother to take me shaking home. Same result for that matter at the dinner table if my father over supper tried to cure or mitigate my ailment in the recommended way, i.e. through calm discussion of what measures had been and would be taken in the unlikely event that the worse comes to worst. Our fallout shelter was to be the cellar, already handily stocked with jars of strawberry jam, pickled cucumbers and beets. My sister would be responsible for bringing down the bedding and such canned goods as were kept upstairs, while my father and I would go out to the garage for the several cans of white kerosene he had bought together with two hurricane lamps for this very purpose and then . . . but it was no use, long before his officially calm face had finished telling its story across the table I was flipping thrashing clean out of my chair, flailing onto the floor, bucking bronco of gibbering fear no doubt like the horse Jim McKay will not ride in public but tames in secret later on after all. I was that sure we were all of us going to die.

There are pictures—photographs, you see them practically every day—of what we call Third World children, often from some place our government is for some multitude of almost entirely bad reasons trying to control, like Southeast Asia ten, twenty years ago, Central America today, children you know have seen and been through any number of things, torture massacre rape you name it, looking back at the lens and you with this absolutely flat opaque gaze, triumph and scar, which you then take to be the very sign, sure and authentic proof, of all that they have suffered and endured. I never looked like that in my life. My grandfather may not have known what it was that made me such a baby, but he could hardly avoid noticing that soft ceaseless flutter, lack of focus in my eyes. Once at last we were inside the city and parked, the women went off to shop at the big downtown stores, Hengerer's and AM&A's, and left my grandfather in charge of me for the duration of the afternoon. I would stand in the parking lot watching them disappear down the street, Grandma in her black Sunday coat regardless of the weather, my sister's face glowing in the joy of clothes to come, my mother moving briskly, slightly ahead of them, guiding them along; then at last I would raise those eyes of mine at Grandpa's, he would lower his at me. To his credit I will say he made some effort if not to appear enthusiastic at least to hide his embarrassment at being with me in my shame. He would swivel the dangling keys in his keychain back over their ring to the palm of his hard red hand; he would whisk them into his pocket then take out his handkerchief, honk at his nose. All this to buy one last moment, to be reconciled to his duty: then he would nod, and we would start off on our way.

On March 24, 1958, in response to Sputnik and the poor or addled public response to the state-sponsored call for more and better science, education in general, defense spending in particular, *Life* magazine began a *vital*

*new LIFE series, Crisis in Education . . . with the story
of two schoolboys, an easy-going American and a hard-
striving Russian (shown in exclusive pictures taken in
Moscow). The difference in the atmosphere of learning
provides a disturbing measure of America's school trouble.* That was me all right, at least to all outward appearances the soft easygoing American boy wandering
the street beside his grandfather taking no more notice
of his surroundings, paying this new edifying environ-
ment no more heed than would any earthworm stunned
by an electric shock. There might have been fights on the
sidewalks, picturesque street vendors, quaint shops or
dazzling emporia, I let it all just blur and slip by. But *Life*
magazine had it wrong in my case, it was not really my
easygoingness that corrupted me, clouded the atmosphere of my learning, kept me from being a hard striver
like my Russian counterpart. The real reason Buffalo,
New York did not appear was that I was watching only
my grandfather's grim set face as he pressed forward
through the crowd, grabbing onto that face, holding on,
letting everything else slide past, otherwise I was still too
scared on the one hand of what might happen, on the
other of what I might do. That is why from all these
walks through the downtown section of Buffalo I recall
only two images aside from that face; one a composite
picture drawn from several trips of him sitting high and
impassive on a black shoeshine boy's chair, the other
more distinct yet anonymous of the yellow and black
striped triangular sign designating Fallout Shelter on the
marble entrance to some building or store, both of which
come along with the remembered feel of keeping myself

standing up, moving forward after him, maintaining my stomach/chest/arms/legs under control.

Once we got to the movies themselves, though, my memory improves considerably, that panicked amnesia lifts like a fog. I could draw you to this day a sketch of the pattern in the carpet in the lobby of the old Century, paint the plush deep red of the curtain across the wide Cinerama screen, hum the soundtrack theme of *The Vikings* and recite the plot from beginning to end. Everything starts there and moves outwards, obviously—from the confidence, the trust you have in the plot, the way you know that with Kirk Douglas and Tony Curtis on their side the Vikings will win out no matter what, and if they're after England it's for a good reason, like the English threw King Ragnar (Ernest Borgnine) into a pit full of wolves, and if Prince Einar (Kirk Douglas) makes the leap over the ravine to the main gate of the English castle and starts using the axes the Vikings were throwing at it a minute ago to climb up, he's going to make it to the top and let them inside, you can bet your life on it. It makes you feel the way Clem Rasmussen, farmer of Thatcher, Idaho, felt when he told *Life* magazine *I don't believe there's very much danger now of an all-out war, but if it did happen I think we would lick them all right. I simply don't believe the Lord would permit those Russians to come over here and take everything.* It gives you a sense of belonging to a fair, decent and exciting story world, which I think everyone likes. I realize now that even my grandfather, stern and hard as he was, might have been ill at ease in the city also, might have liked this feeling as much as the shoeshine itself; I remember once or twice tearing my eyes away from those giant struggles working themselves out to find his upturned face as relaxed by wonder and trust as my own. Today of course you can look back and see all kinds of other things too, e.g. violence and sensitivity, as in *The Vikings* when Prince Einar (Kirk Douglas) loses his fight with Prince Eric (Tony Curtis) over Princess Morgana (Janet Leigh) because he just found out Eric is really his brother so he cannot bring himself to hack him to death and Tony Curtis gets to kill him instead, whereas in *The Big Country* Jim McKay (Gregory Peck) in spite of his principles finally has to strap on his gun once the schoolteacher he now knows he loves, Julie Maragon (Jean Simmons), has been taken prisoner by the crude Hannasseys (Chuck Connors and Burl Ives), you can see how all these things hook up with all this other stuff back then too, like easy-going American versus hard-striving Russians, confrontation vs. cooperation, and the need to protect the peace-loving freedom-seeking American way by smashing anybody we come up against. As bank president John Sollenberger told *Life* magazine, *Naturally no one is in favor of spending billions if it can be avoided. But we should do it if it appears necessary to our military and political leaders, who know the needs of the nation better than the man in the street does.* But my Grandpa in his good old working-class world of hard work, duty and enjoyment, me in my modern world of idle terror, back then neither one of us had any distance whatsoever on these films, we were like my poor sleeping father's arms being pressed white then filling back up with blood when the pressure or pleasure released and we got up

17

shaking ourselves slowly off and walked up the carpeted aisles and back out blinking to the crowded sidewalks of Buffalo and the waning light of the day, if you can't see that chances are you don't get a thing in this story so far.

We met my grandmother, mother and sister at the Aurora Restaurant, a gleaming bright stainless steel den in which to catch a quick early supper before heading off for home. I remember a kind of corn chowder I liked, little stacks of boxes at my mother's feet, a few other bags whose necks my sister kept wringing in her lap and my grandmother sucking her coffee up through a sugar cube held in ruined teeth, clucking and nodding her pleasure as well. The three of them told Grandpa and me all about their shopping day, new fashions, wins and losses for the season or the year. But they never asked us about the movies, were they bad or good, did we like them or not; it is like what I just told you about the landscape, inside it versus out. Instead, my mother asked my grandfather if *I'd* been good: and even then, for whatever reasons, out of a fading warm attachment of shared dream or what, even on the one day I'd really set him off he still answered with the same low voice and nod of the head. He behaved himself fine.

The ride back was uneventful, so this happiness in the Aurora Restaurant is the best fadeout image I have of our trips to Buffalo in the late '50s, back when all five of us were still together and alive. But before moving on to the close of this story as a whole in the '60s, I should say what it was I did that one time that got his goat. It was right after one of those big spectacular movies as in the examples I have given, and we were on our way out, still wrapped in that pleasure of triumphant events when out of the milky light pouring in through the doors beyond the candy counter, on past the ticket-taker letting in the five o'clock crowd, a dark small figure my size in a thin cotton jacket and jeans swam up and asked me with neither threat nor deference, very simply, if I had a nickel to spare, because if I did he could get some Mild Duds. My hand plunged down in my pants pocket as much to dismiss the interruption of my trance as to fulfill what in that same condition seemed a perfectly reasonable request. Then from out of this same fog came the long strong arm of my grandfather, wrenching my hand away from that other dark outstretched one, pushing me suddenly, smartly ahead down the last stretch of rich red carpet to thick plexiglass doors, my grandfather's low voice cracking in fury and fear about my own baffled and now at least equally frightened head, proclaiming, it seemed, at one and the same time *Get out of here!* to the receding astonished black boy and *What's the matter with you?* to me.

This last you will notice is the same at least partly rhetorical question my sister posed as we stared at my puked-up Frosted Flakes on the grass the morning of that first trip: *What's the matter with you?* Which you will note in both cases carries a covert reference to a state of nothing being the matter, an implicit standard of moral and right. In effect my taunting sister told me being scared of the city was stupid or worse, whereas my grandfather said only a creep or idiot would fail to recoil from the touch of a black. In my own mind now these two lessons in trust and fear good and bad seem impossible to square, but I could be wrong. For all I know it could have been handouts not blacks he hated or feared, I'll never find out: long before I went off to college to learn to root out alternate meanings, contradictions, ambiguities, etc., he was dead. Through the year of 1959, we found out from my Grandma later, he came home whitefaced from work and slept badly at night, but showed up at the union hall every day, piling up the requisite time and bucks for retirement until finally one day in March 1960 he nearly fell off a fifth floor scaffold with his hands clutched to his barrel chest. Four more heart attacks spaced themselves through the next year of bedrest and bitterness, insurance plans cheating years of paid premiums, a pension reduced for early retirement, a stack of medical bills and no work, a long body wasting loose and slack, a stern silence slowly worn away by his belief he had to pay to the last dime or stop being a man. At the very end he took to mumbling, moving his square stubbled jaw in constant calculation of how to pay it off, in how many months and years; when we visited him those last few weeks, edging into the stale brown air of the bedroom, he would turn his gaunt hollow face from my sister and me as if preferring the clean blankness of the wall.

By the time he died in the spring of 1961 a line of heroes á la Jim McKay was dying out too, along with *The Big Country/Vikings* kind of story; so there was that much less to keep me from acting either crazy or stupid, out of misplaced trust or excess fear. Take for example Cuba, even back in 1958 if you look at *Life* you see already we were having some problems there, what with jaunty corrupt Batista on the one hand young and exciting but red-tinted Castro and his brother Raúl on the other, how do you get a story like that to move in a straight line? The best *Life* could come up with were lines like *A series of bizarre incidents ranging from melodrama to genuine tragedy last week focused a lurid light on the troubles besetting the rich Caribbean island,* etc., until the Revolution won out. Then for a while everything looked okay, like a good story after all with Castro like maybe a young Robert Mitchum, kind of wild but with good instincts down deep and therefore invincible until he started taking over our stuff down there and turned out to be an out-and-out Red after all.

You can just imagine how we felt: how bewildered and betrayed. I remember walking home from sixth grade getting madder and madder over how we'd been tricked, muttering down at the cracked sidewalks as if the *Weekly Reader* story we had just gone over in school were reprinted there, then squinting fiercely off at the silent round hills. Aside from that other night long ago when I found out about A-bombs and ground-zero terror, I suppose this was the first political event of my life. Along with a whole lot of other Americans of all ages and walks of life I had been led to expect one kind of story with one hero and now had to swallow another. It was as though the impossible had come to pass, Gregory Peck turning into Jack Palance, that was what was so *unnerving* about the whole thing. Of course *Life* did what it could to paint Castro in his true colors, and we got a President who people said looked the part and was willing to go after Cuba at the drop of a hat. But they tried the Bay of Pigs, Missile Crisis, plus two three-part articles, one on The Crisis in Our Hemisphere, the other on Communism in general and what we can do to fight back; and still it was like that old story, that good old dependable build, was falling apart. Now instead of those long rising lines what you had were these *outbreaks*—push here, shove over there—from inside this great nebulous bag called the Cold War of Communism Versus Us, which seems like everywhere and nowhere at once, not like World War II, just these sort of like swellings or saggings in places like Laos El Salvador Vietnam, where getting mad just makes things worse.

You could see the difference even in the trips to Buffalo: now that my sister was in high school, unpopular and unhappy, she and my mom and I drove up all the time, practically every other month with or without Grandma in her old black coat. Now, while they shopped more and more desperately for anything that might make my sister look less ugly, pudgy, unmarketable, I was free to go to the movies alone so long as I told them which one and what time it got out.

Plus I should say that things had changed some for me as well. In 1962 I was thirteen myself, and the trips to Buffalo and back were no more terrifying than anything else I might think of or do, since besides that old background of bomb fear I was now prey to teenagerdom's damp miseries too, chiefly those awful swings between the grey ugliness of the world and my own physical grossness, the absence of beauty or heroism anywhere. It made me sick and ashamed when it turned out the Bay of Pigs was our set-up in spite of Kennedy swearing it wasn't and then we lost it anyway; then, when we called the Russians' bluff with our finger on the button in the Missile Crisis, after three days home from school in a zombie state of dread I was proud as JFK himself. But even that victory was nothing like those movies, nor was the President like my Grandpa before he got sick. That was why in Buffalo I kept going back to the Century, seeking the same stars and shows, never suspecting this whole other story was on down South at this very moment with more heroes than you could count, for example black teenager James Crawford bringing his people to the county courthouse getting them registered to vote, and the white Registrar says *Suppose somebody come in that door and shoot you in the back of the head right now, what would you do?* and James Crawford, *I couldn't do nothing, If they shoot me in the back of the head there are people coming from all over the world,* while I was trying to find the same old story in *The Guns of Navarone, Exodus, Magnificent Seven* instead. Once I even climbed up on a shoeshine stand, tried to feel good and strong like my Grandpa was still alive while below a black man bent over and rubbed my shoes, There you are sir though Grandpa was dead and I only felt stupid, laughed-at and ashamed, exactly what anyone feels caught outside or in between two kinds of stories, two different worlds.

Of course at the time I had pretty much zero chance of getting in on the world of those marchers, demonstrators, revolutionaries armed and unarmed from those black people down South to the Vietnamese later

Nicaraguans and Salvadorans today. And like I say, the other old story of heroes and triumphs was going down the drain. You could see it up there on the screen, the way the people in the crew or gangs of *The Guns of Navarone* or *The Magnificent Seven* would be in trouble start to finish, climbing mountains galloping around killing Nazis shooting bad guys blam blam blam, or in the big epic films the way things every so often went into action but most of the time the stars and heroes just stood around. The first kind of movie held my attention, people got shot or stabbed or fell down cliffs every other second, you were scared to look away; but when it's all over there's nothing, you just feel worn out. The other kind of movie made me feel even worse, though, the way the big music first picks you up, giant shapes of boats and battles and processions sweep the screen, you feel like something's really happening: then after a while I realized the story was so poor I had already forgotten in the case of *Exodus* for example who the Paul Newman and Eva Marie Saint characters were even supposed to be. Then I would get up and go back to the refreshment stand and buy as much popcorn, as many M&M's, etc., as I could to take back to my seat and put away kernel by kernel, round candy stone by candy stone, no crunching allowed because I had to stay here a couple hours more before Mom and ugly Cathy picked me up so I had to employ any and all means to stop thinking about myself and feeling miserable, up to and including stuffing my face as long as I possibly could.

Every responsible face in Washington last week wore a tense and somber look, said *Life* magazine on

May 5, 1961, not long after the Bay of Pigs. *The impact of the bitter Cuban disaster was still heavily felt. The news of impending disaster in Laos, where Communist troops were sweeping pro-Western forces before them, deepened the anxiety. The shock of events called for difficult decisions and implied a shakeout of the half-hearted, the routine and the incompetent* . . . I missed having my Grandpa beside me. I hated being outside the story and alone. There were so few people at matinees by then that I could sit almost always in a row completely empty from one side of the high domed room to the other and often did, wishing things were different the whole time. He should have held on till I got a little older and he could see I was okay, not a coward after all or so I hoped, then make me into a man like him. He shouldn't have died like that, with his lips moving and his face turned to the wall. I even went so far at times as to think some nasty thoughts about my father: how if he were with me instead of off at the store making money all the time, if he'd showed up a little more often not just for Sunday TV but like for hunting/fishing/sports, chances are I never would have needed grandfathers and movies to make me a man in the first place instead of the sweaty-palmed fat boy David I was, surrounded by popcorn boxes candy wrappers empty cups, staring bored at the screen, embodiment of all I hated, half-hearted, incompetent, routine.

All of which I know must be true of this story as well, devoid of all but the most unamazing characters in the least vivid scenes strung together in the most bassackwards way conceivable up to and including this triumphant close. Remember *Lawrence of Arabia,* the David Lean movie with Peter O'Toole? In 1963, on one of our last trips to Buffalo as a family, all three of us, I went to see it down at the old Century, and it seemed like just about the worst movie I had been to in my life. All those tiny figures going left to right across the sand versus Lawrence himself acting too screwed up to be anyone at all, one minute playing himself up then putting himself down, leading all these people into battle and slicing everybody to ribbons then acting all strange about getting whipped. Between all that desert on the one hand and not knowing what to think of Lawrence/O'Toole on the other, I had just about given up again and made up my mind to go back to Refreshments for some popcorn candy and Coke, trying once again not to think how alone what a jerk I was all by myself in the row when someone tapped on my shoulder from behind.

Hey man, the black voice said. Hey—you know what's going on?

I sat up. My mind raced in two directions, one which tried to think of the correct manly thing Grandpa would do, say anything and/or get up and leave, the other scrambling for the answer like this really was some kind of test.

Well—I said—see he's getting the Arabs to fight the Turks, cause the Turks are on Germany's side and it's World War I and he's English so he's against Germany.

I paused for breath. What else to say?

Uh, yeah, the black voice said: You care about that? What?

You care about that?

I turned around. He was a few years older than I, maybe sixteen or so; he was wearing a leather jacket and hat. Already I felt so far beyond anything Grandpa would've ever let himself in on, any notion of strength, good, or right that I might just as well keep right on going from here.

No, I said, I don't care. I think it's dumb.

The boy leaned forward. He smiled and I saw gaps between his teeth.

I know a place we could go dancing, he said. How'd you like to go dancing, have a good time?

This was the craziest thing I had ever heard; in fact at first I didn't think I'd heard him right. Then a few seconds later I knew I had and this feeling started in my chest behind my ribs, light and bright as a lunatic sun, and it was all I could do to keep from grinning, laughing out loud, starting to yell or jump on the seats.

No, I said. I'd like to but I can't.

The boy's brow furrowed. Sure you can, he said. I'll show you how.

No, I whispered, and turned away from him back to the giant agonized image of Lawrence the tortured imperialist on the screen. You don't understand, I said: I'm a cripple; I was in this really bad accident with my father when I was real small—and already, as I keep on saying absolutely whatever comes into my head, watching his stunned astonished eyes fill up aghast with pity and fear as I stand and hobbling turn to explain how the random truck plowed in the side of the station wagon, what it did to my poor ankles and knees, I am scraping and wobbling my skewed way across the row of seats delirious with joy, thinking No I can't dance can't tame a horse shoot a gun even think about the Bomb ever get beyond terror yet at that moment I had a sick little story of my own and this is it, this lurching progress up the aisle through the lobby to the street whose life and clamor greeted me at last.

Hello to you too, Buffalo. Hello to you right back.

The first man wore a suit, dark brown with lighter stripes, a burgundy tie. Hunched over and bent on my tottering legs, I was short enough to see more of his clothes than his features, and to have reached his side before he saw me so that when he felt my touch and heard my voice he yelped and pushed me away. I swiveled and swiped with the right claw, the one I kept held out, at a pink poplin coat, tipping my head to one side while speaking my line to see up at the blond woman's face, but jerked back in time for her purse to swish through empty air. I looked down at the ground: nutshells, pigeons, newspaper, dogturds, gum. It was apparent to me that I must have succeeded quite well in looking not only crippled but truly disgusting; already pedestrian traffic had opened around me, leaving me my own pocket of safe despised space, my own little liberated zone in which to drool beg revolve and revolve. *Nicka fuhsum Mok Duhs?* I cried again and again, thick-tongued, as I turned full of a clear wonderful light, squinting up and around me at all Buffalo, looking Buffalo, New York straight in the eye: and this strictly speaking impossible image is nonetheless the end of my tale.

GATOR

Life is not like a movie or a show on tv. Tonight at the end of a rare evening out in the city with my wife, I was accosted on the street by a large young black man in a green fatigue jacket and a grey knit stocking cap. I was outside the restaurant gazing up at a few stars winking through the smog when the night sky was replaced by a large dark face and yellowed eyes held slightly above yet quite close to mine, with sour-sweet breath splashing over me *Ten dollahs fum yuh man lessgo.* From the blend of distraction and urgency in his voice, I figured he was on drugs or alcohol or both, though this was hardly part of the city where you would expect addicts to hang out. But the main thing is, there is no way it could have been Gator. There is no way Gator could still be a young strong man any more.

In any case, the whole thing was over immediately. I managed to say No of course not, the restaurant's doorman bustled up and shooed him away probably long before Gloria was even finished in the ladies room inside. Already, by the time she joined me on the sidewalk, I realized why I felt so shortwinded and shaken up, and why it was so foolish. Because in real life, in the lives real adult people lead, a figure can appear moving toward you, a memory rise from the past without necessarily meaning or leading to anything. It is simply that it's been that long—twenty years, or nearly so—since any black man has been in anything like that kind of close physical proximity to me. Since sitting pushed up against Gator and James in the truck that day, on the ride down to San Jose and back.

It's hard to believe now in the person I know I was back then, at the beginning of the '70s, in that year and a half or so of stupid self-righteous limbo between B.A. and M.B.A. After graduation I had taken my Stanford diploma and moved into town, literally across the tracks, to a two-room apartment a few blocks down from the bus station in Palo Alto, the shabbiest place I could find. I had a fold-down Murphy bed, a battered table, chair and dresser, toilet, sink, and gas stove, and nothing else. Except for my saxophone, sound system and records, of course: at the time I entertained a pathetically vague notion of somehow becoming a jazzman, no less.

So, whatever else was happening, I spent a few miserable hours each day dully trying to play that horn, and a few more in a state of glazed rapture listening to the

greats—Coleman Hawkins, Rahsaan Roland Kirk, and
the immortal Bird—do their stuff on my AR-5's, the top
of the line for audio in those days. And what else was happening? Not much actually, not very much at all. This
was just past the late sixties, the time of the Viet Nam
War, student movement, Black Power and all that, so I
was part of a ragtag community of postgraduate others
who like me had momentarily decided to be, or behave
like, something radically other than who we were. We
wore our hair long and tangled, dressed in colorful rags,
smoked a good deal of grass and took (in my case, mainly
pretended to have taken) whatever mind-altering sub-
stances lay at hand. We hung out in a number of sleazy
low-life bars off the El Camino, places whose owners had
shrewdly adjusted the mix on their jukes to include Hen-
drix as well as the Supremes, Cream along with country-
western, to attract the new clientele. We drank our
pitchers of beer in front, bought and sold and blew our
dope in the parking lots or the men's rooms, and played
a lot of quarter-table pool, by these means deploring the
straights and demonstrating with our presence our soli-
darity with the working and/or lumpen masses whose
members still wandered in from time to time. That, and
killing time while waiting for the Revolution or something like it to get under way, after which something far-
out would naturally develop when all the straight farts in
power were gone. It was like the way I believed that
someday, simply through good will and desire I would
learn—no, discover I already *knew*—how to play the saxophone. After all, we were all cool, weren't we?

That was how I met Gator one afternoon at a place in Mountain View called the Silver Slipper, waiting for me at the end of a line of quarters on the edge of the felt. I had been on a roll of good shooting, giddy with it, taking on double banks and triple combinations and plopping them in, but when I missed a long-green shot on the 6 two strokes after the break, a large black man pushed his wide body away from the wall and shrugged his broad shoulders underneath the battered black varsity jacket as if shaking off some other, less visible coat as he moved into the overhung circle of light and leaned over to shoot. Most people, when they're lining up, you see their faces tighten and close down to the sharp life in their eyes. It's one reason why I still take colleagues and competitors after dinner back through our house to my study, where the old web-pocket Brunswick is installed: you can tell a great deal about a man from the way he addresses himself to his shot and to the game. And what happened to Gator's face was unusual: the eyes softening, face rounding as though in relaxation, big body ambling dreamily from shot to shot. Beneath the rocking of the juke, when he was close you could hear him murmuring his own barely audible scat to the table and himself: *Awright baby, there you go now, gon put you in the side now off that 15 striper need some side action there now here we go* up to the instant of the shot, then resuming again. After the fourth or fifth ball, when it had become clear he was going to run the table, and effortlessly, the gang of longhairs I'd come in with fell silent and just watched. Gator played the 8 off three cushions for his final shot, with a bizarre amount of English on the cue, and I heard a freak named Eddie, an ex-French major with whom I sometimes talked jazz, say "All *right*!"

Gator straightened from the shot, shaking his head in smiling disavowal. "Hey man," I said, as if in reproof: "Listen man, that was good!"

The smile pursed on his mouth, then broke into a startlingly pure and highpitched laughter; his shoulders writhed in a storm of embarrassment and delight. "That was messin round, just messin," Gator said in his high fluted voice. "You wan play again?"

Of course I said yes immediately. In those days, to be invited by a "spade" (it had not yet become officially, universally "Black") to do anything was the highest honor. And again, though this time without the same table-running splendor, he beat me flat. He won nearly every time we played the rest of that whole rainy winter, as a matter of fact. It grew into a habit, a rhythm almost: in the Slipper, the Halfway, or the D&D, whenever and wherever we ran into each other, if and when the house table was free, we would play. I look back now at those stale smoky afternoons in those sleazy places with their gouged wooden booths and concrete floors littered with peanut shells, sour with old spilt beer, and what I see is a black man fresh out of the service with no skills and nowhere to go, a white kid still too scared and proud and self-deceitful to admit his stupid error. Already I could hardly bear to stay in the squalid little box I pretended to call home, listening to music I would never make, or producing squeaks and squawks on my own horn. Already—though I would not admit it at the time, though I kept right on answering the checks I got from

White Plains with abusive prophecies delivered over
the phone, collect, to my folks on the approach of the
Community of the Just—it had begun to dawn on me
that outside that so-called straight world there was in
fact very little community, and no decent jobs. And, back
within that straight world, starting soon, no forgiveness
for those who had strayed.

How Gator came by his money, I'll never know—
welfare, I suppose, or perhaps dealing dope in those
same lumpenstudent bars. I never did find out much
about him, not even his real name. When we sat together
afterwards over the loser-pays pitchers I bought, and I
asked him a question, he gave back the same soft smiling mask with his vague replies. I learned he'd been let
out of the Army not long before, after what, to my
solemn student-deferred nods, he portentously declared
was "some bad shit" in Nam. He'd drifted up here from
Fort Ord after his discharge, and was living somewhere
now in the East Palo Alto ghetto. He might actually have
said more than that which I failed to take in, thanks to
my shambling, overwhelming fascination with the sheer
physical fact of him across the booth or table, blotting
out whatever else I might have heard. The cap of wiry
hair cut so close the scalp gleamed through—no afro
bush for Gator; the brown eyes simultaneously watchful
and open above the broad nose; a flash of silver whenever he laughed, which was often, or ran his tongue
around his teeth for pieces of the peanuts we cracked and
ate with our beer; that laughter itself, high and un-
guarded and, together with his high drawling voice, sug-
gestive of an entranced little boy. All this together with

his size—not tall but so wide and muscled he had that smooth, almost circular gait you see only on very strong or fat men—and, finally, that astonishing, well-nigh literal blackness of his, like layers on layers of blue-black even underneath the skin, all the way down and in.

I'm sure I felt I knew and liked him personally to some degree. Then too, there was the pleasure and honor of having made friends—me, prodigal scion of a Con Ed Senior V.P.!—with a true, untutored representative of the exploited masses/oppressed races, and a Viet Nam vet to boot. Though I was, accordingly, terrified that any moment my bourgeois past might show through and condemn me, I now suppose I needn't have worried. What was in this little friendship for Gator, after all, except for the spectre of a longhaired white boy across the booth or quarter table fooling nobody, manifesting even underneath his slouchiest gestures and grooviest mumblings a doglike gratitude and an abject aim to please?

So early on that spring came a day when Gator picked up the marker on me. It was a blustery morning in mid-April, full of sudden showers and shafts of light. Inside, we were playing call-shot in the warm, mainly empty dimness of the D&D. "I got to go down, do some business next Thursday, down in San Jose," he said as I racked up the fifth game or so. "Been thinkin I could use some help with this thing. Been wondering what you be doin that day and would you be free to come along with me." Behind the almost quaint politeness of the words, his voice dancing on the edge of that high heedless laughter; eyes locked steady on my face as though I were the cue ball he were talking to while lining up the shot.

It was somewhere around our seventh or eighth time shooting pool together, by which time I could give him a run for his money every now and then. And I think I did that morning; I think I might have even won a game or two. At any rate, afterwards we shook on it, out on the muddy gravel of the parking lot. "This comin Thursday, one o'clock or thereabouts," he explained. "I be by to pick you up." I remember the strange dry wrapping of the giant hand around mine, and then how on the way over to my little Vega I dawdled so as to see his old Dodge pickup jounce across the lot, shattering the gaze of the puddles on the sky overhead. I don't know how it is now with all the pollution, but back then early spring in the South Bay still brought giant bodies of cumulus off the ocean and threw them together against an impossibly blue sky, in a way that made it seem anything could happen to your life.

So the following Thursday at one, as agreed, I was waiting out on the curb in front of the seedy clump of apartments where I lived. By two o'clock, though two cloudbursts had come and gone, I was still there in my soaked jeans jacket, sweater, and shirt, on the assumption that if Gator came by and found me missing he would have no way to find me in the warren of walkways, rotting stairs and numbered doors, knowing neither my phone number nor my last name. In that case, I figured by going off to change into dry clothes I would merely prove yet one more example of how honkies always let black people down; so I shook and rubbed myself as dry as I could, and held my post.

The battered pickup pulled up knocking and sputtering somewhere around 2:30. There was someone, another black man, already on the passenger side, an older man in a red flannel shirt who got out when I came around. I ended up hunched mid-seat between him and Gator, with my knees pulled up and my legs spread for Gator to work the gearshift. "Hey," I said cheerfully, trying not to shiver, not to mention they were an hour and a half late: "hey, how's it going?"

The engine noise was terrific. Behind the wheel, his jaw set, his gaze morosely fixed straight ahead, Gator issued a single grim nod. On my other side I felt my ribs nudged by an elbow, and turned to feel a leathery hand grappling for mine. The face I looked into, as dark-skinned as Gator's, seemed at least a hundred years old, a dry, aged, impossible fabric of wrinkles coursing down over brow, cheeks, and lips, with brown eyes so dark and deepset they seemed utterly without whites. His broad smile displayed five or six rotting teeth. He twisted, and leaned so close my ear felt the tickle of the sparse grey hairs on his chin as he shouted into it. "Name James!" was, I think, what he said.

At any rate, I shouted my name back. The old man named James grinned wider and rolled his eyes, as if I had just said something hilarious. For the next several minutes, as Gator, scowling now, maneuvered us through the light traffic, over to the Embarcadero and out to 101, the freeway south, no one actually spoke to anyone else. Yet somewhere around the third or fourth stoplight, I realized James was talking; or, more precisely, that his mouth was forming shapes, making sounds one could feel more than hear through the incessant grating noise from under the hood.

Gator, I told myself, was simply focused on the traffic, and would relax again once we were on the freeway. It would be easy then to find out what I was doing here, what he needed me for, and to strike up a conversation with both him and James, who might have been mumbling to himself as a lot of old folks do, or who might, for that matter, have been singing. The idea of the two of them driving me out to some forlorn stretch of landfill on the edge of the bay where Gator would break my skull open with a tire iron, James would chant over me a while, and then the two of them would leave me atop the compressed garbage, dead, with the white gulls wheeling and squawking overhead—these images were ridiculous, I pushed them away. At the same time, though, I was becoming aware of a certain *odor* wending its way through and over the oil and gas fumes the truck sent up through its floorboards, a rich yet revolting stench like that of a dense warm fertile mud. Suddenly I realized it was the smell of their sweating bodies squeezed against my wet clothes stuck to me like a new damp hide—of their bodies squeezed up against me. My dull anxious fever over what we were up to took fire, flashed into a panic over whether they had already picked up on my revulsion from that scent, their scent, in whatever vibes I might be, had to be, giving off. I tried to control myself, tried to cool out. I pictured the three of us in that truck-cab talking about jazz. I would demonstrate my good will and affection by sharing with them everything I knew about The Hawk, Bird, and Trane. I would fan out for them the thoughts and insights I had otherwise disclosed only to a handful of my scroungy longhaired cohorts in the grainy yellow kitchen light of cramped apartments at 4 or 5 in the morning, after the dancers and the booze were gone and no one could imagine smoking any more dope, when I would slide out the precious albums I'd brought and hidden earlier just for this moment, so that as they played, as the lines and riffs flowed and buckled through the room, I could point and stammer-slur my commentary to my half-asleep, stoned and drunken pals: "Listen, you hear that? His heart is broken"—holding my hand up, waiting for the sobbed note to rise through the dazed exhausted air—"right *here*!"

But the saner part of me even then knew I would not do that; no more than the two of them would kill me and leave me on the dump. All I could do was sit in between them and wait; so that in fact is what I did do, tamping down my dread and terror as best I could, until at last we were on the freeway. And soon after that, heading down 101, something happened—or had happened, rather, but I only then noticed it. Although I rarely listen to any music, much less jazz, any more these days, I would have to say what I felt was something like the sense of release that results when a set of increasingly frenetic riffs abruptly collapses, and some astonishingly simple chord or pulse emerges from the hole that has been left. I looked around me at James' mouthings, at Gator's intent frown, without trying to guess what was on their minds or control what would unfold. I sank back in the seat, felt their warmth on either side of me, drying out my clothes, let their odor fill my nostrils until it became the air I breathed. I gazed out the windshield at the sleek silver of road, its patches glinting now the sun had broken out, at the flow of traffic past shabby pastel apartment complexes and gaudy billboards, at the swooping gulls from off the baylands to our left; and in that same suspended instant realized that James was indeed singing next to me, I could hear it now, barely—half singing, half-moaning out something like a blues.

For such a state of mind, if that is the word for it, I now can only plead the obvious: the times, my youth, my lack of knowledge of the world. At any rate, I was still in that same mood when down around Sunnyvale Gator finally began to speak, high and clear, as if his speaking had picked up on James' song. "Down San Jose," he said, "there this girl livin down there. She the one we got the business with."

"Oh yeah?" I said.

On the other side of me, James ceased his singing and nodded his head. "That woman owin him plenty," he shouted through a crooked grin. "And she got to pay up soon or be in one humongous load of trouble." He cocked a finger at my face: "That the message you got to bring her, man."

Against my left side I felt Gator's arm moving, his elbow working into me as his hand dug in his jacket pocket. What he pulled out at first looked to me to be an old drab fat brochure. His face, however, remained impassive, set straight ahead. "You know a street down here, name Bristol Mill Lane?"

When I said No, he lost his solemnity and James his grin, they both looked suddenly stricken and confused. It was as if I had deceived them, had led them to believe all along I knew San Jose upside down—San Jose, a city no one went to if he could help it, less a city, in fact, than a Sargasso Sea of used car lots and development tracts. Somewhere inside the whole boundaryless mess, I knew, was an old mission town, a few square blocks where blacks, whites, and chicanos alike wandered from bar to bar under smog-powdered light. I had been through there once or twice on a bus, had looked and walked around during the rest stop, that was all; no one I even knew knew San Jose. And when I looked down at the clutch of papers Gator had set across my knees, I saw what it was—a summons and complaint, with the name *Elva Mayfler* typed in the blanks.

I should have called it quits right there, of course. I could have claimed, and with real justice, that I simply knew too little, both of San Jose and whatever they were up to, to be of any help. But no: I had to be cool, to become that much more determined to take it in stride. So I suggested to Gator that we take the next exit, find a gas station, ask directions there. And when we reached a blue-white-and-red Arco just off the ramp, I went right on letting nothing throw me: not the slow, skulking way Gator pulled the truck in off to the side of the station and pumps, nor James' sliding over and down to let me out; not the news that neither the teenaged gas jockey nor his pockmarked older pal had ever heard of Bristol Mill Lane, and that there were no maps, not even for sale; not the information I heard over the pay phone in the booth outside the station, that the San Jose Planning Office had no record of any Bristol Mill Lane.

The sky overhead was darkening with the huge clouds of another rainstorm drifting in over the coastal range, due to break anytime. "That can't be true," I said firmly, reasonably into the phone. "Could you please try again?" The reedy voice on the other end spluttered grudging assent; its owner left the phone to run another check. From where I stood waiting inside the booth I could see the two white guys from the station casting glances over at the rumbling truck off to the side, at the carefully blank faces of Gator and James sitting stiffly in the cab. I was aware of all this; and of how much time we were taking, myself and this anonymous little bureaucrat off doing my bidding on the nth floor of a tall building somewhere in San Jose; and, with a new and really quite pleasant confidence, of how unlikely it was that either Gator or James could have followed this procedure—gas station, phone booth, general information number, Planning Office—through to a satisfactory reply.

And sure enough: a scant minute before closing time, 4 p.m., my Planning Office man got back to me with the location of Bristol Mill Lane. It turned out the street was part of a development so new it had only just landed on the map, the man explained; that was what had made it so hard to find. I took the info he gave me back out to the truck, and twenty minutes later the three of us were moving through one of those new, raw mazes of streets, past yards of scraped earth with little leafless trees tied and screwed down to it, past empty waiting houses as distinct as freight cars on a train. By now the silence over the truck's engine roar was broken only by my directions to Gator—"Right here, take a right; now left at the top of the hill"—and by the *hunh hunhs* of suspicious contempt emitted by James as he flicked his bloodshot eyes from side to side. To my left Gator drove with a glaring watchfulness, his jaw clamped shut. It had been this way ever since the Arco station: we were in enemy territory now, the moment was upon us, it was up to me to get them through this and back out.

I knew which house it had to be when we were still a good half a block away, and not because it seemed to be the only occupied one. It was also the kind of place that virtually shouts out that the lives of those who live there have gone seriously wrong. In the driveway was a twenty foot Chris-Craft gleaming brown and white on its hitch: but out front, there were two broken lawn chairs lying on their sides, their plastic webbing flapping in the warm, stormy breeze, plus a half-deflated children's swimming pool plopped on the dirt, and a rubble of toys and bits of toys strewn down to the curb. And in addition to all that bright ruin, something more: the way in dreams the chosen person or object swims out from the jumbled landscape towards you, shouting *Here I am, this is it.*

What were my thoughts and feelings, then, as we pulled up behind the boat and I got out? In all honesty, I would have to admit I was very excited. In the instant the engine went dead all three of us must have been aware of the storm wind outside, bending the seedlings in the yard against their guy-strings, whistling through the chinks of the battered pickup's cab. For me, like the scudding clouds overhead, it added adventure; for the other two, of course, I cannot say. Gator still said nothing; he was slumped in the seat now, blinking at the wide hands that had dropped from the wheel into his lap. James slid over, got out, and held the door open for me. There were chips of light gleaming in his black eyes, on his mouth either a tense smile or a grimace at the wind. He shifted from foot to foot, almost hopping, and clapped my shoulder lightly as I passed by with the papers in my hand. "Get her now," he said. "Do her up."

So I walked up the strip of sidewalk, stepped up to the concrete slab laid as landing to the front door of the house. As I knocked, behind the ringing in my ears and the whine of the breeze I could hear from inside, unmistakably, the yelping of Fred Flintstone and Barney Rubble, crossed by bursts of massed laughter. After a moment I knocked again, louder, and this time heard or felt some shuffling movement, abruptly swallowed by the bray from the tv. The third time I pounded my whole fist against the door until it hurt. The tv cut out. Perhaps a full minute passed. Then the door opened and there was a woman staring back at me. "Yes?" she said in a weary voice devoid of curiosity or warmth.

"Elva Mayfler?" I said.

The door opened a little wider. She looked around, as if to check what her surroundings might confirm or deny. Following her gaze, I saw hot-orange-and-blue shag carpeting, a lime-green couch and two matching tube-metal chairs, a hanging pull-down lamp and a kitchen divider with inset sink. The carpet was furry with dirt and littered with more toys; I remember in particular a grey machine gun with a cracked stock and red lights blinking the length of its barrel. All along the divider there were empty pop cans, filmy glasses, paper plates with crusts and crumpled napkins, Burger King cups. Yet this riot of things only increased the silence pouring out of that room around us both.

She turned back to me. Her face was oatmeal white with pallid grey eyes, her shoulder-length hair the color of old cornstalks. "Whadya want," she said in the same dull tone.

I think back on it now and still wonder how I knew what move to make and how much to put behind it. "*Are* you Elva Mayfler?" I said again, this time pressing the first word.

Her eyes slid past my face, fluttered around and found it again. "Who you probly need to talk to is my husband," she said. "He's not here right now, he's somewheres else and I don't know—"

"No," I said. "I don't need him." I raised the hand that held the summons and complaint; a rush of exhiliration went off in my chest. "I'm here to give you this," I said.

Elva Mayfler looked at the papers in my hand and seemed to crumple further. With blotchy fingers she plucked at the illegible college insignia on her faded sweatshirt. Then her gaze moved beyond and past me to the truck out in front of the boat. When it came back she had two points of color on her cheekbones and the kind of blue in her eyes that you can see ordinarily only in the middle of a large block of ice.

"Okay," she said. "I get it now."

"That's good," I said smiling, staying with the script. "Then you'll take this."

An attempt at a defiant smile of her own spread her thin lips. "I don't have to take it," she said, opening the screen door, holding out one skinny arm.

"Yes you do," I said. I put my foot in the doorway; I watched her gaze falter under mine, try to recover itself, not quite succeed. "You have to take it," I said. And I laid the papers in her hand.

She looked down at them, then back up at me. For the first time I noticed the tiny broken veins around her nostrils. *Alcoholic*, I thought, quite distinctly. "So," she said, smiling wider but more crookedly, a sort of wavering, feisty leer—"you really like this work?"

I shrugged, kept my even smile on. "It's okay," I said. "I like it all right. Long as you never get too involved in any one case."

A palpable hit: the smile trembled and fell from her lips, her pale face flattened out. She was in the doorway now purely at my behest.

"Thanks for your time then, Mrs. Mayfler," I said. "Have a good day." And, tucking my hands in my pockets, turned and springheeled my way across the junkstrewn mudslick yard, past that hopeless tree and that ridiculous motorboat Elva Mayfler and her husband had no right to, could almost certainly not afford: the way I figured it, after all, they had to be in hock up to their necks.

"So what is it, man?" said James back at the truck, sliding over, yielding me the passenger seat. His old dark face leaned and craned around towards me, mouth trembling with eagerness. "You get her done?" he said.

From where the truck was parked in the drive they must have seen the papers changing hands; yet they still had to hear it from my lips, had to have it confirmed. "Yes," I said to James, and to Gator's dark eyes. "Yes I got her done for you." And when he smiled, when his broad face opened up I felt my own relax too, felt in fact as if I had just released my whole self down into someone's cupped hands, as if we all had expelled in the same moment the same exact sigh.

And this good mood held for quite a while. Gator relieved, James exultant, I myself flushed with pride, I guided them back through the labyrinth and out to the main drag. We found a 7-11, James went in and came out with a half-gallon of Italian Swiss Colony red which we passed back and forth, hand to hand, James holding the wheel for Gator's swigs. I can still recall the sweet thick taste and texture of that wine, and its aftertaste too, like cigarettes and vomit. I have an image of the three of us on the way out of town half-drunk in the cab of that truck, a snapshot taken, as it were, over the hood looking in through the windshield, freezing forever Gator's mouth splayed wide in laughter, James' old face squinched up and thin shoulders heaving, myself caught mid-seizure in lunatic glee. But what was so funny, who said what, that I cannot for the life of me recall.

The next clear thing I do have comes instead from farther on. We are back out on 101, heading north through the long-threatened squall, which has finally hit.

The first flush of the wine has receded and left in its wake a heavy warmth in which we rock, together and at rest. Then, with an almost formal stiffness, James bends over me and points to Gator at the wheel.

"What that woman did to this man here, you don know," he says.

I look at Gator, whose brows arch over his wine-droopy eyes, whose lower lip pushes out, granting his face an innocence-betrayed look so broad I take it as a comic cue. "Oh yeah?" I say, smiling slyly, as much to Gator as to James. "What'd she do?"

"What she *do?*" James' rheumy eyes widen in a pose of outraged astonishment. "What *dint* she do is more like it."

"Okay," I say—still thinking, more or less, he is kidding, but still curious—"what didn't she do?"

James' old face stares into mine so long my breath nearly stops, my earlier anxiety comes rushing back. When finally he nods and bends over for the jug on the floor, I look out through the windshield for relief. On both sides of the freeway the traffic now is rush-hour thick. It is raining harder too, but you can see the limits of the storm in the eerie rainbowed sunlight on the hills up the bay, a couple thousand brake lights up 101. James lowers the jug, wrings its mouth dry, and hands it over. I take a jolt. When I lower it from my mouth, he nods and starts again.

"This man get out of the service now, back here out of a nasty war. Just like they always send us over, get us killed killing other coloreds, every time. This man, though, he come back from that hell feeling strong. Like he gon make it. Like he gon survive no matter what. Then he meet this woman—"

"Elva Mayfler?" I say, incredulous.

His carved face shows no sign that he has heard. "He meet this woman and this woman bring him down. She tell him she love him, she got to be with him. She put her white legs round him, and she hold him, and she squeeze out everythin she can."

Out through the windshield the sky is breaking open to blue, the clearing sweeping down at us as we rush towards it, bumper to bumper, 60 mph. Something in me, maybe just the wine, has started to curdle, some apprehension is on the rise. "This is Elva Mayfler you're talking about?" I say. "Elva Mayfler of Bristol Mill Lane? Doesn't she have a husband?"

James' red eyes lower, their lids half-closing, his mutter scarcely audible over the engine roar and pelting spring rain. "She tell that man she leave her husband. Give up her babies, even, if it got to be, she love him that much. She tell him Go find us a home, use them vet benefits and what money you got. And he don know no better than to go do it. And she get her name in with his on everythin he buy."

We have hit the sunlight finally, somewhere in the middle of James' last riff, but it is not pleasant. The freeway steams with the sun's sudden heat and there is glare off every surface, billboards, buildings, other cars, striking back through my eyes and aching my head. The cab of the truck has turned into a sauna, mixing our sweat with the stench of the wine. Thick drops pop out on my forehead, break and roll down my face. "Wait a minute," I say. "You can't mean Bristol Mill Lane. You guys didn't even—"

James is shaking his head heavily, his mouth all twisted up. "He buy her this house," he says, softly continuing as if I had said nothing at all. "This fine old farmhouse out East Palo Alto with the barn and horses and two acres in back. Buy her that house and all the trimmins. The boat she want, man, all she want. Put hisself in a pile of debt. But the man, he happy, you know? Cause his woman's gon come be together with him. So he move into that house. Move in and commence to wait for her. Call her up on the phone, say *Honey? Honey, what you want is here for you.*"

Trying to follow along, stay on top of things, I close my eyes against that hot dirty light, and put the figure of Elva Mayfler as I have just seen her behind their shut lids. That dead-white skin, skinny fingers plucking at the sweatshirt, thin wavery smiles. This woman met Gator, talked and danced and drank with him, slept with him, put him under her spell . . . this watery-eyed woman, with broken blood vessels around her nose. I try to put the two of them together at bars I knew, in motel beds. Try to give it a sad, bluesy soundtrack, like Bird's K.C. Blues, give it richness, beauty, truth, to make it work.

And all the while James' voice goes on winding into the dull ache of my head. "Wait a week. Wait a month. Wait two months. Call her up whenever he can, whenever it safe. Say, *When you comin, can I see you now?* but she just put him off. *Baby,* she say, *these things take time, you got to give me time, lemme work it all out.* And he wait some more, hangin out there on the line, cause

52

he love her so bad and he in so deep he got to trust her, he got to believe—"

But at this instant I am struck by a thought so clear and vivid that it forces me to open my eyes. We have reached Mountain View; the traffic has thinned; in a few more minutes we should be home. In the dazed grainy light I catch a glimpse of dog whizzing past my window, a brown and white beagle on the freeway's right shoulder. It was lying on its side in a bright pool of blood, its rear and front legs moving like pistons still, its mouth wide open in a howl I could not hear. *I do not have to see this,* was my thought. *I do not have to imagine any of this.*

"So okay then," I said—somewhat brusquely, I confess, but I just wanted out. "So the summons and complaint are to get her name off what Gator owns, is that right?"

"No man," said Gator—and turning away from James' rocking figure. I saw his black face shiny with tears—"I jes wan that boat!"

It is the truth. That is exactly, word for word, what he said. And it is also the truth that in the instant of that wail, I had despite my shock the closest I've ever had to a revelation, before or since. Sitting there in that truck beside the two of them, listening to Gator cry, it struck me that there must be millions, *billions* of such people in the world—people like Gator, Elva Mayfler, old slobbering James. But no one is required to listen to their sordid absurd stories. No one is required to believe, much less understand, what they are about.

As soon as this thought came to me, in fact, I felt a good deal better. It was as though it allowed me to retreat to a dry quiet room from which it was actually quite easy to put up with the rest of James' speech: "Now young man like you, he don get into such messes . . . You know what woman is, how to handle yousself with her," on and on, etc., etc. To all of which I heard myself chuckling, saying "Yes" or "No, not really," the minimum required, while still reciting my *No one is required* to myself. If it did not sound so excessively dramatic, I would almost say I had attained a kind of peace.

Then, by the time we got to my apartment, Gator too seemed to have recovered. He grinned and said he'd see me back at the tables; James laughed and slapped my knee and said "Take care now, hear?" I told James how much I'd enjoyed meeting him, and assured Gator I'd be looking forward to our next game. Only there was no next game, obviously; although I did run into him one more time after that day. It was a good month or more later on, a brilliantly bright warm almost-summer Saturday. I was out at a rustic old beer hall called Rissoti's out behind the Stanford campus a ways, with a woman named Julie. She was a senior Econ major I'd met at a campus party the week before and, as luck would have it, the woman through whom I would soon meet Gloria my wife. We were on our way through the bar's dank interior to the beer garden in back and so involved in a fierce, happy argument over the role of the market in the welfare state that I only noticed Gator at the last possible minute, on the ledge of the doorway to the garden outside.

I had no idea how long he'd been watching; or, for that matter, what it was that had made me turn around.

But there he was, across the dark room, standing at the edge of the table lamp's soft circle of light. He leaned on his cuestick, head cocked to one side, and smiled his soft steady smile at me. Thanks at first to my surprise, and then by design, I did not return it; I looked back without acknowledging him in any way. The blond, black-leathered biker he was playing started to say something, most likely to tell him it was his shot, but stopped when he saw, as I did, the look on Gator's stiffened face. Then that cold gaze broke and his expression changed again, vanished or covered over by that same old dreamy look as he surveyed the lay of the table, resumed his murmur to himself, his stick and the balls. When I turned back to outside and Julie, who was still talking, carrying on the argument, he had already sunk two, a combination and a bank, in a single movement of lowered circling I knew would not end until the table was clear.

That was the last time I saw him, nearly twenty years ago—back before I knew that only an officer of the court can serve a complaint, and back when I still thought, or hoped, that both the times and I myself made some sort of difference. In another few months, without serious misgivings, I applied for entrance to the Stanford Business School; in a little more than two years I was married to Gloria and in possession of my M.B.A. I began with Frito-Lay in Dallas, and went on to Georgia-Pacific in Atlanta. We were happy in Atlanta, and the working atmosphere at G-P was always pleasant, but when it became clear that beyond a certain level advancement was unlikely, I took a shot at, and won, my present position as head of long-range planning for one of this country's oldest and most respected investment firms. I have worked hard for what I have made for myself, my wife and our children, but I am grateful for the good fortune which has been our lot as well. I do not look back on the time in my life when I knew Gator with any fondness or regret.

I do, on the other hand, still enjoy pool—and will often, on a social evening at our home, invite the men of the party to accompany me after dinner to the teak-panelled room here at the back for cigars and some call-shot, as old-fashioned as that sounds. On such occasions, I find I am not fond of those men who have to talk between shots about how well the balls are spread, what their shooting style or my own is like. At best the only sounds in this climate-controlled room are the calls themselves—4 in the side; 7 all the way down—followed by the clicking or cracking of the balls as they collide, the hush of their roll down the felt, their solid thunks as they plop in. Of course I thought of Gator tonight only because it has been so long, because it happened so swiftly, and he came so close. Still, now that I have—and I wish him well, wherever he is—I must admit the thought of running into him and playing one last round of call-shot gives me pleasure. After all these years of practice at the game, I am certain that by now I could beat anyone who talks or sings as he lines up the shot.

DIRTY PIECES

J ust how or when he knew, he couldn't remember. Off
the tv, out of some other mag? Either that, or from
somebody else, like one of the guys at work. Anyway,
there was this big article on the secret files of the C.I.A.
in this month's issue of *P*. He heard or saw about it one
way or another, noticed it at first and then it seemed
like forgot it for a while. But then a few days later, on a
cold rainy afternoon when he had come home early
from work, he left the house again almost immediately
and walked to the giant chainstore nearby where they
sold everything, including skin magazines like *P*.

Such magazines were kept on a special shelf behind
the sales counter in the section of the chainstore devoted
to candy and tobacco and reading material of almost all
kinds except scholarly stuff and outright filth. Across the

counter from him plastic shields adorned each tray of the special shelf, shields painted or constructed to look like wood, each with the name and insignia of the particular magazine stacked behind it. In this way the shields both indicated which magazine was hidden behind each one and concealed the magazines' salacious covers from all who might be unduly offended or aroused at the sight of them (e.g., certain women, religious and/or deluded women and men, pubescent males, etc.). Also, setting the shelf away from the rest of the magazines on display prevents browsing, which could not only reduce their value to a potential buyer, but might be offensive as well to some of the self-same groups, e.g. women and the devout. So, he realized without really thinking of it or breaking it down, this arrangement made both moral and economic sense.

Unfortunately for him, though, the same arrangement meant he would have to take his place in the line of people waiting to pay for their candy bars, paperbacks, and cigarettes, and then, with still others behind him, ask the woman at the cash register for the magazine by name. The possibility of giving up and forgetting about it crossed his mind as he joined the line but he dismissed it. He wanted to read about the secret files of the C.I.A., he was interested in that kind of thing, ins and outs of intelligence work, the morality of doing this and that. He had read numerous other magazine articles on the same subject over the years; at one point, a few years ago, he had bought a paperback on this subject, and taken it with him on vacation to the beach. There was a woman behind him, a young adult woman with a Payday, and behind her a towheaded boy with a scuba-diving magazine from the open shelves off to his right, but he tried not to think, not to be aware of them. He kept his eyes on the grey-uniformed woman at the cash register, a plain middleaged woman with worry lines along her mouth and eyes which lifted only slightly as she offered those ahead of him their change, their purchase in a bag if they liked, their Thank you and Have a nice day. He thought about what to say to explain, how to buy the magazine when it was his turn at the counter as it would be soon, since the line was of single purchases and moved fast.

"Do you have the May issue?" he said. "The May issue of *P*?"

In fact, he could see for himself that the *P* on the special stand behind her was the May issue, from a glance at the edge of the magazine sticking out above the shield. But his question, uttered in a firm clear voice before the plain store-uniformed woman could speak, was part of his strategy, as it was now for him to continue speaking, explaining with a slight pleasant smile as she turned to check the special stand.

"It's the one with the big piece on the C.I.A. in it," he said amiably, as though to remind her. "The one on the secret files of the C.I.A.?"

She lifted a copy from the stand and put it on the counter; he caught a glimpse of brown water-beaded skin, a green background. Her own face was blank; he could not tell whether she believed him or not. Possibly men came in every day and made excuses, invented pretexts for buying these magazines from her and there was no way to convince her that he was different, his reason was real, in fact he wasn't interested in the pictures and fold-outs and fantastic imaginary letters with their ridiculous scenarios, only in the C.I.A. article. Possibly she just didn't care. "Will that be all?" she said, looking over his shoulder.

"Yes," he said; and then, in a last attempt to demonstrate his innocence, "um, how much is it?"

She told him, and he paid. She rang it up and slid the magazine into a thin brown sack, and thanked him and told him to have a nice day. He moved away and the next customer came up, the young woman with the Payday whose presence he had excised from his mind. He kept the magazine in the sack, held it swinging slightly from his fingertips all the way home. Now he knew what he was going to do with it when he got back. Really, he had always known. And afterwards, when he was through, he would sit down and read the piece on the secret files of the C.I.A.

His girlfriend in college lived with her best friend R, a short plump woman who chain-smoked, spilling flakes of ashes on her clothes and everywhere about her, who spoke and acted always with a sort of brusque, desperate cheer, who had no boyfriend and few dates. He understood why this was so; she was a certain kind of virgin, raucous and coarse and frightened, lank-haired, short-nailed and plain. But perhaps because he knew her through his girlfriend (who was lithe and supple, an aspiring actress he had courted ferociously, winning her against all odds), because he could see the secret acts of kindness R performed for her friend, his girlfriend, sharing her class notes (for his beautiful girlfriend was not too bright, a fact that bothered him at times), sleeping on the living room floor when he stayed overnight in the apartment, driving both of them back and forth to each other in her battered VW van, eventually he found himself attracted to her too.

This, at any rate, was the reason he could come up with most easily at the time. But there were at least two other reasons as well. One which eventually he had to acknowledge you can probably already guess: she was plump and big-breasted and had a nice packed ass, and he liked that, especially in contrast (or complement) to his girlfriend's willowy swells. He had always liked that better actually, he realized. Always liked big breasts, handfuls, plenitude, plunging in the soft wealth of it, grabbing it, sucking it, yes what the hell are you doing with this other skinny selfish passive-aggressive-no-good-in-bed-not-very-smart girl anyway, he asked himself. But when he thought of breaking up with her, he stopped, he could not do it. He had worked so hard, so ardently to get her and now she was his. She said she wanted to be with him all the time, she came over when he was studying or drinking and talking to friends, and sat in his black easy chair in the corner and waited until he was done and they could go to bed, which he no longer cared to do with her all that much. She clung to him physically, grabbing his arm as they walked across the quad or down the street, as if to hold him back. He knew what would happen if and when he ever tried to break it off; he could see her beautiful face all red and hot and teary, see her outstretched arms, hear her cries. Having won her over so completely, he understood that if he dumped her he would be a total shit. But all that only made him want R more.

And there was another reason too, one which accounts as well for why he wanted her in such a pleasant, confident way: R adored him. Adored them both really, just the idea of them. He could imagine her in the apartment when they were not there, leaning her head over her desk, pretending to read a book, take notes, but really picturing the two of them wherever they were, out watching a movie or walking back through the snow holding hands. He could imagine her out on the Navajo rug on the living room floor, hearing their soft, discreet lovemaking sounds. But she adored him most, first, foremost, you could tell that too, from the way her voice got louder and louder, her talk faster with more rough obscenities, her laughter breathier and more uncontrollable whenever he was alone with her. R truly admired his intelligence, his developing ironic stance; R liked his looks, his hands, his lean sharp face. There were moments in the apartment, even with his girlfriend there, when he could feel R's gaze on him like fragrant heat. That was a part of it too—the part he never, even afterwards, admitted to himself.

So in this way their time together passed until the school year was over. They dispersed for the summer to separate homes and jobs, and reconvened the next year as though nothing had changed. Yet there was a difference. Though R still laughed and smoked as much as ever, still wore sweatshirts and jeans everywhere, she was no longer a virgin. Over the summer she had met someone at the lab in Cambridge where she was a research assistant and had her first brief affair.

It was nothing serious, his girlfriend told him, explaining in whispers, snuggled up to him on his cramped single mattress in the dorm. R and her fellow researcher had decided from the start that this would be a fixed-term contract, a friendly time. What R said mostly about it, his girlfriend said, was how glad she was not to have to worry about her stupid precious virginity any more. But she, his girlfriend (with her thin arms and legs all tangled up with his, her exquisite face smiling in the dark), she thought that was not the whole truth. Hadn't he noticed R's occasional spells of brooding silence, the sound of a new, soft note in her voice? Didn't he think that R was probably missing this guy, whoever he was, at least a little bit?

Sure she was, he said. She'd have to be, wouldn't she, he said, patting his girlfriend's long black hair, waiting for her to fall asleep so he could think of her, R, all by himself.

He got the magazines, three of them, soft with age, handling and the damp lightlessness of the places where they had been stored, from a kid in his class who was so bold and sarcastic to teachers, so hairy and skilled in phys ed, so feared and admired by everybody, including him, that he knew the kid would have to have a few lying around. His own boldness in approaching the kid and asking about it—for they hardly knew each other and he was slow-witted, hairless, everything in fact that this kid wasn't—astonished him, as had the kid's own sudden solemn seriousness in the locker room as he agreed to the request. The kid had looked up from the thick bush of black hair he had been ostentatiously toweling dry, had broken off the dirty song he had been singing in his tuneless shout, and fixed him hard with fierce eyes as he told him the rules. Yes, he would bring him some magazines tomorrow, he would give them to him at the beginning of U.S. History, their third period class. But if he got caught with them by anybody and gave the kid's name as their owner, or if he didn't have them back by Friday at the beginning of that same third period, then the kid was going to beat his ass: understand?

He said he understood. The kid went back to his toweling and his song:

> *She's got freckles on her BUT*
> *she's nice*
> *She's got freckles on her BUT*
> *she's nice*
> *All the sailors give her chase*
> *cause they like her naval base*
> *She's got freckles on her BUT*
> *she's nice*

So he got the magazines, three of them, for two days.

They were down in the cellar now behind the stacked mason jars of beans and jam, where he had hidden them that first day, right after school. Now the problem was when and how to get some time alone with them. His mother was home all the time, his sisters were always around after school, his father came home from the store at eight and sat around and watched tv with his mother until it was time for bed. There was no way he could go down in that stone cellar with the laundry sink and canned goods and stay down there for a while without somebody wondering what was going on. Besides, he knew whatever might happen between him and the magazines was not going to happen standing shivering in that wet stoney cold down there. In his joy at getting them and his relief at successfully hiding them he had let all of Wednesday go by. Now it was Thursday, Thursday night, and his father and mother were watching tv and his sisters were working on a dress and he would have to have the magazines back tomorrow or have his ass beat, which was no problem since he could always make a quick run down there and put them back in his notebook: but how was he going to get some time alone with them?

There was only one way, of course. That night he lay in bed for hours, more motionless than if he had actually been asleep, until the silence of the house itself became a high constant sound; then he eased himself slowly out of bed. At the doorway to his bedroom he paused until the sound was in his ears again before pulling the door open and stepping out into the upstairs hallway leading to his parents' and sisters' rooms a few yards away. His bare feet pressed each step against the wood before putting his whole weight on it; if the floor creaked or groaned, they sought elsewhere. So it went with the seventeen steps of the stairs as well. By the time he reached the living room, though several steps had shrieked and exploded, no one upstairs seemed to have stirred. He moved more quickly now, almost at a normal pace, to the kitchen, down the cellar stairs, back up again into the living room. He listened for the silence one last time; there it was. He turned on an end-table lamp, sat down on the couch, and started leafing through the magazines.

He knew, of course, that the women would be naked and sprawled out in these magazines, and he knew that they were exciting. And he knew that he himself felt excited sometimes at something or other, a word or a song or a story that gave you an idea somehow of what it was like, how good it must be. So the hope was that the pictures, when he got to them, would both focus and increase his excitement, the way it seemed to do, as far as he could tell, for the kid who owned these magazines and for other kids his age and for men. Maybe he might even get some idea of what was really going on, what it meant, what he could and should do about it from here on in.

But when he got to the pictures, nothing happened. Nothing. He did not even get stiff, not even when he squeezed it with his thighs, pressing the way he did under his desk at school sometimes, not even when he took two of the full-page spreads from the magazines and stretched them out over his lap.

He stared at them for a long time. One was leaning back on a bench or something, with a big pillow behind her; she was a brunette, with fancy curly hair. The other, a blonde, lay looking up from shiny sheets in a disheveled bed. You could see all their parts except between their legs, which the angle covered for the brunette, the sheets for the blonde. You could see they were supposed to be looking at you. But still nothing. Nothing at all.

And what if these things, these pictures in these magazines, what if they didn't work for him the way they did for everybody else? What did that mean? He paged through them once more, flapping his legs, tasting the panic at the back of his mouth. He read the cartoons, the letters about penis size and premature ejaculation. No good.

Finally he closed the magazines and stacked them on the floor beside his cold bare feet. He tipped his head back against the couch and stared at the ceiling and thought grey wordless miserable thoughts. Then, before tiptoeing back upstairs, he hid the magazines in his notebook and walked over to the family bookcase, to try the only thing he knew of at the time that could give him the excitement he wanted and needed in a regular, trustworthy way.

He took down the dictionary and opened it up to the words and meanings he had discovered there over the past few weeks and months. *Eagerly desirous,* he read. *Inclined to lust or wantonness,* he read. *A ring of color, as around a pustule or the human nipple. Union in sexual intercourse. Concupiscent, lascivious, areola, copulation,* he mouthed the words against the ringing silence; and though his legs were shivering with cold, his feet were numb and icy, he could feel it happening, sense the swoon of excitement, see himself getting hard.

*   *   *

Always one, at least one, in the concourse at the terminal, the line at the bus station, on the bus or train or plane. Or if you're not going anywhere, you don't travel, they're behind a counter, walking past you on the street, a waitress or secretary or somebody you meet through your work at a conference or something. And they walk past you or give their report, hand you your drink or your goods in a bag and look at you or don't when you look at them that way, the way you know shows through whether you mean it to or not. What would this one be like? What if you were doing it, right in the middle of it, right now with this particular one right here? And you know they can see the questions, the scenarios, running through your eyes.

He got on the bus from the airport to town, about an hour's ride away. Sure enough, there was one halfway back among the old ladies and soldiers, college students, small-time salesmen with their rumpled coats and shiny suits. It was too dark to tell much about her for sure but she had good eyes, a nice face anyway. The seat beside hers was empty, as were both seats across the aisle, and for a second after the first flash, question, look, he imagined sitting beside or across from her. But what then? Nothing, probably; and besides, he was tired from the flight. The last thing he wanted to do was talk to anyone. In an hour or so he'd be back with his lover, having supper, going to bed. So he stopped at the row across and behind her, threw his suitcase on the rack, sat down and cracked the dumb book he'd been reading on the plane. Then, as the lights went off and the bus got under way, he heard her and looked over from the corner of his eye.

Her lowered head was cocked sideways. She was smiling broadly, waving a hand towards herself. It seemed to him, from the gesture and the way her mouth moved, plus what reached him over the engine noise, that she was making a slight exclamation, saying "Hey: hey: hey." For a second he thought she must be signalling to whoever had the seat in front of him, across from her. Then he remembered there was no one there. "Hey: hey: hey."

Well, what do you know. It was for him.

He stood up, stepped forward in the aisle, and bent over her. This close he could see she was foreign, Arabic maybe. Real cute, too. Nothing's going to happen, get those fantasies out of your head. "Yes?" he said.

Her giggle was high but throaty. He could not make out what she said next, so he smiled and shook his head. When she repeated it, he caught a little more although her English was not very good. "Do I want some money?" he said as the bus lurched onto the freeway ramp and almost knocked him off his feet.

She laughed like a schoolgirl, with her hand over her mouth. "Nooo," she said and repeated it again, this time slowly and loudly enough that he caught it without believing that he had. No, it had to be "money." And maybe she was getting the pronoun wrong too.

This stuff didn't happen in real life. "Do you want money?" he said.

Another fit of giggles. Then, motioning him to lean over more and closer, she breathed the word into his ear. "Noo-kee," she whispered, laughed and pulled back and pointed to the empty seat beside her, staring back at him with her first expression, head cocked and eyebrows raised.

Jesus Christ, he thought, and sat down. She picked up his near hand, guided it inside her coat, pressed it against her breasts. Her other hand danced over the top of his legs and down to his inner thigh, near where he was automatically, ferociously hard. There was no one immediately around them, he realized, before or behind, and he had never ever been more excited. All the stories he had ever read or heard streamed through his head. He reached under her blouse, around to her back, his fingers scrabbling for her brastrap, jesus jesus jesus. She twisted away, frowning, then leaned forward to kiss his cheek, her round face glowing with mirth.

"You be nice now," she said. "You be good." Then both hands reached back between his legs as she laughed again and thrust her breasts back out.

So it went on, a bit at a time, until at one point her brastrap was unsnapped so his hands were directly against them, while under his overcoat her fingers had unzipped his fly, taken it out, and were now caressing it. For a while he tried to move his hands, one of them anyway, behind the waistline of her jeans and down, out of some crazy, desperate hope that maybe if she got excited enough too, just started breathing a little harder, panting more, then maybe somehow, somehow, by her sitting on him, not moving too much, with his coat over both their laps, maybe it would keep on working out and they could do it right here yes baby yes yes. But when he tried she only pulled away again. "Be nice. Be good." Followed by her giggle, hands and body closing in.

Early on she had asked him his name, he had answered and asked her for hers. It turned out to seem like hardly any name at all, just a collection of syllables, unpronounceable, which was how he liked it anyhow. This way it fit right in with the rest, kept her anonymous, a pure gift even after she had started talking, whispering through her caresses, in between her sighs and giggles: how she had come here from her country of Iran to go to college, that was what her father and the governments still thought, but she had left school in Florida to come ride around and have some fun. She had brothers in this city they were entering now, two brothers with their wives living together here and she would have to stop and see them here or everyone would be too angry at her though she did not want to because they were so bad and all the time wanted to have sex with her and would not let her out to have fun while she was there.

"And you know," she was saying while he clutched and squeezed and prodded, lost in his desire to push things ahead: "you know a person from my country must be careful. Savak is everywhere, even here. A person from my country must be very careful, very good."

Did she really have these brothers here, were they really as horrible, as sick as all that? Even at the time he had to admit it was a little strange, her saying stuff like this to an almost total stranger, in the middle of their grappling, this incredible scenario playing out. Maybe the whole thing was a little crazy after all, just another stupid fantasy. Besides, they were coming down the main drag now, only a few blocks from the station. The possibilities for really doing something were rapidly approaching nil. Finally she pushed him away decisively, albeit with another kiss. Okay with him. Already a sick weakness had replaced the ache in his groin. He sat back and watched from the corner of his eye the pulse of streetlights across her chubby, serious face bent over the huge leather bag she was rummaging through. This whole thing had really been stupid. He was even a little ashamed.

She had found a stub of pencil, she was writing slowly, like a child, on a torn slip of paper. He looked away, out the other side of the bus, but as they pulled in to the station she pressed his side and called his name: "Hey: hey."

He turned back and managed a polite but pointedly detached smile. She put the slip of paper in his hand. He could feel his lover waiting outside in the crowd by the station door. His kind sweet beautiful lover. What the hell did you think you were doing, what's the matter with you anyway, getting involved in a thing like this? "Will you call me?" said the chubby Iranian. She had stopped smiling now too; her lips were trembling; she was nervous too, he supposed. According to her crazy story, there were two nasty-ass brothers out there waiting for her. Savak agents of the Shah as well, for all he knew. Maybe she wasn't weird or crazy after all. But the thought did not make him feel any better.

"Call this number please and make a plan with me to have some fun?" she was saying.

Yeah, sure he would, he told her: but mainly just to get off the bus and away from her as as fast as possible, and forget about the whole sick sordid thing.

The only problem with the skinmags that first time, of course, was that he didn't yet know how to read them. The way in the photographs their legs were cocked or bent or spread, their breasts pooled and rested, pointed or hung, their mouths smirked or pouted, the eyes invited boldly, coyly or hungrily, the hair was long or short or straight or curled—he did not know all that was speaking to him, telling him different things. Or the same thing in different ways, different dialects not all of which he ever learned or came to like. For example, the sunny happy West-Coast-style ones with pert perfect breasts and long limbs out on the beach or sunporch, the ones who said things in the copy like Good sex is like back handsprings or a sauna, these were not for him. He liked them shorter, paler, milky almost translucent white inside half-dark apartments sitting on chairs cupping their white heavy breasts, dark eyes looking back out at him chock-full of lust.

Just after getting out of college he found one like that in a skinmag he kept around a long time: long wavy brown Rossetti hair, a rainbow butterfly tattoo on her thigh, looking out smoldering from the middle of a twilight apartment loaded with rich dark ferns. She worked a long time, almost without fail. But when and if she didn't, by that time there were other pictures too, based on the real women he had been with so far: L, R, K, even, in a pinch, his high-school girlfriend C. Some better than others, but they each worked every now and then. You took what you could remember of being with them, putting it in, and before and after, and mainly just speeded it up, made it like they were really hurting for it, loving it, getting it jammed in quivering right away with your hands and face all over their breasts, their tits with their breaths sucked in their heads snapped back their bodies pushing hard to cram it *up in* until it shook on out, flew into his fingers shot out on the floor.

The only difference came just afterwards. With the real ones, he would instantly remember something about what it had really been like. Sometimes a memory of heavy sweaty limbs, a gust of perfume, a particular body smell; other times, of the long, intimate conversation that had to follow. More often, though, it was something of what actually doing it with them had been like, how she looked under or over or beside him at the time, how and what she really moved and at what speed. A brief, true memory that forced him to realize and admit right away that whatever he had been seeing and thinking and feeling about L or R or C or whoever had never really happened much like that at all.

And the worst of it was, when you did it this way every time you changed it, made it up the way you wanted, you always eventually remembered less after- wards. Less good or bad, pleasant or unpleasant, until fi- nally L and R and K and C were all used up too, sticky cards in a worn-out deck. That was why the ones in the magazines were really better. It took some time and money to find one that spoke to you, but once you did you were better off. They lasted longer, plus then you weren't using up the memories of women you had really been with, C and K and R and L and whoever else, some of whom at least he was sure he had genuinely loved at the time. Not that the magazines didn't make you feel dead or stupid too afterwards; just not quite the same way, not as bad.

Starting that fall, then, he began to spend slightly less time with his slim stupid girlfriend, slightly more with bright buxom R, and compensating for these new proportions by extending to the girlfriend a sort of absentminded tenderness to which she responded with pathetic intensity. He no longer ignored or neglected her for long stretches while she sat in his dorm room. He would get up from his desk every so often and walk over to the recliner chair, stroke her hair, say her name. Now he too, like R, helped his girlfriend write her papers, contributing a paragraph here or page there. Now when they made love he knew just what to do and say. It was like working the combination on an old family lock, circling to the number without so much as looking at the dial, knowing it so well you can think about something, anything else the whole time and the padlock still clicks open: and she never knew the difference, she was that dumb.

R, on the other hand, he was sure understood almost everything he was up to. Casually, almost unconsciously, they had come to know each other's class and work and study schedules better than his girlfriend knew either of theirs. In their drop-in visits to each other when his girlfriend was not around, on the nights at her apartment they would stay up reading and studying long after she had gone to bed and fallen asleep, the two of them in fact discussed her and his relationship with her quite often, and more and more frankly. Eventually he told R the whole story, everything he felt. R understood. She agreed that her friend was childlike, yes, even childish in some ways, but wasn't that part of her charm, what made her so wonderful in her own way? And their eyes would meet and hold; they would laugh nervously, harshly, without quite knowing why.

He could tell R had grown up a lot over the summer, and he told her so. She had really matured. In response, she smiled as if about to break into her old anxious laugh, but gave him back instead a serious, searching gaze. They crouched together on the Navajo rug, smoking R's cigarettes and talking about a whole widening range of subjects: books and ideas and life-plans, family problems, relationships and all that. Some nights when it was really late and they were really tired, they gave each other back and neck rubs, longer and longer ones, first over then under blouses, sweaters, and shirts to the flesh itself. He would do it first to R, then R to him; the other way around, he was too afraid of what would happen, what effects and reactions he would go for when she'd gotten to him first. Though actually, as it turned out, her massages were not really all that erotic. She pressed down too hard, using too much muscle; but still even just the contact with her skin made it pretty hard. He had to slow down, breathe evenly, keep himself from doing anything really stupid, anything he would be ashamed of later, with his poor defenseless girlfriend in the bedroom a thin wall away.

Still, it had to happen sometime. He knew that and figured she did too; and this is how it finally came to pass. In the middle of that winter, after a few months of this, he got what first seemed just a bad cold but developed quickly into some kind of wicked full-body flu that confined him to his bed in the dorm. The second day, when his fever was at its worst, his girlfriend was there the whole afternoon. She bought some juice and made him drink it up; she kept soft music going on the stereo. She sat beside the bed on the old black recliner and practiced her new hobby, knitting, while he drifted in and out of his aching, sweaty sleep to a blend of easy harmonies and clacking needles, domestic sounds which made him grateful for her presence and her love.

Between this gratitude and the hot fog of his fever, the thought of R never crossed his mind. Yet half an hour after his girlfriend left for rehearsal that evening, R was there, shrugging her coat off and throwing it on the old black chair, laughing her hoarse hearty laugh at the sight of his pitiful self all scrunched up under the sheets, unscrewing the top of the pint of good whiskey she had brought and handing it to him as she stretched out beside him on the bed and, soon afterwards, began to rub her hands across his bare achy chest as the whiskey floated straight up in his head until he reached over and pulled her on top of him.

It took less than fifteen minutes that first time, start to finish. Afterwards, he smoked a throat-scalding cigarette with her in the short moment they still lay together, joking as if nothing had happened, everything was just the same. Which was more or less the truth as far as he was concerned, he realized later, after she had put her coat back on and gone: true in a physical sense, anyway. He still felt hot and achy and exhausted, only more so, thanks to coughing up great hunks of stuff from that stupid cigarette. It had all gone too fast, he had been too sick to control himself and pace the whole thing, but at least it was started. And he liked the way just a few seconds afterwards she had rolled over, off and away to the edge of the mattress, and lit up a smoke while tossing off a crack about special nursing care.

But then why should he have ever worried about that anyway: what she might say afterwards, what she would expect? She knew full well what the deal was, how he was stuck with her best friend. How many times had they talked about that very thing? She was coming into this with her eyes wide open, knowing exactly what the story was. How to work things out from here might get sticky now and then in terms of logistics, but that should be all. Once he kicked this stupid cold, everything looked like it could be just fine.

Back with his lover again, eating the special dinner she'd prepared for his return, stealing upstairs with a marvelous fresh urgency to her bed, still a part of him felt dirty and ashamed. This was a fine woman he was with here, smart and sensitive and caring and a lot else, including good in bed. There was no way he was going to jeopardize such a serious, adult commitment to such a woman for some degrading, meaningless sex with some screwed-up chubby Iranian whom, in a moment of weakness and stupidity, he had allowed to paw him for her own private neurotic reasons on the bus and who by now was probably feeling ashamed of herself besides. He was old enough and smart enough by now to know the value of a strong, mature relationship, and the risk to it of catting around in search of some stupid, illusory, free, no-fault jumps in the hay with a total stranger. There was no such thing in this world as free, as no-fault. Life was not a fuck book, all those letters and scenarios were so much bullshit. In a week or so, once he stopped feeling so bad about it, probably there would be a funny story to be made out of the whole weird incident, to be shared over a few beers with his best and closest friends. Right now, though, the main point was that he was home. He had everything you could ever want with this woman right here. And even if this other strange woman did think to look up his number and call it, ninety-nine chances out of a hundred she would get no answer at his place, which since he had all but completely moved in with this fine woman his lover and begun to make a life together with her, he still paid rent on but almost never used. Then, since he'd told her nothing about where he worked or what he did, that was it, there was just no way.

So things fell back into their daily round. He got up the next morning and went to work, got back at night around the same time as his lover, made supper with her, talked about the day, then watched tv and went to bed. He fed her cats, brought the garbage cans around out front on Wednesday, filled out a few reports at work, received and deposited his paycheck, paid his car insurance premium, etc., etc. No word the whole time from the other one, the Iranian on the bus. Now that his relationship with his lover had grown so strong, so solid, he ordinarily only stopped off at his apartment once a week to pick up his mail, make sure no one had broken in, that kind of thing; but now he started dropping by on his lunch hour and/or after work on his way home to his lover, just in case. There was still no way he was going to use the number in his wallet she had given him to call. If she was really serious about wanting to "have some fun," serious enough to find his listing in the phone book and call him, *and* if things worked out so that when she did he actually turned out to be there, that was one thing: whatever happened would not be his fault entirely, plus nobody would ever know. On the other hand, damned if he was going to betray the fine, sensitive woman he lived with and loved by calling up some strange, probably deeply disturbed stranger from the Shah's Iran of all places whom he had met once briefly on a bus and asking her if she wanted to come over to play out a sordid fantasy of cheap, meaningless sex which never happened in real life anyway.

On Thursday morning, a week and a day after their meeting on the bus, he called the number she had given him from work. A young man answered, speaking in a heavy, fluidly accented voice—one of the awful brothers, probably. He stammered out her name as nearly as he could remember, and waited for practically anything to happen—pistol shots, shrieks and cries, dark guttural laughter—on the other end. The young man's voice released a stream of intense language in which he heard the sound of her name correctly pronounced. Had he gotten her in trouble, was the brother angry, what kind of strange scene was he getting into here?

"Yes. Who is this, pliss." It was her on the phone, speaking in a low suspicious voice.

He gave his name. "You remember me?" he asked.

"Yes," she said

In the intolerably awful silence that followed his mind was like an empty, pitilessly floodlit stage. "Are you having a good time?" he said at last, idiotically.

"Yes," she said. "Very nice."

"How much longer are you staying?"

"I stay here until Sunday, I think."

Another pause. She was not going to suggest anything. For that matter, under the circumstances she probably couldn't. The brothers would be standing right over her in the kitchen. He was sure it was the kitchen; he could see the Armstrong tile on the floor, the smudged yellow walls, could smell the layered, half-repugnant cooking smells, sense the brothers' lean grizzled faces and sharp close eyes. He could feel how, finally, it was all up to him.

"Are you still interested in getting together sometime? I mean, if you're not too busy between now and then?"

"Wait, pliss," she said. Then, much more distantly, he heard her talking in her language to one of the men in the room, one of her brothers: only what if they weren't? Or, for that matter, if they were anyway, but this was all part of some kind of strange Iranian plan to trap the American, him, in his apartment, knock him over the head? One of the dark grizzled men, her brothers, would rush out from behind the bedroom curtains, bash his skull in over her, she would roll out laughing, they would take everything and how would he ever explain it to his lover, the cops, the folks at work?

"Tomorrow morning." She was back on the phone, speaking English. "Eleven o'clock in the morning is a good time."

"I have to work." He heard the hardness in his voice, but damned if he was going to suggest a night and fall even further into their hands, and have to figure out some excuse to tell his lover. "I can't take off then," he said. "Look, maybe this is just going to be too difficult, you know?"

"Saturday morning," she said.

"Okay," he said. "What time?"

"Eleven o'clock. Do not come here. Come to corner of—" and she gave him two street names he'd never heard of. "I will be standing there."

Friday night he took his lover out to dinner and a movie and a classy bar for drinks. By the time they got back to her place it was two in the morning and they were both drunk, but he still forced his body through the ritual. They made sodden love until somewhere around 3:30, then collapsed. When he woke up after ten the next morning, the desired effect had been achieved. He was sick and tired all over. He could not imagine even talking with this wacked-out Iranian much less going to bed with her or anyone else.

"Honey," he called out towards the bathroom, where she was. "Listen, honey, I'm just going to throw my stuff on and go over to the apartment to do a few things, I'll be right back."

"That's the way it is," his father said: "For a man the urge is stronger. Which doesn't mean you shouldn't do whatever you can to keep it in your pants, or feel like you can just poke it anywhere you want, figuring the girl has got to keep you in line. But if you do go around with the wrong kind and find one that's just as happy if you do it as if you don't, then you got trouble. Next thing you're married with a kid and a job at the plant. Thirty seconds of ecstasy, a lifetime of misery. And I'd hate to see you ruin your life over some woman. You hear what I'm telling you, son?"

"Yes sir," he said; and from then on wondered, when he saw them, looked at them, what was going on in their minds, what reasons they could possibly have for wanting to do it with him. Could there be one, this one right here behind the counter or walking past him down the street, just one who really just wanted to do it like in the magazines, have some fast hard screaming sex just for itself? What if they were doing it right now, this one and him? After they got done, what would she want, what else would come up, what reasons appear?

"I want you to stop that," said a lover once to him.

"Stop what?" he said though already he knew, and had shifted his gaze.

"I want you to stop looking at other women when you're with me."

By now they were well past the intersection and the one he had been looking at, with the nice ass and legs. He had his eyes steady on the road straight ahead. "What do you mean?" he said with a smile. "There are lots of women out there. I don't look at some of them, I'll fall over them. Or run over them, which would be worse."

"Listen," she said, turning in the car seat so he had to look at her, had to see the two spots of red high on her cheeks. "If you want to go off with one of them, go ahead, I don't care. But don't sit beside me driving down the street staring around like a kid in a candy store. You know how that makes me feel?"

Yes, yes, he could see her point, he admitted it freely. And so soon learned to quicken, expand, and adjust his gaze so that when they were together he could dart his glance off to the side, shoot the look and ask the question, even sometimes receive a reply. Or at least catch a brief glimpse of them anyway, each of them moving past the corners of his eyes, what would this one, that one be like if he were with her and they were doing it right now wham wham thirty seconds of ecstasy, what would she want afterwards?

Two episodes, lessons in how you never know what's going on, can never tell what they want. The first starts years back, at the end of a long boozy party at a friends' house, when L, a blonde with hard good looks he has been eyeing all night comes up to him and says, "Can I leave with you?"

"Sure," he says. "Where you going?"

"It's up to you," she says. "But any motel will do fine."

So he took her to the local Holiday Inn and must have done all right, because the next morning, while she's getting dressed, she tells him in the same deadpan way she's married but her husband's away on a job for a month or so, and does he want to get together again?

So for the next three weeks or so, working around his schedule (she had no job, no kids, all the time in the world), they got together after work a couple times a week and on weekends. Pretty soon it was straight routine—walk in the door, put a record on, take off your clothes, get on the bed—and they got to be pretty good together, doing it hard and serious without a shred of fake intimacy or confessionals or declarations before or after, just the thing itself, zip zap, and she went home. But then—and this is the funny part, the part he thinks about—then in the last week before her husband's back, they start doing things differently. A few nights, they go out to dinner, before or after. They start using endearments, honey, darling, love, while doing it. On the last afternoon before the husband's back he even takes off work, picks her up at her house and drives out to the seashore where they walk barefoot hand-in-hand along the crashing surf then sit wrapped around each other, watching the orange sun go down.

"It's going to be hard," he says. "I'm going to miss you, love."

"I'm not sure what I'm going to do without you," she says. "How I'm going to last. Maybe I won't. Maybe I'll have to call you up and have you come for me."

"I'll be waiting," he says. "I'll be there."

The thing is, they both know damn well none of this is going to happen. They don't even want it to happen, neither one of them. But they go ahead and say it anyhow, himself and this tough blonde who must be going through this whole thing for at least the fiftieth time. Of course they never saw each other again, he never heard from her or tried to reach her. But it's like there was this ritual they had to go through; that's the funny thing.

And then, on the other hand, there's T, whom he met at another friend's place a few years later, at a time when a woman he really loved had just broken off with him and he was really hurting, alone and in pain. He had stopped off at his old friend's place on his way back across the country to see his folks at Christmastime, had arrived to find an old college friend of his friend's wife already there. T was quiet, small and slim, well-built with wide blue eyes and flowing chestnut hair down to her waist; she practiced vegetarianism and transcendental meditation, was concerned with non-violence and the Eastern non-materialist way to knowledge, happiness and truth, and she stayed up to tell him about it long after their old friends had retired, until he finally saw the light and began to take off her clothes. From then on, every morning and night of the next three days they engaged in the same wordless coupling, during which she lay almost completely motionless beneath him with the same vague otherworldly smile on her face, which he imagined was meant to seem sublime and transcendental, though it really looked a lot more like the soft-focus pleasure on the faces of the West-Coast types in skinmags (Good sex is like backhandsprings) as far as he was concerned. Still, even so, it felt good—all the more so since his girlfriend had just cut things off—and he felt lucky to have met her so casually and coincidentally, and grateful for her easy, natural solicitude, for doing it with him so sweetly and easily right up until the morning they all took him out to the airport where he waved goodbye and left her standing at the gate alongside his old friends.

Then, months later, he got this letter from her. This first one was like the way she talked, full of stuff about working things through and finding the center along with some details on her job and the weather. The second, which he got about a week later, was more or less the same, though this one ended with the suggestion that he call or write back and stay in touch. The third, two weeks later, was a five-page denunciation, written front and back in a nearly indecipherable scrawl. He was a a jerk, a pig, a fungus, the epitome of the Western World in its compulsion to use up and destroy and move on. Then, after that one, no more.

Very different women, L and T. Very different times. But still you can see the point: the differences just make it stand out all the more. When you come right down to it, there isn't a one of them in real life that really wants it just for itself, no matter what the skinmags say, no matter what you'd like to believe yourself sometimes.

A cold gusty morning, with the sky spitting hard frozen pellets. He drove carefully over fresh patches of ice on the strange streets; the address she had given him over the phone was in a new subdivision of ugly tract homes.

Now that he had given in, now that he was really going through with this, the surprising thing was that he felt neither much excitement nor much fear. Whatever happened, happened. He was that far off limits now.

At the designated corner was a short figure wrapped in a blue nylon parka, walking briskly back and forth across the street. He stopped the car. The figure spotted it and came over. It seemed to be her, peering out from under her furry hood. He made no signal to her, no move to open the door on her side. When she got in anyway, even then it took him a second more to actually recognize her, and not just because her face was not altogether as he had remembered: it was more like the bus had never happened, they had never met before.

"You did not call me," she said. "You did not want to see me again."

He put the car in gear and got moving. "That's not true," he said. "I called you eventually. How come you had me pick you up out here instead of at your house?"

She lowered her head and smiled the same coy smile she had on the bus; now he remembered it all. "I tried your house sometimes," she said. "You were not there. Were you with your girlfriend?"

"Yes," he said.

Her smile disappeared, her plump features pulled into a pout. "You do not like me," she said.

For a moment he thought of not answering; of letting the silence hang until she started yelling, telling him what an asshole he was, making him turn around and take her back. But finally he spoke instead. "Aw, come on. I like you. Why the hell do you think I called you if I didn't?"

After all, he was thinking, you're in this far—as her face broke into a grin, a giggle, and she wriggled over from her seat and slid her tongue into his ear.

It was freezing inside at his place. Since moving in with his lover, he had only kept the heat on enough to keep the pipes from freezing. But in the doorway she let her parka drop on the floor.

"Take your coat off too, now," she said. "Come give me a hug."

He did. She had a thin shiny stretch top on over tight jeans. He could feel her pressing against his chest and down there below, hear her soft laughter, feel the trembling of hands along her back. Do you really want to do this, is this what you really want? "Where is your bedroom?" she said, and pulled away laughing. "Let's go there now." And when they got there, kicked off her boots, peeled off her top and bra, lay down flat on her back. "Come and get on top of me."

He did. It felt like nothing. He was too cold and she was squirming under him, unbuttoning his shirt. "Do you have some rubbers here?" she said.

He was nowhere near ready. This was a big, grotesque mistake.

He pushed himself up off her. A miscue: she began to unbutton her jeans.

"Listen, now listen to me, please," he said. "I don't think we ought to be doing this. I think I ought to take you back."

"Oh," she said, wiggling and frowning underneath him. "It is true you do not like me."

"No it's not!"

"Good," she said, "come here," and buckled his arms so that he toppled back on her again.

For some time it went on like this, with her squirming and moaning, reaching for him and rolling her eyes, and him protesting, trying and failing to get up, wishing simply to be back in his regular life with his lover again, feeling more and more like a fool with ice-block hands and not the slightest hint of an erection. At one point he even tried to break out of it by rolling to one side, flopping an arm across her bare waist—why the hell wasn't *she* cold?—and trying to have an actual conversation with her, the assumption being that maybe if they could just talk together, share a few of their experiences like ordinary human beings, he could eventually get her to put her clothes on and sit up, if only because of the cold, and move from that point to getting her the hell out of here. He thought of asking her more about her brothers and her stay with them but that seemed wrong, they still frightened him and besides what if she just started blabbering again about how all they wanted was to have sex with her? It would have to be something more distant, more neutral. What else was it she had talked about back on the bus?

"Is Savak," he said, "the Shah's secret police—are they as bad as people say?"

Her eyes widened; she became very still. "Why do you ask this?" she said.

"Oh, I don't know," he said. "Just interested, is all."

She rolled on her side too, and peered flatly at his face. It looked like his tactic was working. He smiled back at her, an amiable, encouraging smile.

And she dropped back laughing again. "You are so funny," she said. "You are just being silly with me. Come here, put your hand here."

From then on, it just made matters worse. While he continued his ridiculous fumblings, pushing away and falling back down again, pecking obligatory kisses on her throat and face and twisting his crotch out of the way of her hands, she accompanied her own grotesque sighs and wriggles with a running monologue like the one on the bus, only much weirder now. Savak cuts up your tongue, puts wires on your breasts and down below there too and in your teeth, and puts electric shocks to you, Savak is everywhere and can do anything, put out your eye with sticks, shoot you in the daytime right here in America in front of very many people on the street, until he realized what was going on was she was doing this because she thought he had invited her to, thought he needed it to get turned on, horror stories for Christ's sake interrupted only by her horrible fake moans and pants and sighs and Come here now, come here.

That, when he figured it out, was the last straw. A rush of blood came to his head; he sat all the way up.

"That's enough," he said. "Really now, I don't want to do this." He turned away, slid to the edge of the cold bed and began to button his shirt: "I think you should go back now," he said.

He kept his back turned for a while, looking down at the floor. When he stood and turned around, she had her bra and top and boots back on, and was standing across the bed from him with a stoney expression on her fat brown face.

"All right," he said, "let's go."

In the front room they put on their coats. Already he was feeling better. Ten more minutes in the car and that would be that. He could go back to his lover with a clear conscience, having done the right thing. All he had to do now was take the few steps to the door where she was standing frowning like she hated his ass as much as he had hated hers a few minutes back; open the door; walk out.

So he walked to the door. Put his hand on the doorknob. Turned his head to look once more at her sad angry face. This was it, it was over.

He felt like he ought to say something anyway. After all, it wasn't really like it was all her fault. She had just thought here they had a chance to do it, get together and have some fun with no way they would ever see each other again, nothing serious or complicated, just the thing itself the way you always think you'd love to have it, as close to one of those fake letters as you could ever get, probably. He owed it to her to say something, for god's sake. He had been the one who turned it down, after all.

She had her parka zipped only partway up. She was less than a step away. This was it. He put his hand inside the coat, under her top, and drew her against him.

"Hey," he said, "I'm sorry," as she started to laugh, as she pushed herself against him down there where for the first time he was ready to go.

On the way back into the bedroom with this wonderful, terrific excitement, laughing together with her, he even remembered that yes, he did even have a Trojan, gotten god knows when, too far back to remember. Was it still there? Stepping out of his clothes in a sick, shivering blur—she was stripped already, on the bed giggling, stretched out lolling for him like a dream—he moved to the dresser, opened the drawer, scrabbled down through the socks and handkerchiefs. God, there it was. This is it, here we go.

"Come on, sweetie," she called from the bed as he slipped it on. "Let's go," she said as he got on. "You love me now. Do it to me like the big Savak man."

Who had a big long one who could do it to her many times over and over, she told him in between her moans and pants and sighs. Then about the Russian sailor, very big, very strong. About the big American black man. She ran through the stories in between her squeals and cries the whole time he was doing it to her. He tried not to listen, shut out the sound, just keep on doing it, pushing it like it was going on in total silence with the sound off, just the thing itself without these ridiculous stories which she must have thought he liked and wanted with her impossibly weird mind. But he could never quite shut it off, make it go away; just the same old thing over and over, until the best thing to do was get it over with, finish it off fast, which was what he finally did.

She gave a last squeal, grinned and laughed: "You like that, huh?" She was out from under him already, on her feet and getting dressed.

He got up too, more slowly. He went into the bathroom, peeled off the rubber, threw it into the trash. That was that. "You take me back now, okay?" she called.

In another half hour he was back at his lover's, getting ready to go on a grocery run with her. He felt shitty lying, telling her the pipes had frozen at his place, he had to clean up, that was what took him so long. He felt even more depressed the next day when it really hit him just how grotesque, sordid and ridiculous it was. It took a few months for him to get over it, stop feeling quite so bad. Still, eventually he was able to use it the way he had wanted it to be at the time, with the Iranian pleading for it, twisting around and moaning and gasping with no stories attached. Though of course right afterwards he would feel ashamed again and remember for real and wonder what the hell must have happened to her in real life, the same way he did with all the rest of them. Though certainly she had been crazier than most.

His childhood, occupation, a physical description, a name—this part of his life exists alongside and beyond all those other facets, playing over and behind them like continuous background music on a tape. A tape always going behind his "real life" as citizen, worker, family member. A tape which says the same thing, plays the same music over and over again, which he hears whether he stops to listen to it or not.

Still, the tape was not always there; or at least was not always playing. And I wish I could go back to that moment when the excitement he wanted located itself only in those words in the dictionary—though even there not "naturally," of course—and start from that point to piece together the story, such as it is, of how he learned to read and use the magazines, learned to make up similar images and stories for himself, how and when he first began to act on them. The problem is how to put it together, and how to weight each incident: the talk between himself and other boys and men, heard, overheard, and guessed at; the peeks at other skinmags and paperbacks and certain library books; the hidden and overt messages of school and family; the ads and movies and dates, and all the other stuff that comes together in the tape.

Such a story is beyond me, if only because I can neither make it up nor use any more of my life and the lives of others I know than I already have. But I can give you another metaphor for what it would be like if I could write it: for how it would move, what it would show. It would be like the record, the physical record, of a series of cuts in the same spot. Some of them the slightest, barely perceptible scratches; some little nicks; some quick sharp slices; others, a few, deep gouges of the knife, creating and keeping open the same wound, the same raw incurable sore whose pain is always with him and whose smarting he has even grown to enjoy enough that he now keeps his own sore open, he can even, by now, cut himself.

And he knows now how to read a skin magazine. First, you do the letters to the Forum or Advisor, whatever they call the section of supposedly true first-person narratives of various experiences of doing it in various ways with various people from strangers to friends to fiancées, Laurie and Valerie and Susan and Nancy and the hitchhiker by the side of the road and the lab partner at college, the cb freak and the seafood lady and the nylon stocking fetishist, the one who wants to do it with two at a time, one black and one white man or her best friend Marge, etc., etc. Read them over quickly, looking for the right stories and the right passages, the most effective combinations and scenarios for you. Then, also rapidly, flip through the pictures farther in. Note the ones with the right sizes and angles, positions and decors. Then go back to the right words and stories from the letters in Step 1. Then back to the pictures from Step 2. Back and forth, back and forth. If you get stuck and it isn't working, either go back to 1 and 2 again, look again at all the letters, through the photographs, make a few other choices and go from there; and/or think of someone you have actually been with, in the way that I have previously described. Listen to the tape. Feel your sore. You'll get there eventually.

"You know," R says more or less out of nowhere, "I've thought a lot about what happened back then with us. I was actually upset about it for a while. You were pretty shitty to me back then, don't you think?"

It is years later, a long time since he saw her last. He is in one city, R in another, thousands of miles apart. But ever since they dispersed after graduation she has kept in touch with him through Christmas cards, a note on his birthday, a phone call once every six months or so. Over the phone she tells of her struggles in graduate school and with men, her two abortions, her dissertation, her funds and scholarships and odd jobs and drinking habits and changes in cigarette brands; in the easy, funny patterns of their old conversations, she keeps him filled in. Though when she asks what his life is like he answers with less, avoiding in particular any mention of past or present lovers—it never seems right somehow—he is always just as glad to joke with her as ever, to listen to that same hard hoarse laugh followed by the newest account of her life—delivered, as he pictures it, with a cigarette perpetually in her nervous hands or mouth, breathing her short spumes of smoke into the mouthpiece of the phone.

Yet now, in the middle of this call she has jarred him out of this easy, affectionate routine. He cannot even recall what she was saying a minute ago, just before this— something about some new woman friend of hers?—or how she got them to this moment, so sudden and bewildering is his panic. Panic, yes, as if the familiar snug walls and soft carpet of his present apartment had suddenly turned into the deck of a tossing boat: panic, and the flood of exact, unretouched reminiscences rising up in front of him.

All the times and places they had done it, that winter and spring of senior year—back in his dorm room, her apartment in her bed and on the Navajo rug, in the shower, outside in a little patch of woods, once even in a classroom building late at night, up in the lab where she worked. Wherever they were, whatever the hour, his time with R was always short. He had still not broken up with his girlfriend who knew nothing about what was going on with him and R, who was always coming over later, after classes or rehearsals to stay with him at the dorm, since now staying over with her in her apartment, with R camped in the living room out front, was unimaginable given the way things stood. And yet alone with R, knowing how little time there was, he still could never bring himself to lunge at her, fall into her, wrap her in an embrace when she appeared in his doorway, the second after their first step into the woods. He always had to wait until the last possible moment, joking and talking with her about classes, careers, the girlfriend, the screwed-up parents, the weather, practically anything at all until they had turned around and come back far enough to see the road again, twenty feet or so off past the trees, until she was actually putting her coat back on in his doorway and the chance was almost past. Half the time they would be in the middle of saying goodbye before he would finally make his move, push himself against her, kiss her face and neck, lift out the tucked ends of her blouse. Then always the rest was silent and fast, though he had to undress her completely. She made almost no move to help herself, just lay there breathing hard and staring at his smiling face with wide still eyes as he uncovered her, moved on her, into her, feeling her breasts which always felt so good, so big, more or less exactly the way he wanted them, and trying not to think about the girlfriend coming over soon, any minute now, possibly finding them here, catching them at it just like this with his hands on R's big breasts moving inside her with her wide eyes still on his face and her rough breath, holding and moving just like this, trying not to think but thinking anyway, to slow down but pushing too hard and fast, squeezing and pushing below those still eyes with her coming over any minute, so good that then before you knew it it was over, he was done in five minutes, maybe less. For a few seconds afterwards, they lay quietly; then rolled apart and started cracking jokes again. In another few minutes R got up to dress and leave. And that was the way it always was.

Actually even at the time he had felt ashamed of himself. Guilty for cheating on his poor helpless girlfriend (who'd driven him to it, but still); guilty too for always getting so excited, cutting it so short. Even back then he knew it took girls longer, you had to hold yourself in. And knowing it that much better now, thanks to the other women he has been with since, makes him feel that much worse yet. But the worst of what he knows as he stands in the kitchen trying to think of what to say right now, is this: that he has been waiting for this phone call, these lines from her, for years.

So now it has happened, you have to answer. Through the dead silence comes the hum of the refrigerator, soft sighs of the late night traffic outside. What do you say, shit-ass?

"You're right," he says. "I've thought a lot about it too," he says. "I feel guilty about it," he says. "I've thought of writing you," he says. "Once or twice I've thought of even trying to say something about it over the phone when we're talking like this," he says.

"I guess," he says.

"I just didn't know," he says.

"How," he says.

"Well," says R—and her voice is softened, thousands of miles away—"well, it's over now. I mean, we're past that now, I know. I guess I felt I had to say something about it, anyway."

"Yes," he says, "yes well I'm really glad you did." And in that moment of purgation and relief—for her tone seemed to contain its own hint of guilt too now, along with its forgiveness, almost as though they really were back together—for the first time since the phone call started his hand beneath the bathrobe unclenches its grip on his shriveled little penis down there.

Already by the time he got home he had made up his mind not to use the bedroom. For one reason or another, time pressure or laziness or whatever, he didn't feel like taking off his clothes and lying down in bed. Instead he drew the skinmag out of its brown bag in the kitchen, threw the bag in the garbage can under the sink, placed the magazine on the counter and began.

It seemed as though every time now, whenever he looked there were fewer and fewer letters, before you knew it they were done. As usual, too, half of them were so stilted, so ridiculously exaggerated or so far from the kinds of things he liked as to be unusable. But the first one was all right, about this woman the guy met when he was a student, and another one about this Arab woman this guy met while he was in the service who liked to do it everywhere, get it everywhere, all the time.

So when he got to the pictures he was well under way, he had his coat off on the chair and his pants unzipped and pushed down and his hand down there where it was already good and hard. The first set of pictures, two woman on a sailboat, lesbians, didn't do much for him. Neither did this month's feature who had big heavy breasts all right but was supposed to be a cowgirl from Texas or something, lolling on hides, swinging ropes, grinning way too much with full white teeth in her tanned happy healthy face. He considered going back to the letters but went ahead: the third one was better, best of all even though her breasts were not real big, the way she pushed them up and petted them was good, she looked like she liked it in the shots of her leaning all greasy with sweat or oil with legs spread back against the orange wall, on the bed with her tongue out and her nice ass up in the air asking for it, begging for it he could have finished it off right there but in spite of the time—a glance at the clock over the sink, 4:45—he turned back to the letters again, looking for something, some passage he remembered, not exactly what it said or just what was going on but where was it now? All the letters seemed stupid, same words, same actions over and over again. The one with the Arab wasn't it, the one with the woman at the party wasn't it, they all did the same things with the same words and he was running out of time, looking over his shoulder at the clock every two seconds now, 4:48, 4:50, trying to find that other one, the one about the student, by the student, where was that? He was really almost out of time, turn back to the blonde, look at her shoving out those tits ready to go, asking for it put it in with her tongue yeah baby jesus yeah *up in.*

He kept it off the magazine, just barely. The paper towel dispenser was within reach on his right. He tore one off to wipe his hand with, another two for the counter and floor.

The paper towels went into the toilet, got flushed away. He zipped and belted his pants and took the magazine into the living room. The article on the secret files of the C.I.A. began on page 41. By a little after five, when his wife got home and crossed the room to kiss him hello, he was reading about dirty tricks in Nicaragua over the past eight years.

"What are you doing with that thing?" she said when she saw it. "Did you actually buy one of those?"

"Hey," he said smiling into her half-ironic scowl, "hey, they got a big article in here on the secret files of the C.I.A."

"Sure they do," said his wife, turning away. "Plus a bunch of other fun things."

"Come on," he said. "Give me a break, will you? You know I'm interested in this stuff."

Across the room, by the closet, her face stayed skeptical but softened. "So how is it?" she said.

"I'm not done with it yet, I got it on the way home so I just started reading it just now," he said, watching her with half an eye, his lovely wife—really, she was—hanging up her coat, putting it away in the closet. He stayed quite still in the chair while she went first into the bathroom, then into the kitchen. There was nothing there for her to see or find. He had left no traces, he was sure. In a moment she came back with a glass of something, sat down on the couch, turned on the tv news with nothing special on her face that he could see.

He looked down at his lap and saw he must have closed the magazine when she first came in. When he spread it open again now, wouldn't you know, there was the one he had used, the shot of her there in the sauna or whatever it was, acting like she was all excited, like she was staring him right in the face. It made him sigh and shake his head. How stupid. What a fantasy. He even thought of saying something, maybe even showing her. But there she was, his sweet wonderful smart sensitive wife sitting there on the couch sipping her drink and watching the news, why show her any of this stupid stuff anyway? After you told her you got it for the piece on the C.I.A.?

Instead he found his place, picked up again and read through the rest of it, slapped the magazine down when he was through, and smiled back when the noise made her look over.

"It was okay," he said by way of answering the question in her eyes. "Honestly. It had some good stuff, it was actually pretty good."

THE ANGEL OF DAD

Max the Rad, galumphing home, saw his dead father strolling down the other side of the street. "Rad" here is short for Radical; Max was 35; his father, who'd died of an embolism eight years before, at the end of his fifties, looked connotatively not at all like his old living self, although the flushed face and heavy body were unmistakeable. In mortal life a rumpled figure in nondescript suits shiny with synthetic fiber and prolonged wear, he now appeared a virtual fop in grey wool slacks and blazer, white shirt open at the throat, limber walking stick (rattan, perhaps?) atwirl in his left hand. And the sly good nature of his glance across the street, amused assessment, droll tip of the head—none of this was in character, none at all.

Max the Rad nodded back, monkey see monkey do; his father smiled, walked on. Around Max, to his left and right on this tree-lined street of the smug college town where he lived, a woman flapped her elbows in a grey sweatsuit, a scrubbed squad of young Republican males ambled past fresh from their latest class in death-bound rationality, business or engineering; across the street, as an older couple in matching beige sweaters looked on, his father turned his face over his shoulder and winked back.

"Jesus," exclaimed Max the Rad under his breath, the sound no more than part of the jolt his whole self had just received; and, as instinctively, turned and walked away. Through the first bleak and then bleaker seventies into this decade's new ice age he has had to learn how to bracket anomalies, small miracles of political will, squeaks of collective transcendence, without either wholly discounting them or getting too charged up. The result was a cautious skepticism made of equal parts of plodding on and tune-in-later, muted millenarianism and despair—which attitude could, with some stretching, cover even the sight of one's dead father heading south on Emerson Street.

So Max turned his attention elsewhere, off over his head to the yellow leaves stirring in the breeze pulled off the ocean and over the coastal range each evening of late summer, early fall, to bank down the heat of these baked plains. *It's okay,* thought Max the Rad to the cuticle of moon at the sky's edge, *Wait and see;* and without pausing for a reply, bent his dogged long steps home.

*   *   *

This happened on a Tuesday night, the night of the Women's Study Group, as he was reminded mid-meal by Angela. "Out by seven," she said, leaning forward, resting her arms on the table. "Don't forget."

Her face was hard, her dark brows knit, conveying the same no-nonsense she could dish out at the end of any meeting, when it came time to divvy up the tasks. Once, just after hitting town, Max had found her humorless and high-handed when they'd first met inside a new group opposed to CIA recruiting on campus. Since that time, five years ago now, it had been god knows what all—doomed community coalitions, public employee strike support groups, committees against cutbacks and racism, for jobs and reproductive rights, you name it and Angela was there doing the work, making things go. Since so was Max, at a certain point a few years later it only made sense for them to link up as housemates with Carol and Jill, two other members of La Causa and her friends, in this funky frame house at the student ghetto's dilapidated edge. By that time, of course, he had long since come to understand her brusqueness as a function of an intense focus on the long and short run both, a desire to make (finally) a revolution and to wrap the business up fast before it drove you out of your mind. Yet just now, sitting down to eat, looking forward to telling them all about seeing (or hallucinating) Dad, having a light, caring laugh and letting it go, that same abruptness felt like a slap.

Max took a spoon of glop—cheese-beans, it was called—washed it down with a glug of milk. No good; the rage kept wriggling around, a hot hunched shape low in his chest. Slowly he raised his eyes to his three house-mates, dark poised Angela looking back wide-eyed, waiting for his answer, Jill and Carol dipping spoons to and from their bowls, detached as cats. Problem was, everyone still remembered the night six months ago when he barged into the living room having clean forgotten, thus interrupting the group at a particularly sensitive moment, in the midst of their sharing all their stories of sex with men ever endured against their wills. His grin slowly fading in the face of their appalled collective outrage, lesbian separatists Mickey and Jody from the north of town standing stiffly, brushing past him, walking out in protest—a bad scene for all concerned, which no one wanted again. *Macho shit,* he was thinking even now, stroking milk from his moustache, *just the very kind of thing* but came out with it anyway, knowing someone at their next house meeting would call him on his sulking and justly so. "I know that, Angela," he said. "I'll be out of here on time, dear ladies, never fear."

To his surprise Angela herself said nothing. It was Jill who put down her spoon and took over instead. "Seems to me," she said, softly, "like I'm hearing some hostility there, Max. Want to talk about it some?"

"No," he said, picking his own bowl back up. "Thanks anyway, but no."

"It's okay then?" said Carol, off to his right. "You feel all right about it then?"

Another swallow of milk. Still the anger, but now blended with some guilt. "I feel all right. Thanks for asking. I feel fine."

He finished the meal quickly, and went up to his room for his coat. By the time he came back down they were done too. So he helped Carol pick up while Angela washed and chef du jour Jill went off upstairs, probably to watch her TV. "I'm looking at the Community Calendar," Angela announced as if not a second had passed since the conversation had broken off, and proceeded to read from the pink chart drawn up and distributed monthly by the local DSA folks, posted on the corkboard over the sink. "You can go to the County Commission meeting at the Law Enforcement Building at 7:30. Or to Christians for Peace at the Methodists at 8 o'clock."

She put a glass in the drainboard, wiped her hands on her khakis, turned around and smiled at him her dry humorous smile. "Hot dog," he said, trying to respond in kind. "Developers or warm hearts." But he was sure they could both hear the edge still in his voice; he could watch the good will wither, their faces closing down. Carol looked over at Angela; Angela shrugged; Max looked down at the frayed collar of his denim jacket, white with age. "Well then," he said, "have a good meeting. I'm off to the Roost."

And strode down the hall as fast as possible without running, back outside into the sunlight's glaring finale for the day, skid of swallows, clamor of finches hopping in the shrubs up against the dingy house. Destination set, bootheels chunking the pavement; Max the Rad, six feet tall, ginger hair flowing over his collar, marching off straight ahead. East on 1st, past Emerson, Hawthorne,

Dana, Irving, etc.—there was always some such system in these college towns. For almost a year in the mid-70s, back when environmental seemed the only action around, he had lived in a Northern California town where the north-south streets were hardwoods, east and west explorers, trappers, big-name knaves and brigands from a century ago. Another place, this one in Nebraska, simply lettered east-west and gave north-south to former Secretaries of State. Blaine and H, Dulles and A, Crockett and Cherry, Huntingdon and Oak. Shoe clerk, CETA trainee, dishwasher, nurse's aide. And the Revolution still ain't happened yet.

"Exactly," said his father. "So what've you got to show?"

As if he had simply stolen up, reached your side, and matched his step to yours. All of which (how natural it seemed) being what made it so bizarre; that and the note of unwonted geniality in the old man's voice, which Max sought in vain to match. "I could ask the same of you," he calmly murmured, or tried to.

"So go ahead and ask," said his father, unruffled, patting his thick sides. "I'm here, aren't I?"

"So'm I," said Max. "Is that what we're talking about, degrees of substance on the reality scale? I thought you meant things like washers, driers, automobiles."

Yet his father failed again to rise to the bait; he shrugged, looked off pensively, shook his head. "There's a middle level," he said. "A connection. You call that a job you got, sitting on a stool in a hippie bookstore? Where you live, is that a home? Anybody care here if you fall over dead? Would you like me to go on?"

The quite obvious political objections to be raised here fluttered away. Instead Max stared at the merry brown eyes under the raised brows, violet shreds of broken capillaries splayed across cheeks and nose. He himself was gasping for air, mind snapping like a windowshade released in cartoons. He forced himself to look away and found they were already past Bryant, nearly downtown, moving through a fringe area of gas stations, Burger and Pizza Huts, suck-it-up desert belt of interchangeable parts backlit by twilight's last glare. He thought of the beer waiting for him at the Roost, how good it would taste in a moment, and, bolstered by this thought, began his reply.

"I believe," he said, "a brief review is in order. We can start by agreeing you did indeed work your butt off. And that you did so at least partly to give us a good life. And since this made you unhappy much of the time, you made other people miserable at work, came back to your nice home in the suburbs miserable, and made us miserable too. Let me remind you that my mother your wife had no fun for years at a stretch cooped up in a tract house with us, the TV, and an infinitely refillable scrip for Elavil. And now you come back wanting to talk ontological security? Don't make me laugh."

But Max's father was not laughing; just the opposite. The brown eyes whose gaze in real life had always been opaque now shown with clear trembling tears, forcing the realization that it was he, Max the Rad, who was yelling, waving his arms, being a crud. Then, to his own further astonishment, he was stretching out his arms, drawing his father into something like an embrace.

Beneath his hands, through the layers of clothing, he could feel his father's body shudder regularly as if hiccuping, sense the obdurate bones afloat in his dead flesh. With a twinge of shame he realized just how glad he was the street lay as still as a pond. Maybe now, with no one else around, was the time to ask questions, get some information: how the old man got here anyway, ins and outs of life after death, whether this appearance was a special or the first of a series. On the other hand, that seemed like so much male chitchat on stats and techniques, right down there with sports and cars. What you really want to know is what happens next.

No sooner asked than answered: already, with a fresh dapper smile, his father was pulling away from Max's hold. "What you were wondering there a minute ago," he said, brushing his front smooth, "think of it like graduate school. You finish up, you graduate, in your particular case you get so hot to change the world you just drop out, whatever—you think that means you have to stop learning too? Same with dying. Or put it another way—you stop growing you're already dead. It's the truth of the capitalist world."

And with that, stepped jauntily back the way they came, leaving Max staring after with the evening breeze a chill gale force against his stricken face, scarecrow body, bereft self. "Dad!" he cried out. "Dad! Dad!"

A block away, no more than that, beneath a used-car lot sign blinking off and on, he waggled his hand. "See you later, boy," Max's father was calling. "Take care."

*   *   *

Though the Roost was no more than another dank woody bar of students, hippies, misfits and the slightly crazed, there were at least other people, people he knew, who knew him, sitting around the scarred wooden tables smoking cigarettes, drinking beer, talking whenever they could pry their eyes away from the TV over the bar. For a while he spoke with silver-toothed Soni in her bedraggled peasant blouse; later, boney Ryland, blinking watery blue eyes; later still, dark moonfaced Eva, chainsmoking as always, booming out her harsh clanging laugh. Those three and then a few others, people he had worked with, seen at demonstrations, tried to organize. It was hard not to recall this as they talked, having pretty much the same conversation every time. How's it going, what're you up to these days; then, a few minutes later, You still living over on 14th, how's that working out, still at the bookstore too? Not a word about politics past or future, local or world; nor did Max display any interest in their exciting personal lives. It got to be a kind of stalemate, he would just sit there at whoever's table, let the conversation drop, watch their eyes drift back to the TV until they figured out that was what you were doing, watching them, at which point they generally left you alone to rummage through your own movies from long ago. Working in McMinnville with the migrants, preaching La Raza, talking union at the nail factory in Culver until you were canned, proletarianizing yourself but still taking acid, back when any minute it could still come down, how many years ago? And still there over the bar after all was Johnny Carson with his first guest the Lovely So-and-So, the foul cackle of Ed McMahon.

117

At some point Max the Rad looked around him at the other tables and chairs, recognized nary a soul, tried and failed to count the pitchers he'd consumed. It was time, he figured, to get on back.

So then, outside, he was making his way past a litter of storefronts and houses, beneath a chaos of stars. In his head a numb buzzing like a fluorescent light, his rangy body a carcass of wet wool. Under the light on his mind's floor were odd scraps of words he could pick up and put down as he pleased. *Pessimism of the intelligence, optimism of the will, el pueblo unido jamas será vincido, you lose til you win. It stands to reason,* he was thinking—only in his present state it was neither thought nor exactly what he meant—*the problems of three little people don't amount to a hill of beans . . .*

In his house—home?—the front room was empty, unlit except for the fishtank in one corner, the Agrolite in the other over Jill's small shelf of potted herbs. It would have been Angela, though, who before the meeting came in and picked up the place the way it looked now, like a goddamn leftie *House and Garden,* folding the afghan on the battered couch, piling the magazines and papers on the packing crate beside the armchair. Good old Angela, getting things done. Aspects of this her ordered world swam toward him as large heavy motes through which you have to chart a path upstairs to the place where you sleep, a.k.a. your room, across from Carol's and Jill's. Clothes fermenting on the floor, sheets and blankets twisted on the futon, bookshelves of paint cans and pine boards holding paperbacks whose every beat-up cover he can see without looking, whose titles he knows by heart. *The Whole World is Watching. The Wretched of the Earth.* The problems of three little, five little, million little. While out on the airstrip Bogie touches Ingrid Bergman's smooth warm face. And down the hall beyond the living room, past the staircase, a bright seam of light edges Angela's door.

"You seen the movie *Casablanca?*" he said, pronouncing with as much care as he could.

When he'd first knocked and walked in she'd looked up startled from the clothbound book she'd been writing in. Now she set down her pen and slid her chair back from the small walnut desk. She was wearing her own robe, he had seen it, her in it around the house a thousand times.

"It's after one, Max," she said. "I don't want to discuss movies now."

"Okay, sure," said Max. "Right. Fine." He did not feel at all drunk any more. Angela was shelving her journal in place atop the desk, amongst a short neat row of her canonical works, Simone de Beauvoir, Marge Piercy, etc. She was standing up, pushing her chair in, on her way to something else. Her expression remained severe but her cheeks were rosy. Long as they had known each other, after how many years and a kajillion meetings, it only struck him now, the effect of that sharpness together with that very nice skin.

So when she looked back over he tried to thoughtfully furrow his brow. "I'm feeling bad," he said.

"I'm not surprised," said Angela, smiling, folding her arms across her chest. "Tonight was not your finest hour. But I don't think anyone's permanently upset."

119

"It's not that," Max said. "Not just that, I mean. It's where that came from, why I did it." Yet now, even looking away from her scrutinizing eyes and smooth skin, down at the patterns of her rag-rug on the floor, he could not go on with his explanation, this new need had opened up so crazy strong and fast. "Angela," he said— astonished by the forcing of his gaze back up to hers— "could I just be with you tonight? Would that be okay?"

A whole lot of time seemed to pass. She stared at Max so hard, with such a steep frown, her look was like a glare. Could it be she was seeing him now as he had seen her? Was she trying to figure repercussions for the household, implications for their Bread and Roses group? Or trying to see in your face, through your own eyes, what you mean/feel/want? Finally she moved two steps forward with her expression basically unchanged, bare forearms extending straight out from the level of her waist.

"You should know I'm nervous," she said as her fingertips touched his elbows. "Not to say scared. Are we talking about really just sleeping together and that's all?"

She was holding him, he was holding her. It felt wonderful even if they were both shaking some, the way their bodies were just like that. "I'm not sure," he whispered dry-mouthed, eyes still shut. "It's been a long time for me too."

But already she was pulling away, leaving only a soft echo behind. "So what was that about *Casablanca*?" she said, tapping his butt. Then she was moving around the old iron-frame bed, yanking down the sheets. "How about if you go wash—you smell like a brewery—maybe get yourself a shave as well? Then when you come back you can get right in here and tell me all."

Which was no doubt how a part of her—a part of them both—must have wanted it to be. Only it did not happen like that. What happened instead, that night then three times more in the following week, was that he came back to her room from washing up and got into bed and they went at it staring at each other as if it were anger, that intense. Age and weight dropped away, even names; then afterwards, when he remembered that he ought to say something, start getting things clarified, sleep closed over him before he could think of word one. Next morning he would wake head jangling at first light, still entangled with Angela Patillo, no idea what it meant. While he tugged and slid himself loose she would sleep on, her lips parted open, making dreaming sighs of gentle protest so unlike her official waking self he was both moved and shocked as he threw on pants and shirt, grabbed his boots and went up to doze another hour or so on his mattress in his own room, dreaming light uneasy dreams. In the one he remembered most clearly afterwards, he was sitting across a table from her—a kitchen table, it seemed—and in response to some indication or request, raised his forearms from the table surface where they had been resting, and felt her terror and amazement with his own at the sight of the dark cool subsoil dotted with green liverwort along the white undersides, entrenched in his skin. Meanwhile, at the real kitchen table a real hour or so later, the four of them got through breakfast same as always, reading the paper, listening to the radio, mumbling to each other on the news and weather, this and that until it was time for Carol and Jill to go off to school, Angela to Community Services, Max his stool at the Rainbow Bookstore. Then as the week wore on he began to sense a problem. First it seemed as though she was having trouble looking at him when they met with the others around the table; then it became clear she was looking away. Finally, Thursday morning, after their most recent night, he brushed her side as they stood together at the stove—his oatmeal, her scrambled eggs—and felt her flinch, watched her face go hard and blank.

"What is it with you people," said his father, "you don't date any more? Why not take her out, spend a little money on her, have a good time?"

Though the bookstore was tiny, Max had been too engrossed in the new Murray Bookchin to have seen him come in. He simply looked up at the sound of the voice and there he was again, dead Dad across the counter, his cane neatly hooked over the wrist of his right hand, a French intensive gardening paperback in his left. For a second Max toyed with absurd possibilities, either going back to his own book and hoping he would leave, or something more drastic—shutting off the background tape of New Age sea and synthesizers, informing everyone, his father and, over by the Mysticism section, the brown-haired girl and her overalled friend, that the store was closed as of right now.

Instead, though, like a good boy, he shut his book and sought to calm his double-timing heart while composing his reply. No sense playing into the old man's hand, letting him get you all freaked out. "It's not like that," he said, with a patient smile. "I tried pulling anything like that, she'd eat me alive."

His father gave a little shrug and snort. "What'd be so bad about that?" Then quickly raised the hand with the cane. "All right, just kidding, just kidding."

They paused, both uneasy, Max still trying to keep down the—what?—*irritation* he felt unfolding inside him. As if, were he to consent to it, let it grow, it might blossom into something utterly different, something else. "What's with the cane?" he said finally, randomly, trying to keep the heat down off his face.

"The cane," said his father. "What's with the cane." Softly, musingly repeating it, the dumb question they both knew it was. "Just an affectation, I guess," he said. "All my life I wanted some kind of class."

"Is that right?" said Max. "I never knew that."

"Neither did I," said his father. "In those terms." He snapped the gardening book shut like a wallet, smacked it against his other palm. "Besides," he said, "we never talked, you know that. I yelled at you, you took off, I died."

Another pause. The brown-haired girl and her hulking friend nodded at them on their way out, Max and his father sent back identical vacant smiles, then lapsed into sad shyness again.

"So tell me about the girl," his father said finally. "Angela. What's she like?"

"Well—" Max tried honestly to think. "She's from Lawrence, Massachusetts, where they had the big famous strike in 1912. By the time her parents were grown the place was a wreck, all the industry was gone. She grew up in some of the first projects ever, living there with her folks, who were basically unemployed most of the time, and her brothers and sisters, and her Grandma, who was in on the actual strike, she found out later, but who wouldn't even—"

"Hey," said his father. "I'm not asking for credentials. I want to know what you think of her, who she is to you."

"That's what I'm trying to tell you," said Max. "She's political too, it's important to her too. I'm trying to tell you how and why that is."

His father shook his head. "Not interested," he said. "That is not what I'm here for."

It was like old times, almost. They could almost have been back in the tiled kitchen or out on the patio, Max could see himself, his young and confident self in jeans and the old Keep on Truckin' t-shirt, standing on the grotesque plastic lawn they'd put in sometime since he'd left for school, his crimson pudgy father in one of those white wrought-iron chairs yelling at him as he stood there hardly listening, easily living in the truth. All the advantages, our hard-earned money, just throw it down the drain. Only now he was no longer yelling. Now he just stood there waiting, dead.

"All right," said Max. "I don't know what she's like. We've worked together three, four years, we get along, we live together with a couple other people in this house. But I don't know what it means, our sleeping together. I don't know what she's like. And that does bother me, yes it does."

Like reciting a confession, a prepared statement, looking down at the worn all-weather carpeted floor. Like being old and heavy and a little kid again, all at once. When he looked back up his father had stepped over to the Handyperson section to reshelve the book. Dully, as depleted as if watching TV, Max watched the slender cane bow under his father's weight and snap straight again until the old man, half-turning, looked off and up as if sniffing the air.

"This stuff you got on here," he said. "How come it never changes?" He was smiling, albeit a smile mixed with rue, as he headed past the counter, register, and Max, moving for the door. "You used to tell us our music was boring. Now you listen to this?"

"Boss wants it on," Max said. "It's for sales. Don't accuse me of liking this stuff."

"Okay," said his father on his way out. "So what do you like?"

As an exit line, infuriating. Yet Max found himself ticking off his options long after the store door had tinkled shut. At the moment, for obvious reasons, anything Latin American was hot, from Peruvian flutes to demo sing-along; there was women's music, okay to like if you were non-patronizing; reggae or rap if it was non-sexist, selected New Wave. But the last music he had really liked, the last made for him . . . He had to admit it went back to the Stones. Stones and Beatles. Nasal snarling Dylan, too cool to live. Moby Grape, for Christ's sake. Phil Ochs before he lost it, the Doors before Morrison died. And the Airplane, of course. *Look what's happenin' out on the street . . .*

125

The next night, at the meeting of his Bread and Roses group, he was still flashing on it, feeling how far it was from there to here in Harry's apartment where they met week after week, month after month, trying to think of something possible that might matter, bigger than just holding tight, more effectual than nudging the other ragtag groups—anti-nuke, anti-interventionist, that was just about it—along. Partly given this impasse, partly because it was still late summer, not yet fall when things might once again pick up, the group was down to its hard core, Angela, Carol, Jill, Harry and Max himself, lounging on the stained and faded batik pillows on the floor. It was Harry talking now, Harry, Carol then Jill sharing announcements which were virtually zilch. To Max's left knelt Angela, frowning down at the bare wood. Carol announced running into Dale from the Freeze who was trying to put up a phone tree, did people want their numbers on too? Jill and Harry both said something, Harry took a piece of paper from his shirt pocket and wrote something down, Max looked away from Angela who would not return his gaze, and went back to Harry instead. What had Harry been into back then?—back somewhere in Michigan, Lansing or Ann Arbor, Max seemed to recall. These days Harry was nearly bald on top, with a little belly pushing his ragged jeans' waist, red eyes from staying up too long, too many days making the rounds with posters, fliers, exhortations after working nights as a janitor of the Tidee Town Laundromat. At this very moment, in fact, he was talking again, sad impeccable Harry, in the absence of other new business expounding his favorite themes concerning the old vexed question of how to make contact with the Real Working People of the town.

"Door-to-door canvassing," Harry was saying, stubby fingers poking stale air. "Find out what the workers want and need in their own words, then bring them together to go out and get it." What music would Harry like now? Max wondered, then realized what without looking he'd known all along. There was no stereo, no tapedeck, no records in this small dark studio. Only a transistor on the counter by the sink, and that most likely for the news. Nor had old Harry ever been known to have a lover. Nor did anyone know what old Harry's parents were like.

"What we need," Harry said in his flat fervent twang, "we gotta have a good survey instrument. And that means we can't, I mean we shouldn't, make it up ourselves." To his right Carol was listening, nodding encouragement, next to her Jill was practically asleep. When Max shut his own eyes he saw his dead father smile and shake his head. When he opened them again they were on Angela's bowed figure; and then for a sharp shocking instant he was with her, in her all opened up, but she still would not look back. There was no air moving in here, it was almost foul. The clock on the bookshelf said eight forty-five. The posters on the walls, Harry's single indulgence, matted framed and glassed at no small expense, said day-glo Viet Nam, khaki Wounded Knee, pastel Three Mile Island, black-and-white Greensboro massacre, blue and red and gold Nicaragua and El Salvador.

"We've got to avoid class bias at all costs. So the first step is to *find* some workers, *talk* to them, *ask* them—"

"Harry," Max said, "how bout if tonight we cut it a little short? I'm tired. I want to go home."

Harry stopped talking. At first his mouth stayed open, then it turned into a sneer. Everyone by now was sitting up straight. "Max, I think that's really bad process, interrupting like that," said Carol, off to his right.

"Really, Max," said Jill, wiping her long hair from her face. "I was really listening. I want to hear what Harry has to say."

All this time, with contemptuous indolence, Harry's small hands scratched his belly under the faded brown t-shirt. "Max the Rad," he said softly, sneer still on. "Max the big Rad. Where are your big ideas now?"

By now Angela was making no effort to conceal the fact that she was crying. Tears slid down her face and dropped to the streaked pillow, their landings audible in the awful silence. Then, swiftly, Max was standing, joints cracking, stepping over to her, kneeling down. He put his arms around her; she neither flinched nor relaxed; her skin was hot to the touch on her shoulders and arms.

"I don't have any big ideas, Harry," he heard himself say with astonishing ease. "Except the Revolution seems a long ways away. And spending my whole damn life trying to find it, crack it open, isn't making it for me any more."

He could have gone on, told them about his dead father, taken them too into his arms to hold and be held.

But Angela was tearing herself loose. Flustered, he made a soothing noise, then saw the fury on her face and let go instead. In another second she was standing stock-still in the doorway, turned back to the four of them, lips quivering, not as though crying but seeking the words to make a statement through the confusion on her face. Then, with Max behind her, she was out the door, tripping down the porch steps.

"Angela!" he called and, when she just went faster, broke into a lope. Within a block he had reached her, put his arm around her waist.

"Get your meathooks off me," she said, shaking it off. "I'm not your property."

"I know you're not," said Max.

She stopped and turned to face him, hands on hips, jaw set. The pupils in her eyes were flat black discs. "Sure you do," she said. "That's why you sneak in and out of my room, so nobody knows. Then, when I break down at a meeting, come on over and stroke down my hide. Hey," she said, "it's a great relationship. I understand it perfectly, and like it a whole lot."

"That's not who you are to me," Max said. "Not what I mean."

His voice so low it was almost a whisper, aching all along his limbs. They were stopped at the corner of 5th and Cooper. Angela's face darted up and down the street as if checking the traffic, though there was not a moving car in sight.

"I'll tell you what," she said, turning away again, her own voice choked and harsh. "When you do have it figured out, let me know. Until then, just stay the hell away."

Max the Rad watched her figure growing smaller, moving off under streetlights which had just winked on. When it was clear she would not turn around, would not beckon within any pool of light, he turned away too, heading randomly westward toward the better side of town. For a time he moved through census tracts of blue-lit boxes inside which pale faces floated across from their TVs. Then bent his steps southward, cutting across campus, past black windows of brick classroom buildings, students drifting to and from the computer center's bright humming hive. On Fraternity Row he paused on the sidewalk to gaze in upon a chugging contest, young smoothfaced managers-to-be stomping and chanting and swilling down beer. Somewhat later, brushing past other young blank faces glued to video gamescreens, pressing buttons to blow things up, he went up to the counter of a 7–11, squinting in the hard flat brightness of its lights, assailed by all the goods on their shelves. On the sidewalk outside with his Monster Cookie he was approached by a three-coed squadlette in designer jeans with Walkmans clamped to their heads. One of the three, with short blond hair, a flash of dazzling teeth in perfect line, tilted her bright face towards his cookie as they passed, said *Mmmmmmm* and rolled her eyes. Then they were beyond him, the glass and silver of their carefree laughter already faint as if far away.

By the time he reached downtown the traffic lights were all blinking yellow, and a stiff wind, the first lick of winter, had begun to blow. Max groped through the streets, feeling his limbs becoming heavy aching stone. Finally he stopped to rest and after some further passage of time came to understand he was looking through the window of a men's store at the smooth hard eyeless faces of the dummies in their blazers, sportshirts, hats. *The point*, he told them, *is not to understand the world but to change it. The personal is the political. If you're not part of the solution, you're part of the problem. Yankee, come home.* They did not respond.

Later still, he was down by the river at the east edge of town, and a light rain had started to fall. Its drops reached through the leaves and branches of the ghostly sycamores and birches over his head until his shoulders were damp, ginger hair misted, face and hands stiff with cold. From down the bank and out beyond the trees came the ceaseless rushing of the river, glimmering wherever its currents eddied and swirled. Back in his head— way back in his head—Janis Joplin was singing a blues he couldn't have named. In the corner of his eye, a sense of movement up the footpath. The murkiness took shape, suitably attired in a herringbone wool coat. He took his place beside Max, so close their shoulders touched. They stared at the invisible river without speaking a word.

I'm not surprised, said Max. *I knew you'd show.*

Bright boy, said his father. *Always were. Tell me what you see, bright boy, when you look out there.*

It took a while to answer; the words came slow and hard. As if not words at all, but pieces of the stone inside him, cracked and levered up to light. Even then, at the moment of their silent utterance they seemed to change, lose their colors, be no longer what they meant. *Nothing,* said Max the Rad. *Babble. Waste of motion. Murderous rush.*

His father lowered his head and tucked in his chin, rolling jowls slightly over the coat's collar. *And that's all?*

No, said Max. *Also death. I see death too.*

This, said his father, *is what I would call a very depressing view. And undialectical, if I might add.*

Come off it, Max said. *Remember who you are. An objectively unpleasant person living at best a useless life. What do you know about dialectics?*

You keep forgetting, said his father. *I'm dead now. I'm in you now, I know a lot more. Theory is grey, my friend,* he said quoting Lenin quoting Goethe, *but green is the tree of life. What do you think that was you felt, back then when it was so exciting and awful and you woke up every morning thinking Today's the day? That thing so much larger than you, that was just the Revolution? What you think you were tapping into, boy, what power is that?*

For a while Max looked down at the dark ground and said nothing, not even in his head. Then, slowly, he drew his hands to his mouth and blew them warm.

All right, said his father. *Don't say it. You don't want to lose, but you know what it is.*

Max the Rad closed his eyes; listened to the rain's music, heard the river run.

Got it? said his father. *Okay, then, I'm taking off. Call your mother sometime, why don't you? She'd be real glad to hear from you.*

*   *   *

The cold rain had settled into a drizzle whose steady hush subsumed the river's sounds, as Max moved back over the gridwork of streets. In no time at all he was coming down the sidewalk towards the house whose bright front windows stood out like a ship's lights. Two cats broke yowling from the shrubs on his way up the porch steps; then he was standing in the living room, completely drenched, looking back at them: Jill glaring from the armchair, Carol from one end of the couch; on the other, Angela staring simply, stonily, at the TV set from Carol's room. On the tube poor dead Belushi was running rampant, bouncing antennae atop his head, *Best of Saturday Night Live;* around the living room, not a flicker of amusement on a single face.

"Angela?" he said, wiping rain from his brow and cheeks, smoothing wet hair against his skull. "May I speak with you?"

Her eyes flitted up and over him, then back to the TV. "Sure. What do you want?"

From the middle of the room, where he still stood dripping, he raised his eyebrows first at one then the other, Carol to Jill. They looked back like unfriendly scientists. "Alone?" he said.

Jill and Carol looked over at Angela. Angela's hand scrabbled in the bowl beside her for a few last kernels of popcorn. On the TV now was a Diet Coke commercial. Angela brought the popcorn up to her mouth.

"You've done enough talking for one night, don't you think?" Carol said. "Angela's been very upset—"

Max the Rad paid no attention. He waved the back of his hand to Carol, took another step towards the couch, and squatted down. "Angela?"

Angela stopped chewing; swallowed; looked back into his eyes. In another minute she sent a shaky smile left and right. "You can take off now," she told Carol and Jill. "I'll be okay."

History, it is written, *is what hurts, what refuses desire;* so what happened from the time Jill and Carol left the living room remains unknown, at least in its details. We know that outside the rain continued; inside, in the tank across the room, the little fish swam round and round; on the unattended TV eventually the channel signed off, leaving roaring snow behind until tomorrow's *Good Morning America,* the resumption of the bloody craven song. By that time they'd agreed to have a relationship; agreed to consider, if things went well, sharing bedroom space or more, depending how that went. By that time Max the Rad had moved up to the couch and snuggled in beside her underneath the afghan. Their conversation turned into sleepy murmurs and gradually stopped. By that time through the snow on the tube, in Max's mind, beyond the steady rain his father walked off whistling and spinning his cane, thinking to himself *Good enough, good enough for now. . . .*

PLUS YOU

I.

Mark grew up in the suburbs. A medium-ritzy neighborhood, two-car garages, plenty of lawn. Houses mostly real modern—glass, hardwood floors, split-level tricks—but some also of the older kind of classy house with second floors and sometimes shutters. Or like those really old windows with iron frames running through dividing them up, or those kind of rough plaster walls and red curving Spanish tile things up on the roof. Where he lived with his family, though, was one of the modernistic ones.

It wasn't bad growing up there in the suburbs, mostly Mark didn't think about it one way or the other.

Not until somewhere in high school, when you'd be like laying around hanging out with Tommy, David and whoever, getting messed up on some weed or whatever at somebody's house. Then at some point they'd pull their eyes away from the tube, look around the room like it and all the stuff inside it had just shown up out of nowhere, and say Man I gotta get out of here, you know? There's nothing happening, it's driving me crazy, you know what I mean? And then, when they said that Mark realized Yeah he did know, he'd been feeling that same thing, that same low dull noise in his head. And he started coming out with the same sort of thing.

So the way the singing thing started was this one guy Allan, who they hung around with sometimes and whose father, everybody's orthodontist, ran around all the time in white deck pants and an Alfa Romeo being Mr. Divorced Superstud—this guy's son Allan had all these old-like classic 45s, he'd been into it since he was like nine. So one day after school they're over there at Allan's listening to this stuff—they meaning Mark and David and Tommy—and they've all like called up their parents' houses to say Yeah, they're having dinner over at Allan's, Yeah Allan's dad Dr. Swigart is there, and Allan, who like desperately wants to hang around with the three of them on a regular basis has practically smashed in his old man's liquor cabinet so they're pretty well wasted on scotch and ginger ale, laying around on the pile carpeting, sprawled around the Swedish living combo, when the next record drops down the spindle and Allan—to impress them, whatever—begins to sing.

"Under the Boardwalk." Original version, by the Drifters. Allan takes the bass line, instrumental on the cut itself. At the time, with his weird pale fatty face, clunky glasses, chubby cheeks, he is a goony sweating guy, almost pathetic. But drunk enough at that moment to take a chance (which, Mark thought later, much later, who knows how long he'd been practicing?), smeared enough not to give a shit how he looks or how it sounds, just go right ahead. And what do you know? It sounds all right! They're laughing at him and everything, but it sounds pretty good! Next thing you know, who was it, Tommy? is up in his chair, filling in on the chorus, Allan's grinning like a fucking madman—*Under the boardwalk*—Tommy's rolling his eyes—*Out of the sun*—floating it up there, hamming it up, Mark and David're laughing their asses off . . .

Under the board-walk	*We'll be having some fun*
Under the board-walk	*People walking a-bove*
Under the board-walk	*We'll be fallin' in love*
Under the board-walk	*BOARD WALK*

And it sounds great. *Feels* great. An hour later they're doing the whole song front to back all together, no need for backup from the record any more. Kidding around between takes about calling up some girls, trying to get them to come over so we can lay this on them, impress the shit out of them and then get down. But no one actually makes the calls; same as they've forgot all about Allan's dad's booze. So when Allan's dad drags back in early thanks to slow action that night at the bars, when he sees the cabinet doors hanging open, Johnny Walker on the coffee table more than half-dead, when he blows up and starts ragging on them, it's like they can hardly remember when that drinking and stuff happened, who did that. They just stand there around the living room, watching him go. He's really pissed, he's yelling and screaming, you can see him tearing and tugging at the chain around his neck with the gold tooth on it as he talks, watch his skin darken up beneath the tan, but it's like they can hardly even hear what's coming out. And then the moment the rant stops Allan kicks off the song, they hit it again. *Oh when the sun beats down, and burns the tar up off the roof . . .* And before it's over, Allan's old man is smiling and laughing, getting off on it, you can see he's completely blown away.

Which is not what it's about, though—not at first. They're almost bashful about it, there at first. Even Allan plays it cool at school, doesn't come up hanging on them, trying to sit down and eat lunch with them or anything. No one even lets on to whatever girls they are seeing at the time. For the next couple months or so after school they get on over to Allan's, he spins a cut, they listen to it X number of times, play around with it, divvy up the parts and go to town until it's time to split for dinner back in their respective homes. Then, after dinner, get on back, pick up where they left off. Only not to Allan's house exactly, not for long. At this point they're still so—well, *shy*—it's their secret, they don't want anybody, not even Allan's old man, coming in on them again.

140

Lucky thing it's spring, warm enough out they can walk down the street to its dead-end circle, out back of the ring of houses there to the patch of rocks and trees that got left in when this neighborhood first got made, umpty-umpty years ago. *The Great Pretender. Silhouettes. Blueberry Hill. Chain Gang. You Send Me.* Mark standing with the other guys there in the woods, the dark, rocking with it, joining in and laying out to make that rocking in that place halfway in between the bottom bass pulsing from Allan and that high silk gliding out of Tommy, pushing that motion but resting in it too, not looking around at each other's faces or anything at all except the stars up through the trees, if there were stars.

What they were doing was doo-wop but they didn't know it. Except they sort of knew or at least had a feeling it was pretty much black. You knew the voices on the originals, they were mostly black; plus the whole idea of the thing you were making and how it felt to make it moving together in that way, brought a soft-focus image to your head from who knows where of black men, three or four or five of them casual but cool, duded up, swaying it out on some gray kind of street like in a city, a ghetto more or less, some time who knows how far back, how long ago now. Nothing sharper, more filled in than that. No notion how it came out of the dark mouths of bars and bright light of churches, up from the blues and over from worksongs and down from Jesus, becoming in the process not just its own newest juice of joy but also and as dearly yet another transmigration of known sweat and pain to unknown grace. Plus something more specific yet, a way of being present, *having* presence with your brothers without beating ass or getting your ass beat in turn, in and by the gangs on the street. The joy, yes the four of them could feel that, singing out there in that patch of woods. The other stuff, the rest of it, slid right on by, as taken for granted in its illegibility as the sound of their voices drifting up to the folks in that dead-end ring of big split-level houses, white upper-middle-class men and women who you can bet must have some time or other come into their kitchens or back bedrooms hearing the noise floating up from out back, down in the trees, thinking it was strange, or nice, or whatever, and letting it go at that. Allan, poor dorky Allan, was the only one of the four of them who even knew it had a name. *Doo-wah,* he thought he'd heard it called once, in one of the used record shops in the city where he picked this shit up. But when none of the others showed any interest in what you called it, where it came from, he played it smart and let it drop.

One thing you get for getting out of history is no memory, no memory at all. The whole point of doing it here at first, this first month in the spring of his junior year, the whole charge of it's the way it doesn't come out of or fit in with anything else he knows. That's what counts—that and the sound itself, making that sound. So Mark will never remember these times, this joy, except for those traces of it that get stuck to what comes next. Years later there will come a night when he is lying beside Amanda, the woman he almost marries but doesn't; and he will dream he and Tommy and

David and Allan are arrayed in a clearing in the jungle, standing up on something like a big lily pad so each looks out on a different zone of the same deep gorgeous fearful green against and into which flows what comes out of their bodies, not just their mouths but their eyes and ears and cocks and every place else. Nor is what comes out just music. It is also a rich endless print or pattern, it is as much coming into them as going out. It is what makes the jungle, what makes them. It is all there is. The single source of this dream in Mark's life is this time when he sang doo-wop in the woods outside everything else before or behind him, for everyone and no one else to hear. But he cannot remember this moment; it is out of time; there is nothing it goes together with in the rest of his life.

When he wakes up, after the first few seconds he can hardly remember the dream. With the guys from back in high school, someplace wild. Beside him he can feel more than see Amanda's body shift, twisting the sheets in her own dream. Another moment, and his eyes are used to the moonlight in the room. By this time he has been living in this house for several years, a modest ranch-style actually older than his parents', not to mention less costly, less expensively furnished. Yet the space feels basically the same: smooth walls, doorless rooms, plate-glass windows, smooth enclosed dry even air. The space and air he has been moving in all his life, only thanks to this dream he's just had Mark is conscious of it now, together with the soft scratchy feel of the carpeting under his feet. He goes over to the window, draws back the curtain. There is the back lawn, bare and silver in the moonlight, sloping upwards, unadorned by anything. Though he has already forgotten even having the dream, he is mindlessly happy nonetheless, his heart pounding against his ribs a wild tattoo, a terrible yearning and sense of loss. At this moment, standing here by the window, Mark is twenty-six; he and Amanda have been together nearly three years; he believes they will last. He has an O.K. job; a home; a decent life. Yet when he closes his eyes once again he sees the ad he once starred in, himself in the ad.

II.

They called it Parrot—a new line of men's shirts. It was being put out by a much larger outfit, which at the time, without letting go of their core denim-maker image, makers of the overalls and jeans and brass-button jackets you buy formfitted for your rugged life and/or work, was trying to slide over, open up a few more directions as well. Especially in the 17–22 white male slot. Not only as its own market but as what you might call, demographically speaking, the bellwether for all white males 15–35, mid-income and up. From the start marketing research had pushed for *exotic, flowery* (ergo *Parrot* as well) for the line; a portion of the subcontractor's big Malaysian plant had been retooled and was now into production; their customary agency, Bishop's and Co., had been brought in on the project nearly two years back. Now the business of the Parrot Creative Group at

Bishop's was to put together the new theme for the line. The first impulse running through the eight of them in the CG was to go with the obvious, play the bird thing. But where they finally came down was on letting the visuals do the bird—go with something looser, more open and adaptable in the lines. Which, said the client firm, the makers of tough denim-wear, was fine by them.

What specifically they finally tested out and got approval on was this:

> *Pick it up and wear it*
> *Lookin' good, it's Parrot*

Which had the right kind of snap—something *sure* there, something *what the hell*—yet still left lots of room for scripts and scoring: already, all along, given the name and target audience, everyone was agreed this whole campaign would be heavy on the music side of things.

So by this time, a few years down the road, they had the basic theme line; the music tag from Anders-Robinson, the composing firm Bishop's used a lot back then; plus a number of variant settings—one more-or-less reggae, one New Wave, heavy metal, and one doo-wop—to go with the scripts: eight scripts for thirty seconds apiece, five of which were now in the can, the sixth of which, the doo-wop number, was ready to shoot.

When there came one of those freaky twists that happen sometimes. The white doo-woppers from Brooklyn which Bob Towers the director and his people, together with the Creative Group, had settled on as scanning best (most wholesome yet hip) of all ten or twelve groups the agency people had sent over, were coming back from some private party out in the Hamptons and got side-swiped by a truck, some crazy semi, run off the road smack into a concrete embankment on the Long Island Expressway. All dead, of course, just like that. Cops figured must have been maybe 3, 3:30 in the morning, Sunday morning, less than two weeks before Day One of the shoot.

So, first thing Monday morning, one of the Brooklyn doo-woppers' parents called the agency, the agency called Bob Towers Associates, Towers' assistant notified the Parrot Creative Group. In light of the fact it's taken something close to two weeks to find any group with the right proportions of clean-cut versus funky, there was now some talk in the CG about just scrapping this spot altogether. Do a mock-nostalgic sock hop instead, Phil Marston suggested, early rock 'n' roll. That means a new theme arrangement, Ogden said, glancing over at Ray Edwards from the client company. That means time. I don't want to second-guess anybody, or speak for Ray here, but I imagine even if they say O.K., they won't like it really. That's the kind of thing that comes back to haunt you in the relationship, down the road.

O.K., said Art, I have to tell you, I never understood why not in the first place, come to that. Haven't we been talking lip-synch here all along?

Art is young, younger even than the rest of them, a mere twenty-five. He has some good ideas but too often lets his enthusiasm get the better of him, forgets something core. Which is why he's on the Parrot account, by no means the hottest or biggest thing at Bishop's, not even close; and even here his appointment is provisional, whether he knows it or not. Now, after this his newest gaffe, silence reigned briefly in the conference room. Marston craned his head back, looked up at the soundproof tile, as if noting it for the first time. Ogden pressed the last crumbs and flecks of cream cheese and bagel onto his fingertips, lifted them to his mouth and licked them, thorough as a cat. You do that, Arty, he said blandly, you got a format problem with the titles. Remember the titles? He leaned across the slate-topped table, issued a wide winning smile: What we got scripted in and client-approved, what we've done in the first five? On the twenty-second mark, before the logo? In the lower lefthand corner, the name of the band?

Up to this point Ray Edwards has kept quiet, waited to see what they come up with before trotting out what he has. First, because as representative of the client company it is not exactly his place. Second, because what he has is such a wild hair. But now that it's clear they're going nowhere fast, what the hell. O.K., he says. I got a wild-hair idea. It's probably real stupid. It probably won't work.

Down the table from him, on either side of the fruit-bowl and coffee-pot, Art's and Phil's faces clear to blank receptive screens. On the other end Ogden smiles again, a tighter smile, and cocks an eyebrow: Well God knows we're cold, Ray, he says. What do you have?

Mark and David and Tommy and Allan—the Skipstones, Ray calls them, cooking the name up on the spot. Because even though by this time they were singing together in public (insofar as suburbs have public space) they still hardly thought of themselves as a band. Word of what they could do spread later on that same spring, when they started fooling around after school. Out in the parking lot leaning on their cars, not Mark's little Honda but the bigger cooler cars, David's Camaro, Tommy's Mustang, Allan's Firebird. Cock your ass against the edge of the grille or sit up on the fender, one leg out straight, one hand on bent knee; yourself there in the middle, other guys lined up against the car, snapping their fingers, tapping their toes, as together you jump in. Watching the other kids, feeling them gathering, moving from their cars towards the one where you are. Everybody, hoods to preppies, standing around the car watching you sing; you watching them watching, seeing what they see. The four of them still told themselves it was strictly for nothing, just a goof, but it was more than that now. Since the first head had turned and looked up— *Hey isn't that Mark?*—the first recognition of yourself posed with the others in the car's shiny finish. No more hanging out at night in the woods, no more new numbers, though Allan still pushed for it every now and then. Thanks to the parking-lot appearances, they first got asked to a few kid parties, kids their own age; thanks to them, plus Allan's father talking it around, the adult crowd caught on. They did no more than forty minutes max, that was all they had; kids their age thought it was a kick, people their parents' age sometimes cried and went ape-shit. Mrs. Gallagher sobbed on Mark's shoulder, said it took her back to boarding school, up in her dorm room listening to some radio station from Detroit. Mrs. Hyland invited them all back the next afternoon, and when only David and Allan showed up blew them both off, they swore it was true. They started wearing white tuxedos with big black cummerbunds to the parties. They tried to do their bit around 9:30, 10 o'clock, be out by 11 before everyone was bombed. Drive away with something like $75 apiece in their pockets, more than they knew what to do with, every week. So Ray Edwards, who lives a few streets over from Mark, sees them at the Whitson's a month or so back, and stores them away out of sheer force of habit. Because who knows what might come in handy in this business, one minute to the next?

We'd have to give them a test, Ray's saying now, but they're in the ballpark. One of them a little googly, maybe, but that might play too. I swear to God, he says, smiling around, that's what I thought when I first heard them. My God, I said, how's that for a bunch of fresh-faced kids?

Bob Ogden looks left and right over his glasses at Marston and Art. They look back like two animals surprised by a third at a waterhole, with an alert opacity which Ogden knows from past experience signifies a very neutral form of assent. He himself has half a mind to reach for the coffeepot on the tray in the middle of the table, or some Perrier, something to press back on the cottony fatigue at the back of his head. But no, just wrap it up instead. No harm in trying anyway, he says. At least while we check with the agencies again, see what's there. How soon, Ray, would you think we can get them down here and over to Towers for testing? Got a best guess?

The four of them, the Skipstones, took off school the next day, came down on the train, so keyed up they could hardly even joke about how stupid the whole thing was. Though when Allan broke the silence at one point near Cos Cob to say Why not be the Skipstones for real? Like, you know, go ahead and make records and everything? they told him to forget it, just shut the fuck up. They took a cab from Penn Station to an address in the East Fifties, down by the river, an old squat pile of brick which seemed to have strayed upstream from the Brooklyn docks a century ago. Inside, past desks and office cubicles, where a bored pretty woman with jade circlets in her ears takes them through another door and down a corridor that could have been their high-school basement, unpainted cement blocks for walls, small heaps of dustballs, wood shavings, empty cans of beer and soda, heating pipes running overhead. Their guide stops abruptly, tosses her head at a door on their left. In there, she says, and takes off. The room they enter makes Mark flash on a TV movie he saw once on Hitler's last days in the bunker. A long beatup blue couch along one wall, a chrome chair with padded seat and back, like part of an old kitchen set from the fifties, a videocam with monitor attached, an operator and a young assistant to Bob Towers, the director, whose offices they are now in. The young assistant, Victor, wears a rust-colored shirt, a black scarf and jeans, an outfit Mark thinks ought to look stupid but somehow doesn't. Maybe because Victor himself has this sort of European look, an anxious air in his high forehead, arched brows, thin ironic lips which curl upward and open into a dazzling smile. O.K. kids, he says without introduction. We'll take you one at a time, then all together. I want to see you stroll across the room like this, doing this move—he demonstrates the walk, the simple jive movement of the arms—and I want to see lots of happy-to-be-here, real upbeat but with determination too. Like basically three-quarters great-to-be-here, one quarter moving-ahead, moving-on-up. So who wants to go first?

One week later they are in a sound studio, sitting on stools, earphones clamped to their heads. Through the phones come the snap and lilt of the rhythm track, plus each other's live voices toned down low. That way, even if one of them screws up the rest can keep going, there might be something to save in every take. Dan the sound engineer explained that to them when they first got in. Now, after each take, they take off the earphones and wait for the verdict from the control room. Through the glass they can see them in there talking, Dan conferring with Art from the Parrot CG who holds a stopwatch on each take, with Ray Edwards' assistant from the client firm, and with Ernie Bush, the mid-thirties black man from Anders Robinson who worked up the doo-wop setting for this ad. A little too loud on the *oh baby,* fellas, Dan says over speakers set in the corners of the soundroom. David, I need you crisper on those middle notes. Mark, you're a hair late on that second entrance. Got to have more push on that bass line, Allan. O.K., guys, don't go dead on me now in the center, you're going a little dead. It keeps on going from 1:30 to 5, you'd think you'd get tired or pissed off. But Dan Litton's voice behind the smoked glass remains uniformly patient, understanding, slightly sad, the air in the soundroom cool and fresh, its cream walls soothing to the eye, so much so it is easy to forget not only the others in the control room but the other guys here singing with you, in the swoon of slack attentiveness with which Mark sings time after time, take after take, guided by Dan Litton's soft steady uncomplaining voice. Until finally over the speakers comes instead of that voice a brief and startling splash of applause from the control room. O.K., we're done, Dan's voice says, loud and brisk. I'm sending Sally to the deli down the street. Who wants what kind of sandwich, soda, beer?

Every so often people asked him about it afterwards: what it was like to make an ad, be in an ad. People who'd seen him in it at first, back in high school; who remembered it, in college; who'd heard about it somehow, from somebody, after that. But by the time you told the steps—tryouts, recording session, shoot, the parts he was there for, plus editing and sound mix after that—

they'd had enough. So the only one he ever really told about it was Amanda, and only that one time. Back when they were first lovers, during those weeks when you are so open you tell everything. Sometime—a day, two days before?—he'd showed her the video, watched her laugh and lean forward—My *God*, I remember this! Oh my God, that's *you!*—as he strolls out of the crowd of extras, point man of the Skipstones, his sashaying group, and the camera zooms in on his handsome happy face, savvy self-mocking wave of hand in pure blue air, *Pa-ah-ar-ruht bay-ya-bee*—Amanda's mouth open as if a little out of breath. Now, on this weekend afternoon when he tells her, really tells her how it was, they are lying in bed, his bed, having once again made that slow climb, that amazing journey from easy touching and soft laughter up through the hunched urgency of their respective comes and back out again. He is there with her, lying beside her, feeling their sweat cool and vanish in the autumn breeze coming in through the window, smelling her smell, their lovemaking smell, in that same breeze. Once again he thinks of the ad; of her having seen that ad. He raises himself on an elbow, looks down on her. Her eyelids are closed. A corner of her lush mouth twitches. Out of her comes a low private noise, something like a sigh.

You know what the funniest thing was? The thing that really stays with me about being in it, I mean? It's how incredibly *hot* it was like the whole time, the tryouts and everything. This was like in early May, the tryouts and everything, you'd think it wouldn't be so bad. But that May there was this freak heat wave, it was horrendous. Every day we were down in the city it was like ninety degrees, ninety-four percent humidity, including the day of the shoot. We drove out in the vans to this big field in Flushing Meadows and piled out. The crews started setting up this like big picnic table under the trees with fruit juice, Perrier, fifty-seven kinds of little sandwiches, stuff like that. Other people're rehearsing the extras, showing them where to go, how to move, and making us all up, especially like the four of us, Tommy, David, Allan and me. It's like only 8:30, 9 in the morning and already steaming, everybody's pissing and moaning, Allan said he thought he was gonna faint, it was like utter pandemonium with thirty-five, forty people running around all sweating and drooping, unhappy as hell. Then this guy Bob Towers the director finally shows up, and he's like this really handsome guy. Sort of craggy face like he's from out West, California or someplace, and he's wearing just like carpenter pants and a blue workshirt and a Reds baseball cap; and he comes over and picks up about six little sandwiches and looks through this whole crazy crowd running around freaking out over the heat, and he looks right at me sitting there by one of the vans, on this little campstool? And it was so weird, the way he keyed on me and I responded. It was like one of those moments when you're looking at another person and it's like absolutely clear. I'm telling him yeah I'm right here; I am totally up for doing this ad. The heat wasn't fazing me, I hardly even noticed it all along, since like the first train ride down for the tryout. It was like I knew all along we were going to make that ad, even knew—this sounds weird, I know—we were going to make it with me out front, the way it turned out. Don't ask me how, I just knew. And I was right. Isn't it amazing? Anyway, that's what I was telling this guy Bob Towers the director with my eyes. And I could tell he was taking it all in. He nodded his head, a little nod I couldn't even've picked up if I hadn't been watching so close. He was nodding at me, telling me he knew. Then he looked over and said something to his assistant Victor, the guy who tried us out. And Victor yelled out *O.K. let's take places now.* And we were done in like three hours. People said it was the smoothest group-musical shoot they'd ever even seen. Bob Towers came up afterwards and shook my hand. He said—these were his exact words—*You were great; this is going to be a really tasty ad.* And I just smiled, but I thought *I know, I know.* That's what happened, Mark said, looking straight into Amanda's gold-flecked eyes, which had opened as he spoke. That's how it really was.

III.

How she loved him back then! How poignant, how keen the attraction of his simple earnestness, combined with the gorgeous corny pathos of his tale. Come here, baby, she said, and drew him to her with slender arms strengthened by daily curls with fifteen-pound weights, pulling his head down to rest without discomfort against her sternum. This was a little more than three months after they had met at the giant Christmas party for main office employees of the conglomerate for which Mark now worked, had been working since graduation from college. She was there at the party because while still in college, a quasi-Ivy League school like Mark's but a notch or so higher, she had figured out she'd have to make money without a steady job until such time as her photography caught on, and so had switched her major to Computer Science, minoring in Studio Arts. That way after graduation she could come to the city, find the right agency and hire out as a troubleshooting temp with supreme computer literacy and allied skills—which was, in fact, how it had worked out, and how P&W, the conglomerate hosting today's Christmas Party, with interests ranging from nose cones to beef, had called on her services often enough to invite her as well.

She explained this to Mark as they sat, quite by chance, at the same back table of the midtown nightclub-restaurant P&W'd engaged for the evening, having separately stumbled in late. He kept asking her questions, seemed genuinely interested, said very little about himself. His face, she noted, was strikingly handsome, almost perfect except for a little extra space around the eyes. He asked where she lived in the city, wanted to know what her photographs were like. She told him about both: the transitional neighborhood of vacant-lot rubble, shooting galleries, Puerto Ricans and young white professionals, a dangerous, thrilling DMZ she was proud of herself for living in; the series she'd just finished, of mental patients in the upstate hospital where her psychotherapist father'd put in time on the side of his private practice. *Gosh*, he'd said when she was done, over the campy music of the old dance band up on the stage, they sound really neat. I'd really like to see them sometime, you know? In the cab with him twenty minutes later, when she started freaking out—what do you know about this guy anyway, what kind of risk are you taking, what if your shots remind him of Arbus, the way they do everyone else?—she played back that sweet silly *Gosh* to herself, and relaxed. And when they got to her apartment, where she had the new series mounted, in spite of the crowding, on the walls, he looked at each a decent amount of time, then told her he liked them all. The color shots especially. He said he really liked her colors, the way they worked together in the shot. Nobody had ever said that to her before. He said there was one whole set of them he particularly liked, the ones of patients sitting around the rec room, he said he really liked the way the pale whites of their skins sort of blended in with but played off the blue of the walls. Not one word about Diane Arbus, no trace of art-crit mumbo-jumbo or self-consciousness. Even the way, when he finished, he blushed and looked down at his shoes gave her another rush of pleasure, head to toe. They were sitting close together on her little couch, drinking some bad Greek brandy which was all she had on hand. She was thinking how open, how unassuming, how handsome he was when at that instant from out on the street came a single horrible shriek of fear and pain that broke the mood. For a while they listened in silence to the ensuing silence; then he stood up, said it was time to go. He put on his coat, walked to the doorway, she accompanied him. Well gee, he said, thanks for the photographs and everything. I mean, it's been a really great time. That was when she reached up for him, and they started to kiss.

Back then, in those early days, the two of them did what young lovers of their class and caste do inside the city: went to movies and museums and Jamaica for a week; went out dancing, listened to music, ate out a bunch. Of course she saw and admitted he was not very verbal, obviously. Yet there was something subtly subversive, even perverse, not in spite of but *in* his smiling inarticulateness and bland good looks. He'll say something like "I guess I didn't like the story much" when we're walking out of some, you know, *Senegalese* film I've dragged him to, she told her friend Janet one May afternoon that spring, over gelati at Livecchio's. He'll say it and sort of hunch his shoulders and give a little laugh—you know, embarrassed, like a kid, but also sort of looking sideways at you, to see what you think. And all of a sudden you realize he's right, it *is* a really dumb slow boring story. You just didn't want to admit it, is all. And it's like that smile and look of his are telling you he knows all that and it's O.K., you can disagree with him if you want or need to. But he's going to tell you what he thinks anyway, and just see how you take it from there, you know what I mean?

Janet nodded, said Uh-huh. Basically, though, she was keeping her mouth shut, except to spoon in mango ice. She had met Mark twice, once at a party given by a couple of gays she and Amanda'd known in school, the other time when, walking home half-drunk after a horrible public argument at the Lisboa with her then-lover Greg, she'd run into Amanda and Mark on Broome and Mercer and allowed herself to be swept off, distracted and calmed with soothing chatter and yet more drinks. Amanda's chatter, that is: as on Janet's first encounter with him, subversive Mark had said virtually nothing, had seemed a perfectly complacent stick, with the kind of good looks that made you want to smack his face. Yet Janet loved her friend Amanda, they went way back. So she smiled and kept on nodding and eating the ice, pressing it up with her tongue against the roof of her mouth, until it made her entire head ache.

Wow, she said gasping, that's cold. Listen, yeah, he sounds terrific, like he's really good for you. Yet even so, she could feel as much as see her friend's smile clouding: not enough, not convincing enough, you've got to say more. Didn't you tell me once, she said, leaning forward on the marble-topped table, he told you this wonderful touching story about being in some ad?

Like all they kept of the whole scene at Flushing Meadows was the grass but even that looks weirded out. Not the color so much, but the way it sort of ripples in with the rest, the sky this kind of blue you never saw in your life and this crazy smiling cartoon sun spilling these sort of rays like you might have drawn when you were in grade school if you were drawing with light instead of crayons. Which is part of the joke, the fun of the ad, the way that sun looks; and which, for a second, piece of a second, is all there is, just that. Then the space starts to fill up with people coming in from either side and also like just showing up out of nowhere from the middle, moving towards you flickering different shades, whole different unreal colors in synch with sky and grass and music, Allan's voice—BAH-dop bu-BAH-dop buh Dup bup bup BOUW BOUW—*kicking in—*

Later on—two and one half years later, to be exact—when Amanda told her how moving out of the city and into this house in Connecticut with Mark had been the stupidest biggest mistake of her entire life, Janet remembered the reservations she'd eventually tried to voice after all at Livecchio's that day: whether it all wasn't happening too fast, whether Mark wasn't in effect asking her to give up too much, why in the world they had to be so grotesquely conclusive as to buy a goddamn house, etc., etc. Then Amanda had glared back and sulked; now, three years later, over hot-and-sour shrimp soup, she was saying the same things herself. It was so self-destructive, I can see that now, she was telling Janet. Like taking on some awful, stupid moth-to-the-flame dare. I didn't want to say to myself, Look, you've stopped taking your stuff around to the galleries, you haven't shot anything new for a year, you're scared you don't have it anymore, or never did. I didn't want to think about what it meant to move in full-time with him in terms of either our relationship or my work. She turned her head from side to side with an air so intensely melodramatic for a crazy second Janet feared her friend had flipped over some paranoid edge, was hallucinating being surveilled by the Chinese waiters. And you know what *really* makes me mad? Amanda said, fixing Janet in her wild stare. I already knew, I *knew* I was going to do better than he was. I was already tired of those everlasting stories of those wonderful nights with his buddies the Skipstones driving from gig to gig over hell's half-acre in their glorious Cadillac. I already thought the whole thing about his stupid ad and how he made it and all that happy horseshit was just plain tedious. God help me, Janet—she said, delicately removing a lemongrass strand from her mouth, placing it at the edge of her plate—I was even tired of the sex. But I was so scared to admit that to myself, you know what I mean? And now, she said, picking up the rice bowl, setting it down and, to Janet's amazement, beginning to cry—and now it's too late.

Which, of course, Janet told her, it certainly was not. So the relationship had cost her five years, come on, she was still just twenty-seven! Though back at the office afterwards Janet wondered just how upbeat she'd been able to sound. For one thing, in her heart of hearts there was something which, for all Amanda's anguish, whispered to her that her friend had indeed brought it on herself. For another, she had to admit there *was* a certain problem now with Amanda's looks. There were wrinkles starting to show at the corners of the eyes, a discernible roughness to the skin, especially around the temples and at the edge of her rather sharp chin. Plus what was worst—that sallow weary air, that negative aura, her body's sagging in the restaurant's cane chair. Then too, these days Janet herself was having her own problems with Larry, but had not, the entire lunch hour, been given a single chance to get a word in edgewise about them. Which, she thought, scrolling up the next personnel review, was understandable, but still—

Allan had gone to Williams, majored in English, followed it on through Yale Law to a junior partnership in a nice old midtown firm. Tom, electrical engineering at MIT, followed by a Stanford M.B.A., off on the West Coast now with RayChem. Out of Dartmouth's Amos Tuck, David collared a position inside Dun and Bradstreet's Long-Range Investment Planning. Ray Edwards, first assistant to the V.P.-Advertising for the parent firm of Parrot Styles, had retired last spring, yet still asked Mark's mom and dad about him, how he was doing, whenever they ran into him at the liquor store or country club. As, for that matter, did George Rosshalder, now also retired to his Tudorized mansion at the end of Brook Tree Lane—George, ex-V.P.-Personnel at P&W, thanks to which Mark had his job in Vacation Benefits, his shared office off the north-central hallway on fourteen, the job he was stuck in for the rest of his life. His father was thinking of closing down his own mutual funds consultancy in a few more years' time, his mother said. Neither asked how his work was going anymore; but they always inquired about Amanda, how she was, how things were between the two of them, making it plain, repeatedly, how much they liked her and the house, whose down payment they'd supplied, after all, whose financing his father had worked out with the bank and countersigned.

A story he never told Amanda or anyone, of how he got his copy of the ad. Outside it was mid-February, a mean wind knifing down raw icy streets; in here, inside this old brick building, Robert Towers, Inc. was the same as ever, even the young men and women at their desks still dressed in flower prints, bright pastels, light summer clothes. He felt silly in his gray wool worsted with red tie and vest, his scalp itching with dandruffy sweat. How could it be so much warmer here than in the P&W tower where he was supposed to be at work that very minute? Where they had him stuck in the same fourteenth-floor office with some cocky little twerp, thinks he's King Shit cause he comes from Amherst College, gets to play around with bonus schedules in the Philippines, South Korea, places like that, until they move him on up, leaving you in your Vacation Benefits place. The young woman he had talked to here at Robert Towers, Inc., had spoken to him curtly, punctuating her speech with sharp little jabs of her slim hand. She was wearing a tight sleeveless dress in a zebra-striped pattern, a pearl and pop-top choker, a button which read BORN TO SHOP. The people at Bishop's, she said, had been quite mistaken in sending him over, if he was interested in acquiring a tape of the ad in which he had appeared he would first have to write to the client company, it was their property after all. Then, if the company grants that permission, get in touch with us again and at that time we'll haul it out, reproduce it and charge you an appropriate fee. Across the wide room from himself and the young woman, at the head of the corridor down which, with the rest of the Skipstones, he had once been led, two male figures in Hawaiian shirts were earnestly conversing. One of them, Mark thought, seemed an older yet more relaxed version of the Victor with the wavy hair and high smooth forehead who had first coached, then tried them out that day. But even if it were there was no use calling out Victor's name, crossing the room and shaking hands, asking if Bob Towers were around. What he ended up doing was what the woman told him to; he took down the name and address she gave him, wrote the letter and followed it through; and accordingly, eventually, for $25, got from Robert Towers, Inc. a dupe of the spot.

A story he did tell instead: about the Skipstones, the dark rainy night they all ended up edging out the back door of this ramshackle roadhouse outside this upstate Podunkville in the Hudson Valley as it became clear, unmistakably clear, the crowd was there only to fight— breaking bottles, busting chairs over heads, the whole crazy shmeer. He told it to her in bed in their new home in Connecticut, two weeks or so after they first moved in. At the time they were quite stoned, had smoked up deliberately to dispel what she called the sheer throat-stopping weirdness of moving in with each other, out of their city, into this house which was now weirdly theirs. It all came from some movie about this fifties rock band he'd seen once on TV, he meant to tell her it was just a goof, nothing close to that had happened, they had never even toured. But she laughed and laughed there beside him, held her chest with both arms and rocked against him, laughing till she cried. Ah God, she said when it let up enough for her to speak. She was leaning against his side, head on his chest; he could feel her short gasping breaths warm on his skin. So what kind of car did you guys tour in? she whispered. That was when he made up the '56 Cadillac, white, with huge grillwork and fins.

Like the song and the crowd have been there all along, maybe thirty, forty of them now, who knows? All wearing Parrot shirts whose patterned checks, stripes, lightbulbs, ducks, kites, guns, you name it, flash their hot colors in time. Above the shirts the colors of the faces have been dulled down towards the background, all except for Tommy and David screen right in the front row, Allan screen left, plus you in the center, leading the crowd, throwing your head back in perfect rainbow happiness crowing it out

When you want to be cool   (bah-bah-bah-bah)
When you want to look fine   (bah-bah-bah-bah)
When you got that spe-shul some-thin in mind
       (wah-wah-wah-wah-oh-YEAH—)
Still moving closer, everyone closer as if about to spill out of the screen—

The morning Amanda tells him, over breakfast, that she wants to leave comes fourteen months and two weeks after his dream of being with the other boys out in the jungle. She says for some time now she has felt their relationship has stopped growing or going anywhere. Such growth is a two-way street, she admits, but she no longer feels she can give the relationship the kind of attention and commitment it deserves. Although it embarrasses her to say so, even to herself, she confesses his lack of advancement in the company is a problem for her, which it probably wouldn't be, she says, if it weren't for her own anguish, guilt and uncertainty over her retreat from— no, abandonment of, let's face it—a career in art, now that she has let herself be drawn up into the corporate ranks. A gray heavy stillness spreads inside him at these words, the sound of these things. When she pauses as if flustered, smiles uncertainly and licks her lips, he tries to think of some right thing to say. It is impossible to look at her as he speaks, to deliver any words directly to her, so he stares down instead at the two halves of English muffin going cold on the blue-and-white plate. Maybe, he says, surprised at both the thought itself and its obviousness—maybe we should have a kid? Which it turns out is the wrong thing to have said. As she launches into her enraged response, measuring it out sentence by sentence, blow by blow, he lifts his gaze from the plate and slides it past her, out through the glass sliding door to the redwood deck outside, past the deck to where you can see through the line of leafless trees left by the developers the cold silver of the pond they had put in, and the patches sliding on that silver that are ducks. He holds himself still inside and keeps on watching as she says That's all you can talk about, you and your goddamn Skipstones, No friends except the ones I make, Never go anywhere, all you do is watch TV, I need some companionship, some stimulation and so on while out in the distance beyond the deck the brown and grey blurs glide back and forth until she is done and it is time for you to do what you have to do, get out of that chair and go over to her, get down on your knees and start to beg.

You're all that matters to me. I love you forever. I can't live without your love. Plus there was their combined income, which despite his stagnation was by no means inconsiderable, and their co-investment in the house, which in all its bourgeois functionality she had come to like. Besides, it was probably true that in some ways he understood her more and better than anyone else; besides, from any semi-objective point of view, he remained a strikingly attractive man. Still, while making no commitments herself, she got him to promise there at the table that he would never again in her presence run the Parrot spot or mention the Skipstones. And three days later, still considering, she signed up for two courses, one in Weightlifting for Women, the other Kung Fu, at the White Lotus Center for Martial Arts on the western edge of town.

Mark remembered the little gray fifteen-pound dumbbells in the clutter of dropped clothes, Polaroid snapshots, spread-eagled *Artforums* in her old apartment back in the city, but this was something else. Mornings, as soon as she woke, one half hour on the bench press and exerciser, another fifteen minutes of Kung Fu; ditto afternoons, as soon as she got in the door from work. She moved the light-table, books and equipment out of her room, stripped it of all but a few of her old photographs, moved in weights, bench and light-blue matting; she cleared the trays, chemicals and thick black curtains from her adjoining darkroom, thereby returning it to bathroom and shower. Without saying so, she made it clear she did not welcome his presence while she exercised; nor, for that matter, did he much care for the sight of her red and rigid, squeezing up on the press, or numb and opaque executing her routines. So, with showers and all, that took care of maybe three of their six and a half waking hours together; then there were classes at White Lotus, 7–10, Monday and Wednesday nights. While she was out he would sometimes get the ad out, slap it on the VCR, run it through once or twice, then hide it back away. More often, he just lay back on the couch and watched TV, not the major networks but the scrubby independents coming in via cable from tacky little towns in Jersey or the southeastern shore, the kind that give you lots of local bowling and wrestling, reruns of *Leave It to Beaver, I Love Lucy, WKRP,* diced up with sordid hysterical ads shouted in Spanish and English from endless furniture factory showrooms, used-car lots with triangular pennants snapping in the breeze. He liked feeling he could imagine the target audiences for such programming, the small stuffy rooms in small dirty houses where second-hand shows and cut-rate commercials were supposed to land. He closed his eyes on the bilingual ranting for greatest-hits anthologies, Biblical videos, discount shoes, fast-food surf 'n' turf, and thought with a strange sad contentment of smudgy toys strewn on garish stained carpets, sprung couches, torn and broken recliner chairs all bathed in the screen's fluctuating watery light. On Channel 36 every week-night running from 10 until 3, Waterbed Warehouse brought you Friendly Flickers, showing two great old Hollywood films every night, hosted by your old friend Casey Caxton, who sometimes went on ten, fifteen minutes between one stretch of film and the next, extolling the incredible sale prices of the outstanding merchandise all around me right here in the center of our Waterbed Warehouse, located where Business 84 meets the Dean Parkway, and reading letters from his Friendly Flicker Fans. One came from a woman with terminal cancer, she didn't say where, who wrote to tell Casey how much his presence and show The Friendly Flickers meant to her. Some nights, Casey read out in his nasal, twangy voice, I cannot sleep for the pain, which you take my mind off of with your sallies and jokes. Bless you Casey Caxton and your Friendly Flickers Fan Club for the good work you are doing and the fun. It was letters like this, said Casey Caxton from the center of the showroom of waterbeds and waterbed accessories, folding up the letter and wiping his blue eyes, that gave him too the strength to go on, plus the knowledge that he was on the right path.

Terminal cancer, he repeats, laughing, shaking his head, and then the guy goes ahead and reads the letter. I mean, you don't know whether to laugh or cry, you know what I mean? The hair dryer he has been shouting over shuts off in the bathroom, she moves past him down the hallway in her terry-cloth robe. I think what's weird is wanting to watch shows like that in the first place, she says from the bedroom. Which, for the first few seconds after the initial shock—at the contempt in her voice, at her betrayal—makes him want to answer with yet another story. This one from another recent evening, when she got into bed with him, and, once again, promptly fell asleep; and he lay there beside her a long time, feeling her next to him without touching her anywhere, just hearing her breath and trying to push what he was feeling back down, until he couldn't anymore. Then he got up and crouched over the bed, over the blank mask of her sleeping face, and beat off on the wall-to-wall carpeting. Then he went off into the living room to Casey Caxton, the Friendly Flickers Fan club, the special double feature we have for you tonight, Joan Crawford in *The Damned Don't Cry* and Charlton Heston in *Pony Express*.

So bay-ay-bee—
    Put it on and wear it
    Lookin' good it's Parrot   (wah,wah-ooo)
So bay-ay-bee—
and once again, and again, and again, surging forward moving ahead yet staying in place. The title The Skipstones *in lower screen left, in screen right the Parrot silhouette logo, chorus faded down behind an older, amused white male voice saying* Parrot, at quality clothing stores near you *then the chorus resurging again, bouncing hard, very bright colored lights flaring out*

of the whole crazy world. Then, as a final touch, after the closing chord's burst, the sound of your laughter, your completely happy laughter trailing on another minisecond after freeze-frame and blackout.

IV

Though by now there was no more Parrot—the line was dumped years ago for lack of sales. In a failure situation like that you see a lot of ugly fallout, everybody blaming everyone else; so, inevitably, the Creative Group at Bishop's came in for a certain amount of finger-pointing from the client company's marketing folks, whose basic mistake it had been, in Bob Ogden's opinion, to have come up with a wacked-out line of clothing for a manifestly increasingly conservative target group in the first place. Given their years with the company and reputations for competence, Ogden and Phil Marston had few problems riding out the modest storm that followed, attaching themselves to another product line. Not so Art, whose fortunes continued to decline. As for doo-wop, its free-floating connotations of nostalgic funk had by now shifted over to hip-hop, a youth subculture dating from the streets of Brooklyn and the Bronx in the late seventies involving break dancing, rap music and graffiti, any or all of which could now be reinvoked and represented in suitably transmuted form to tap that circuit, draw off some of that juice, run it through, say, Diet Coke straight to your heart.

But what happened to the music, the singing in Mark's life? It can't all have just disappeared or been diverted, left to float away or get mixed in with all this other crap, the commercial, the job, his relationship with this woman, etc., etc. Isn't there still, way down deep—inside his character, psyche, even soul—some safe and secret place where the music remains as bright and useless as we say all great or real Art has to be? Maybe you can still have him hum to himself in the car. Or while he's shaving, watching the face that is his looking back in the mirror. Maybe he can just hear the music in his head sometimes, a scrap of bass-line or melody as he sits on the train taking him to his job in the morning or back home at night. Or even more random, more fleeting than that: a fragrance of tune, a warbling pulse, the merest sense memory of vibration, trees, night, going by so quick and low that it hardly, hardly registers at all. Certainly not enough for him to think about, ask what it is, where it's from. But just because he doesn't ask doesn't mean it isn't still inside him somewhere, that it hasn't lasted, no one wants to think that.

Casey Caxton is really there just as he promises to be, every Saturday all day. From the entrance doors to the giant Waterbed Warehouse you can spot him in the middle of the showroom floor, inside the same rough-shingled gazebo he comes out of at the start of each weeknight's Friendly Flickers. He is waving goodbye now to a frail white-haired couple whose dazed smiles float over Mark too on his way up through the aisles, past waterbeds and waterbed arrangements of all kinds under steel girders draped with red-white-and blue banners proclaiming SALE! SALE! SALE! There are, as far as Mark can see, not more than eight or ten other customers in the whole huge store, so before he reaches Casey's gazebo he has to fend off three separate young salespeople in black T-shirts with Friendly Flickers on the front, Waterbed Warehouse on the back with the address. By the time he reaches the knotty-pine steps from which Casey Caxton reads the mail and makes his nightly pitches, his initial sense of goofy euphoria has pretty well collapsed. But he still has to say something, now that he is here no more than ten feet away. Mark rests one foot on the first step up, cocks his head, tries to show Casey Caxton a folksy down-home grin. Kinda slow out here for a Saturday, huh, he says. Casey Caxton's pale blue eyes look up and over from the sandwich whose waxed-paper wrapping he's just undone. Pardner, he says tonelessly, you ain't said shit. Mark feels like an idiot to be so nervous. His mouth has gone completely dry, he has to clear his throat before speaking again. I'd like to join the Friendly Flickers Fan Club, he says, and receive my T-shirt and free schedule of the movies coming up. No sweat, pardner, says Casey Caxton, rising from his rocker, drawing a card from the rumpled white sportsjacket over his own Friendly Flickers T-shirt: Just fill in the blanks here and we'll get you all set up. As Mark fills the card out Casey Caxton stands over him on the other side of the gazebo rail smoking a cigarette, wheezing a little with every breath. Amanda is off at an all-day fitness seminar for businesswomen in high-stress positions, there is no way she will ever find out you are here in the Waterbed Warehouse with Casey Caxton, no way he can understand why he is here doing this, standing by Casey Caxton so close if he looked up from the red-white-and-blue Friendly Flickers Fan Club membership card he's filling out he would be staring through the gazebo latticework at Casey Caxton's crotch. Only Mark is no longer filling the card out because he can no longer see to do it, because he has to his shame and horror started to cry. He cannot help it; his shoulders shake, he sobs aloud. A heavy hand comes to rest on his shoulder. What's the trouble here, boy, Casey Caxton is saying: you gonna need some help gettin' out of here? The voice is low and casual, his late-night Friendly Flickers voice. On Mark it has an instant steadying effect. He takes a step back, away from the rail, I'm fine, he says, just give me my listings. Give me my listings and T-shirt and I'll go home. Casey Caxton turns away, reaches behind him. When he turns back holding the goods his seamed craggy face is split by a grin. Congratulations, says Casey Caxton leaning over the rail, placing T-shirt and schedule in one hand while shaking the other. Welcome to the Friendly Flickers Fan Club, you are now officially one of us.

An overcast sky, dull color of gray milk; then, rapidly, with volume up on expressway noise, pan down to traffic on the Deane Parkway. Horizontal pan down traffic shooting past Dick Brown Ford Burger King Factory Outlet National Tire Radio Shack Wendy's CVS Drug, each car with one or more people in it, each headed somewhere. Zoom in on traffic; volume further up on traffic noise in synch with zoom. Then volume down to normal for Shot 2, eye-level long shot from across the Parkway. Asphalt parking lot shiny with rain, a scatter of cars here and there in the grid of open-ended boxes laid out in yellow diagonal rows; giant box of steel and concrete, giant show windows, waterbeds displayed in giant windows under flapping red-white-and-blue banner ALL AMERICAN SALE. All this plus you in the center of the shot, member of the Skipstones, lover of Amanda, salaried employee in Vacation Benefits, member of the Friendly Flickers Fan Club, moving quickly, almost running, for the car. Shot 3 outside car, close shot of hand unclasping unbuttoned topcoat, fishing for keys in coat pocket, other hand still grasping TV schedule, Fan Club T-shirt and membership card. Then traffic sounds bleed out swiftly for Shot 4, silent close-up of face looking up at opaque sky then suddenly down and straight back at the camera as if realizing for one shocking second we are here before getting in the car starting it up and driving away.

ALMOST LIKE FALLING

Towards the end of that year I got nicked again, but I didn't care at the time. Since the first long stretch in '82 work had never really come back steady, so I was used to socking some away for layoffs ahead. Plus with Cindy gone since August, no matter what she used to say about us each paying our way, I had that much more out of every check.

So November 1, got my slip on the way in to swing, four to midnight, and figured All right, I'm out of here. Now that Cindy had the last of her junk there wasn't much left of the old apartment anyhow. And I hadn't seen my friends Bob and Sharon for years.

Cleveland to Boston you can make in under fourteen hours if the state boys look the other way, but I was in no hurry. I could stop anywhere, eat my tuna fish, have an apple, glug one of those little cans of juice I'd brought along; I could pull off at roadside rests and just sit. No way Bob and Sharon would be expecting me, since I hadn't called ahead or anything; not so much the surprise factor as no need, given the kind of friends we were. And of course no rush whatever about getting back.

As it turned out, though, I only stopped once, at an overlook somewhere the other side of Albany. Just a turnoff into gravel most of the way up a hill, a couple of benches, a stone fence to keep kids and dumbos from falling off the edge. I slid myself up on the hood of the car, put my legs into a half-assed lotus. There was a river down there moving too slow to tell, the color of foil when the light was off it, and the trees on the hills and the river flats, with leaves and without, pretty much all the same mousey grey-brown. I took a few balls out of my jacket, the orange ones I keep with me, and went three to four, four to five, and then back down to three, and then quit. Nobody else pulled off to look, and why should they? It was plenty cold and windy, with Lord knows not that much to see.

Anyway, what with stopping that once and driving slow, I didn't get in to Bob and Sharon's part of Boston til after midnight. I knew Bob'd still be up anyway, he always was even nights he wasn't playing, spinning his old scratchy albums and honing his licks along with them. And sure enough—when I got to their street there was a light on up in their place, and when I buzzed it was Bob who came down.

"God," he said in the doorway, "Great balls of fire, Jimmy DeMott!" He grabbed my arms hard, I grabbed back, grinning like mad just like him. "How you been keeping, man? Get on in here, you want a beer?"

Bob does a good job of sounding like he's from someplace like West Texas, even if you know which block of Cleveland he's from. I picked up my bag and padded upstairs behind him, hearing his breathing. From behind, he looked like he might've put on some, but I wasn't sure.

Upstairs in their place, I put down my bag and watched him take a look around the kitchen and living room—basically all the same space—like he was the one visiting. I noticed his beard was different, cut trimmer I think. Then he looked back at me and came back to his grin.

"God damn, god damn," he said. "Jimmy DeMott. What the hell you doing here?"

"Oh," I said, "just got a little forced vacation from the old plant. Got to thinking I'd stop by and see how you guys were, maybe spend a few days if that's all right."

"Absolutely," Bob said. "Great," he said. "Hold on a sec though, would you? Lemme throttle that box."

He went over to where the tv was on, Letterman it sounded like, and turned it off, then sank back into the armchair he must have been in when I buzzed.

"Wow," he said, nodding. "A visit from Jimmy. All right."

"Yeah," I said, sitting down on their old couch, thinking how he must have forgot about the beer. "So how you doing?" I said. "How's Sharon? How're you both?"

Bob gave me some of that deep nodding people sometimes use as a serious Okay. "Sharon's sacked out," he said.

"Yeah sure," I said. "I mean, I figured she would be."

"She's gonna be glad as hell to see you," he said, still with most of his last smile.

I watched him sneak a look back over at the tv as if it were still on, or he was sorry it wasn't. "How about you?" I said. "How's the music business treating you, you gonna be playing anywhere while I'm here?"

"Oh, absolutely," Bob said, with some more of that nodding. "Yep," he said, "you'll get your chance."

He got up from his chair then and started walking, part sideways part backing up through the kitchen towards the bedroom. "How 'bout that—aw shit, what's her name," he said. "Was it Carol? No, not Carol I mean. Who is it now?"

"Cindy," I said. "No, we broke up. Jeez, Bob," I said, laughing: "Carol. Where'd you get that?"

Bob shrugged, still backing, and ran a hand through his hair. "Hell I don't know," he said. "What can I tell you? Alzheimers or something. How long's it been?"

"I don't know," I said, and stopped to do the math: when I first met Cindy, when we moved in, when we came out on my last visit. "Three years, I guess. Almost three."

"Three years," Bob said from the hallway, just outside the bedroom door. He had stopped moving, he was looking at the floor. "Hey," he said, whispering but loud, bringing his head back up grinning. "I can't keep up with your hounddoggin'."

Look who's talking, I started to say, but decided that might not go over so funny my first night in. Besides, Bob was out of sight now, in the bedroom, I would've had to raise my voice. In the quiet just before the furnace started up below us I could catch the scuffling noises he was making in there, then a bip-da-bop of mumbles, hers high and a little grouchy, his low and soothing, like a birdsong you basically recognize even when you don't get all the notes, though I could tell how this one ended just by rhythm and sound, her saying "Jim who?" and him, "Jim DeMott . . . "

Then I heard her sort of sigh and sort of groan like someone going back to sleep; and then, like I say, the heating system kicked in. Bob came back out with some sheets and blankets and we set up the couch. Neither one of us said anything til Bob offered me first dibs on the bathroom. Then I was out and getting settled on the couch and he was in there washing up.

"You doing any juggling?"

Technically in a whisper; but still loud enough to make me sorry for Sharon, trying to sleep. "Oh—" I hissed back, soft as I could—"you know. Not much."

The water shut off. Then, from my spot on the couch, I could see his silhouette lit from behind in the bathroom doorway, toweling his face. I'd been right about the weight; you could see it easy now he had his shirt off, like a sweater tied around his waist. "Well," he said, like a soft sigh, "we'll talk more tomorrow. Great to see you, man."

*　　*　　*

Next day I woke up and didn't know where I was. There was a grey light over everything that seemed like it could have been Ohio. Then I could tell I wasn't home, and remembered about me and Cindy. And then I looked around again and saw the records lined up along the wall, and up over them this poster with a picture of Bob Sharon drew for one of Bob's very first gigs, at the old Alexandra on Clark, back near when the three of us first got together at North Cleveland CC; and then it all came together, where I was, who I was with, and I was okay.

"Hey hey," Sharon said from over at the kitchen table. "New hope for the dead."

"How you doing, darlin'?" I said.

She tapped her smoke against the ashtray and gave me one of her good-little-girl smiles. "Fine," she said. "Good to see you. How 'bout you?"

I picked up my pants from the floor and hustled them on under the covers. "Okay," I said. "Yeah," I said. "Doing all right."

"That's not the way I hear it," Sharon said. "I hear you're out of work and lovelorn."

"Oh yeah?" I said, heading past her for the john. "That's what Bobby told you?"

"That's what I heard from what he said. Listen, you want coffee, there's fresh in the thermos by the stove. Eggs and that stuff's in the fridge, help yourself."

Which I did, but just for coffee, once I was done in the bathroom and dressed. Sharon looked up from the newspaper crossword she'd been doing when I sat down beside her, and gave me a nice smile before lighting up her next cigarette. She was still in her bathrobe, with her sort of squirrel-colored hair—prematurely grey, I guess—falling every which way around a face so round and big-eyed that even with the wrinkles it still made you think of a feisty kid.

"So," she said, wise-assing the words: "you're looking well, at least."

"Long as you got your health," I said. "Speaking of which, when you gonna give that shit up?"

"Hey," she said. "I'm down to Carltons, gimme a break." She took a long pull on the one she had going, let the smoke out in a few spinning O's, then leaned back. "You sound like the jerks I have to work with," she said. "You know how much crap you get smoking anywhere in a hospital now?"

Her being the only one of us to finish up the A.A. degree that got her the blood-lab jobs they lived on, aside from whatever Bob's music brought in. I didn't say anything back; didn't have to. Just sat there and sipped my coffee, looking out at the grey day, while she kept her head cocked to the side, thinking to herself.

"You okay about Cindy?" she said after a while, out of that nice quiet.

"Yeah," I said. "Basically. I mean, she's an okay person and everything. But it was definitely not working by the time we packed it in."

She lifted the Carlton to her lips, took another drag, plumed the smoke out. "She think you're an okay person?"

"Naw," I said. "In her mind I'm an asshole, last I knew."

"Why's that?" she said.

"Because," I said, "she thought we should've worked on it harder. Should've made a commitment to making it work. Should've got married and then me set her up with some kind of post-punk hair salon while I work my fucking life away at the plant."

"Uh," she said, and shifted forward again. A minute later, by the time she stubbed her Carlton out, I'd picked a couple pieces of fruit off the bowl on the table, an apple and a couple oranges, something like that, and started tossing them around.

Sharon watched the fruit move around a minute or so. Not making a big deal of it or anything; just watching the stuff toss from one hand to the other, almost like falling, across and back.

"Well," she said finally, "better get dressed and get moving," and shoved her chair back and got up.

"You working today?" I said.

"Yeah," she said. "Three to eleven. But I need to get a wash in before I go."

I put the fruit back and made myself useful, taking the dishes over to the sink. Had them done and in the drainer and was sponging off the table by the time she was back out of the bedroom in a sweatshirt and jeans. "Bob still crashed out?" I said.

She looked up and over from the basket she was pulling clothes out of, and shook her head no. "He was up before either of us," she said. "He'll be down at the Wedgwood having breakfast with Jean."

"Oh yeah?" I straightened up but tried to keep my voice loose. "Who's Jean?"

It crossed my mind she wasn't going to answer. But she was just sorting their stuff into two pillowcases, darks and lights, before looking back over, her whole face saying No big deal.

"Friend of Bobby's," she said. "Friend of ours, really, by now. They had a thing together," she said, "cou-

186

ple years ago. Now she comes over here, or Bob goes out to meet her. She's a smart person, Jean is, and she's had a rough life she needs to talk over with somebody, and we're it."

All of which I should've picked up more from than I did; either that, or thought more about what I did get. At the time, what I mostly fixed on was how Sharon looked saying it: how her face seemed to slide and sag until it caught up with the grey of her hair. It gave me the creeps, how old she was looking how fast, and at the same time made me so sad I could hardly stand it.

So I started backing up towards the front room, and said the first thing that came to my head. "You got the old poster framed," I said. "The one for Bobby at the Alexandria."

"Yeah," she said. "Family heirloom. You like it?"

"Sure I do," I said.

She grinned and nodded, even colored up a bit. "See you're still up to scratch on the juggling," she said.

"Yeah," I said. "Yeah, well, not really." Then realized I was still holding the wet scrub-sponge in my hand, and came back to the table to finish it up. Sharon lifted one stuffed pillowcase, slung it over her shoulder, and moved for the door, carrying the other by its neck.

"You get that all right?" I said.

"Hey," she said, "you're out of work, remember? Whyn't you get out of here, go down to the Wedgewood, catch up with them yourself."

"I might do that," I said, swiping away at the plastic tablecloth. "You want this paper with the puzzle saved?"

"Naw," she said, half out the door. "Toss it. I can't finish them any more anyway. I don't know," she said laughing, "I guess my mind is turning to fucking cheese," and the door swung shut.

From outside in the late November rain the Wedgewood was like any one of a thousand places off the main drags in neighborhoods back home, somebody's little white house up close to the sidewalk, beer neon winking in the windows, a sign with the place's name hung up by the roof. Probably it'd been a joint like that too, once upon a time. Only now you went in to a place had fresh cut flowers, the real thing, in vases on the tables, and people my age and younger in like sportshirts from the '50s, so old they were new, and leathers and shades, sitting around these little tables eating deli sandwiches and fancy salads with their beers, and music the like of which I have never heard coming out of any juke before or since.

So partly there was this scene, which I wasn't used to yet, and partly the weird deal of just leaving Sharon and bopping down the street to hang out with some so-called "former lover" of Bob's who still comes around and hangs out with them both. I mean, I knew the deal with Bob and Sharon, what with Bob being a blues musician playing around, meeting people, staying out late. They'd been through it before, even back as far as Cleveland, when he was running around a while as I recall first with someone named Judy and then a Marie. I'd sat across the bar and watched him having a one-on-one nightcap with this one or that one at the end of the night; I'd seen the looks on Sharon's face and heard the cracks that slipped out sometimes. But I always figured hey, that was up to the two of them, it was none of my business. Besides, with my track record on relationships, who was I to talk?

What with all this, anyhow, the point is I felt more than ever like I had to stay down, mind my p's and q's. I looked around and spotted them at a dinky smoking table in back: Bob slouched in his Neville Brothers t-shirt, and Jean, this former lover, with both elbows parked on the table and a cigarette crooked in one of her long-fingered hands. Sort of skinny, sort of dressed-up, some red on her cheeks I couldn't tell was real or not. She was talking hard to Bob, like she was mad at him almost, though that couldn't be right, the way he was just sitting back bobbing his head and sipping away at his beer.

I tried to come up with some kind of semi-hip opener on the way over to them, but nothing leaped to mind. Then I was alongside their table and the nice-looking woman named Jean was looking up at me wide-eyed, with her thin eyebrows raised.

"Hey," I said, smiling and feeling goofy. "This music is some weird shit."

"Hey Jimmy," Bob said, nodding. "Jean, this's Jimmy DeMott, went to community college with me and Sharon back in Cleveland a hundred years ago. Jimmy, my friend Jean Duhaime."

She held out her hand, pressed mine and let it go, but what she said went to Bob not me. "You don't have classical back in Cleveland?"

"Cleveland Orchestra," I said, though sounding like I was sticking up for Ohio made me feel even stupider.

"One of the best. Just not used to hearing it in your neighborhood beerjoint, is all."

Then got tripped up again by the grin on her face. "Don't let it bug you," she said. "It's just here to help the new gentry stay impressed with their fucking gorgeous selves. Whyn't you pull up a chair?"

Bob leaned back and shot me a wink. I pulled up a chair and sat down and listened to Jean picking up where she left off. She was talking about this guy Simon she disliked a lot, but was going out with anyway—no, not anyway, but practically because she despised him so much. *Despised* in fact would be a word she probably used together with the swear-words, right in line with the way her hands moved as she talked, bracelets jangling on both wrists, long bronze-painted nails at the ends of her fingers like I hadn't seen in years. The story was, this guy Simon had taken her to dinner with his folks at some upscale town around here, and either at the folks' house or their country club, before or after dinner, she had managed to get so drunk she finally blew the whole scene off and came home in a cab.

It was a fairly funny story, except she'd obviously been on it for a while and was still milking it for all it was worth. "And you know what else that fucking asshole Simon said when I ordered my third one?" she'd say; or "*Then* you should've seen what the *dining* room looked like" and her hard pretty face would flare up like a match. I snuck a few questions in, but basically let Bob supply the feeders, That right? No you gotta be kiddin, etcet etcet, and joined in on the laughter. But every so often, in between one of these little story-ettes and the next, while she was still coughing out her laugh he'd put his fingers on the table and lean forward as though hauling himself in with his hands and say something like So what you gonna say next time he says Let's get together with my parents? or So how much longer *are* you gonna put up with some jerk who doesn't know who you are?

This last word for word, pretty much. And the whole way he said it, and looked while he was saying it, made me feel pretty strange. It was like I was way back there watching them both, my old friend Bob and this lady he was handing out advice to, at one and the same time really close and far away. I was looking at him and the way he was sitting, and picking up again on the weight he'd put on, not just in the spare tire stretching his t-shirt but even in his lips, which I don't recall ever looking at before. Now beneath his moustache and around his beard they were all red and puffy and swollen. And around them it was like his face too had gone all soft and drowsy, gentled down to where he seemed half-asleep.

For a while I tripped off back to the rest of the scene there, looking at the differences between them and either Jean or Bob. The not-so-young professionals trying to look on their time off like revamped fifties hoods, with their hair chopped or slicked back a hundred different ways, whereas Jean, by now on her third or fourth time around the story since I'd sat down, had this long reddish-brown hair, very pretty, falling down over her shoulders, and this tan sweater and slacks combo with a flashy scarf, brown with orange flecks, around her neck. Then there was Bob in his t-shirt and jeans, freckled face,

and curly beard, Bob sipping his glass of beer and handing her another piece of advice about her and younger
guys; and there I was, trying to stay on track, think about
what I looked like to anyone in my nothing flannel shirt,
khaki pants, Red Wing boots, the same shit I have put
on every fall and winter morning since before leaving
school, but getting pulled back to Bob's face instead, that
round pleased face and wet baby lips, wondering *Who is
this guy? Did he always look this way? Does he only
look like this now to you?*

"So, old friend of Bob's," she was saying now, Bob's
former lover named Jean over the lip of her wineglass.
"How far back do you go?"

Again I was flustered, like being called on back in
school when you were totally spaced. Plus also the surprise of how pretty she could get when she turned her
face at you and jacked the smile up all the way. She gave
me a second, then turned away and signalled for another
glass of wine, Bob shaking his head No on another beer.
And just who the hell are you? I felt like asking back.

But didn't, of course; just behaved like a good boy
instead. "Jeez, I don't know," I said, looking over at Bob.
"Ten years now?"

"More'n ten, easy," Bob said. "Lotta time on
the trail."

The barkeep came over with the bottle, poured the
wine for her. I started feeling more comfortable, but still
kept looking mostly at Bob. "Saw something just now
made me feel a lot older," I said. "Sharon's poster for you
at the Alexandria, now under glass."

Bob shook his head, smiled crooked with those fat red lips shut tight. "That's right," he said. "About a thousand years ago."

"You should've seen it," I said to Jean. "People stopped talking, stopped even drinking, just to listen. He blew them away."

Jean took a sip of wine and a puff on a new cigarette, pretty much both at the same time. "That's right," she said to Bob. "And the only difference between then and now is now you're a thousand percent better than you were."

The sort of bent way that came out plus the heavy way she said it made me wonder how much she'd had. But I let it go when Bob pointed over at me. "Well," he said, "you ought to see what all this guy can move through the air."

She rested her cigarette hand on top of her glass and tipped her head towards me, asking. "He means juggling," I said, hoping my face looked less hot than it felt. "He and Sharon're about the only people in the universe who remember I used to fool round with it back when."

"You heard of the Flying Karamazov Brothers?" said Bob. "Well, this guy Jimmy DeMott's *better* than them."

Which, of course, was such a crock it wasn't worth responding to, except to realize both of them had to be half in the bag. Across the room the jukebox had turned to jazz a while back. I turned to Jean again. "What do you do?"

"I work for a real estate firm in the neighborhood," she said. "I'm an appraiser."

"Hear that, brother?" Bob said over to my right. "You wonder why the neighborhood's changing? You're looking at the reason right here."

Half-kidding, half-not, the way that is. He licked his lips—I practically had to look away—and threw us both a sloppy smile, brown eyes blurred and wide, sheen of beersweat all over his face.

Across the room the sax cut out and the Stones came on the juke—"Brown Sugar," vintage stuff. Jean lowered her wineglass but kept her eyes on me, the way they'd been since the last time she spoke. "I don't sell," she said, lifting and squaring her chin, "and I don't buy. I look over properties and guess what they'll bring, and I don't think that makes me a criminal. And besides, I don't give a ripe shit what either one of you thinks."

Bob choked some laughter through his beer; I don't know what I did. Jean tossed off what was left in her glass, and reached over for her coat and a black leather purse as big as a briefcase. "Matter of fact," she said, "I'm late for a place right now, I believe. So gentlemen, if you'll excuse me—"

"Nice to meet you," I said, hauling back my chair.

"Nice to meet you," she said, flashing teeth as she went past. "Hope to see you again." She came around to my other side, bent down and placed a kiss on Bob's sweaty temple. "Knock 'em dead tomorrow night, champ," she said, and swiveled away.

I watched her move through the yups in their decorator oldies, head high and giant purse tucked solid under her arm, but just a little wobbly on her heels. Bob I imagine watched her too. We were both quiet, at any rate, til she reached the front door. Then, as I turned back to him hunched over his glass, it occurred to me that I had a hard time seeing the two of them as lovers; matter of fact I hardly believed it'd happened at all.

"Quite a lady," I said. "She say you're playing tomorrow?"

"Yeah," Bob said. "Yeah she is." He was smiling droopy-eyed straight ahead, as if at something right in front of his face. "Yeah, that's right, tomorrow night. God *damn*," he said, shaking his head and rubbing his neck. "I got up too early, man, I need some more shut-eye. Okay with you if we just go home?"

I couldn't say I had any buzz on Jean there at first. I don't think I was thinking much about her at all. All I remember having on my mind back at the apartment was what to do next, with Bob crashed out and Sharon at work.

At first I thought about putting one of Bob's records on, but that didn't seem right. We used to listen to music a lot back in Ohio, Bob pointing out this or that hook on the guitar, this slide or growl in the voice of this or that black man playing what he always called the "pure and nat-chul blues" for its own sake. *And the lower you go,* he loved to say, *the bluer you get,* quoting one old dead man whose name I've long forgotten while playing another note for note on the guitar—*until you get to it.* But it would have been too weird to play it now, with him in the next room snoring away.

So after hanging around a while waiting for the rain to stop, I decided to give up and go out in it anyway. I

195

went back down the street past the Wedgewood, to the T stop I remembered from my visit here with Cindy. I went down and bought my tokens, read the map and got on the train that connected with the line that went to Harvard Square in Cambridge, where we'd gone one afternoon back then and had a pretty good time. While I sat waiting, then riding, I went back over what I still had of that afternoon: the light and music swelling as the station's escalators brought us up, accordion stuff so corny it was cool, and our arms around each others' waists, still new but fitting right, and fresh sun on everything and everybody milling around on streets squeezed together like spokes in a wheel, thin sidewalks, old brick and black wrought-iron fences of hot-shit Harvard over on our left, and pigeons shining silver off their grey as they strutted around or took off up into the sky. We were walking around like everybody else looking at the stores and stuff, but I kept picking up on all the street entertainment, mostly guys playing music or singing but one doing sleight-of-hand stuff and another couple, farther on, wearing mime makeup and leotards, making balloon animals for the few kids around. And Cindy must have seen me looking.

You thinking about juggling?

I don't know, I said. *Maybe a little. Just wondering how much these guys make on a good day.*

What would you wear? she said.

I don't know. What do you think?

Lemme see, she said, and lowered her chin and pursed her pretty mouth. *Okay,* she said, *I got it. An old torn-up top hat, and a coat with tails and a dress shirt—*

With some gloves, right? I said. *White cotton gloves, so what you're tossing shows up that much better. Plus the hands themselves, people like to watch what's happening with your hands.*

Yeah, she said giggling, squeezing me closer. *Yeah that sounds great. Now, so okay you're all dressed up, you got these—*

Balls, I said. *Make it easy to start with. White and orange balls, start with two and go up to eight.*

Great, she said. *And what's your riff?*

Riff? I said.

You know, she said. *Your riff, your line of talk. It's not gonna work if you just juggle. You gotta talk it up, tell some jokes, keep the crowd feeling good.*

No matter how good I am? I said.

No matter how good you are.

We were almost stopped now, looking right into each other. *Then what can I say?* I said to her. *My street career's over. Cause I don't do riffs.*

It was not the best or smartest thing I could have done, calling it back, but it beat sitting joggling in the train's no-rhythm rhythm, staring over at the cheese-colored faces looking back as if they were taking a crap and I were the bathroom wall. The cool guys and girls Cindy's age or less who got on the last few stops before Harvard looked stupid in their black leather coats, their dangling earrings and reddish dyed hair over white white faces trying hard to look like something had happened to them once in their lives. I heard them talking as they passed me on their way up and out, giving lectures to each other was more like it, and swearing at the rain we

197

were all headed into like it was some sort of personal af-
fliction. Last time around with Cindy, I'd felt okay about
kids like this, like we had some kind of outlook in com-
mon. Now I was too old and too out-of-town, and besides, I didn't give a shit.

So what the fuck had I been doing with her? Tromping through the rain in Harvard Square, I gave that one a
fair amount of thought. A great month or so when we
first got together, followed by about a year half-decent to
good; then through the end last August, pretty much
straight downhill. The last few months we were hardly
talking other than to say like, Where's the electric bill,
Got the keys to the Chevette? for fear the other person
would start back in. Now, just a couple months later it
was almost as hard to remember what had pissed me off
as to get back what I'd liked about her, other than the sex.

I wanted to go have a beer someplace, but the only
bars I saw were trying to be pubs like in England, dark
wooden beams and fireplaces, shit like that, and for that
tradition probably sock you five bucks a draft. So I
ended up grabbing something inside this little mall, a
Chinese place across from a coffee place with lots of
Harvard-type people scrunched up at gnarly wooden tables reading and talking and being intense. I ate a bowl
of stir-fry vegetables and noodles standing up, trying to
get out of my bad mood. We weren't right for each other.
We wanted different things, was all. The point now, from
now on, I told myself, was not to disappoint any more
people, not to disappoint myself.

Back outside, the rain had let up some, but it was
colder and darker. Also it hit me there were no enter-

tainers out, just panhandlers and bums. One guy came up to me just outside the station, at the top of the stairs, his whiskered face running with rain, his tramp suit of half a dozen sweaters, torn suitpants and sneakers stinking of piss and alcohol. I gave him some money, then sat on the train the whole way back to Jamaica Plain telling myself *It's okay, man, it's all right, you can go home whenever you want* . . .

When I got back to the apartment it was somewhere after eight, and Bob was up watching a movie. They had a Boston station you could get on cable, showed Reagan movies every Saturday, he said. Tonight's was from World War II, Reagan and Errol Flynn I think and a bunch of other flyboys busting out of the POW camp the Nazis have them in, stopping off here and there in Berlin or wherever on their way back through Germany to blow up this or that factory, steal plans and planes, and generally gum up the works. I sat on the couch, Bob in his easy chair, same as the night before. Once during commercials he got up and put some popcorn on, brought us back a couple of beers. Later on, when the popcorn was done, we had a few more. Neither one of us said much except for once in a great while, a comment on how dumb the movie was, how what these guys were pulling off could never happen in a million years.

Sharon got in later, down near the weather on the 11 o'clock news. She grabbed a beer too and came and sat beside me, giving Bob's shoulder a squeeze on her way past.

"So," I said, "how'd it go?"

She hauled back on her bottle then leaned forward, the little nameplate still pinned to her blouse. "How'd it go," she said—not mean, just rolling it over. "I don't know. What do you say when you get asked that?"

"Nobody ever does," I said, "Aside from which these days I can't recall what it was like."

"Oh, I'll just bet that's not true," Sharon said. "Not on the basis of my experience." She fished down through her purse for her pack, shook one out and lit it, looked off at the tv. "I'm gonna remember reading blood samples til the day I die."

"Yeah," I said—seeing myself checking the gauges, taking the readings, writing them down over and over on the form—"I hear that," I said. "I know what you mean."

Sharon nodded; took another swig; sat back and gave a sigh. *Saturday Night Live* came on, and the three of us watched it through the first skit, celebrity intro and on into the first real commercial break.

"Whoa," Sharon said, shaking her head. "Not funny."

"Yeah," I said. "Just keeps getting worse and worse."

"Either that," Bob said, "or it always sucked this bad and we didn't notice."

It should've been a joke, I imagine, but instead of laughing we both turned to look at him over in his chair.

"How 'bout you?" Sharon said to him. "How was your day, how was Jean? You two guys have some good time together?"

"Oh yeah," Bob said, nodding his big nod, looking not at us but not at the tv either. Then he turned his big face to Sharon's—to both ours really—and spread his grin across it like a flag. "We hung out after Jean left for a while," he said. "Then Jimmy headed off for Harvard Square while I got me a little practice in."

Bull shit, I thought, and had to bite my lips, practically, to keep from saying it: *Bull shit, man, you went to sleep!*

But I didn't say anything, and Sharon went on. "How's Jean? What's she up to?"

"Not too much," he said. "Dumping more shit on Simon, mostly."

Sharon grinned too, and gave a little chuckle. Then she took a drag off her smoke and arched her brows, doing a Marlene Dietrich over at me. "And what'd she think of our Jimmy here?"

I rolled my eyes at her, at them both. "Get off, Sharon," I said.

"I think she really likes him," Bob said, wide-eyed in his chair. "Yeah, she likes him a lot. Hey, she told me so, man," he said, tipping forward, arms propped on his knees. "She told me she likes you. She said she wants you to ask her to the fucking prom."

And that, for some reason, was what finally got the three of us laughing, like back in the old days way back when.

*   *   *

A little later on, getting ready for bed, the last thing we did was make a plan for tomorrow. Bob said he'd need some time alone to get himself set, which by this point I figured might mean practicing or might not. Sharon said Okay, since she had the day off how about her and me go out and trip around somewhere tomorrow afternoon, take my car out to the gig that night? And Bob said Great but then how about the three of us do a long kickback Sunday breakfast, and we all said Fine to that, and then Goodnight.

But next morning we hadn't been up half an hour, and Bob and Sharon, in their bathrobes, were navigating between sink, fridge, and stove after telling me I couldn't help, when the phone rang and it was Jean. I was over by the table making chitchat with them while I tossed the balls around, just for fun to wake up my hands, the way I used to back then. The phone was on the wall just over my shoulder. I caught the balls and transferred them to the table, plink plank plunk plump, before picking up the call.

"G'morning," I said off the top of my head, "Paddy's Bar and Grill."

"How you doing, Jimmy," she said, like I was an old pal who'd said the usual. "Everybody up over there? Anybody mind if I come by for a minute or two?"

So there went our breakfast. Not in the sense we didn't have one. But having Jean there, which she was in about two seconds flat, all dolled up again in heels and stockings, a fancy blouse and skirt, telling her newest story about the shit she had to put up with poor Simon, wasn't what I'd had in mind. I tried not to act like a dickhead but I really wasn't interested in some awful thing he'd said he didn't even know how insulting it was last night until she told him, that was how fucking snobbish he was, etcet, etcet. I concentrated on the pancakes which were great, nice and light with crisp brown edges, I had about eight. Then I raised my head up from my plate and stood up from the table, picked my balls up off the counter and started in again, while the three of them kept sitting around and Jean talked.

This time through, Sharon fed Jean the straight lines, while Bob sat beside them forking it in through the hazey smile on his face. Periodically the two women broke into regular little fits together, Jean snorting with her hand over her mouth while Sharon's came out in little yelps and whoops. Once you get the basic hand-eye stuff down, the thing about juggling is heft, the weight and feel of what passes through your hands; that's why it's so much tougher to do more than one kind of thing at a time. And by the time they snapped out of it enough to notice I was still in the same room with them, I'd added one aluminum teaball and one juice glass, and taken out two of the balls.

"Jesus," I heard Jean whisper—probably still short of breath from her last fit—"he *is* good, isn't he?"

"Told you he was, didn't I now?" Bob said—as if the thing were his idea, like I was tossing my stuff around on his or anybody else's behalf.

I slowed the tosses down; I stopped altogether. "Hey," I said, with everything back on the countertop, "that was one great breakfast. Those pancakes sure hit the spot."

Sharon gave me a look that tried to read my face. Jean's smile stayed fastened on. "Glad you liked it," Sharon said. "You feeling about ready to get moving?"

"Naw," I said. "Take your time. Whyn't you guys just take it easy, just sit around here, keep on talking long as you like. I'll just pick up these dishes—"

"No, no," Sharon shook her head, started to get up. "We can get them."

"Sit down," I said. "You and Bob made the breakfast, I can wash up the dishes, fair's fair."

Across the table, Bob pushed back his chair and heaved up. "Okay," he said. "Guess I might's well get started."

"Come on, then," Jean said to Sharon as I reached over for the plates. "Let's go in the other room where we can really talk."

So while I cleaned up, Bob got his old Gibson out of its case and sat back at the table, turning it up and humming back to it, and the women kept going out in the front room. When I was done, I folded the dishtowel and walked past Bob to the dividing wall between kitchen and front room. There on the couch Jean stopped what she was saying; Sharon leaned over and whispered in her ear, then jumped up with a bright smile for me.

"Okay," she said, "we're off."

We had our coats on and were set to walk out before Bob looked up from his guitar. I stayed in the doorway as Sharon went over, leaned down and put her arms around him from behind.

"Bye baby," she said, kissing his cheek. "Love you, see you tonight."

"Bye Bob," I said, "check you later, man," and caught Jean's pale eyes as I turned around, sliding from the two of them over to me.

"Have a great time, you two," she said through her halo of smoke. "Don't do anything I wouldn't do."

"Not a chance," I said with my own smile. "Take care yourself now, hear?"

Outside was better than the day before, but still blustery and overcast, as if later on it could start spitting snow. All the way to the T with the wind making talk hard anyway, I was telling myself not to say it; but once we were in and on the platform side by side and I looked over at her, that aging kid's face still tightened up against the cold, it just popped out. "You're not worried about the two of them back there?"

I heard my voice saying it, then drifting off, already hollow, down the tiled landing. Sharon's eyebrows lifted as she looked back at me.

"No," she said—then had to raise her voice, and keep on raising it against the rising wall of roar, the train coming in—"No, nothing's gonna happen. Jean'll sit there a while and listen to him, then she'll let herself out. You know Bob"—by now really yelling—"once he gets into it, he's gone."

The train squealed to a stop, we got on, it lurched and slid us away. Again I told myself *Shut up, don't get into it,* then realized I had no idea where we were going, I could ask that instead.

"So where we going?" I said.

"I don't know," Sharon said. "I was thinking maybe Faneuil Hall, you know that place? It's an old Boston-type place they fixed up so it's all stores now. But it's down by the water, you know, it's kind of fun. That sound all right to you?"

"Sure," I said. "Sounds just fine. Lemme ask you," I said, "is Bob like needing a lot more sleep these days?"

She cocked her head and looked back wide-eyed. "I don't know," she said. "I don't think so. Why do you ask?"

"Cause," I said, "when Bob said last night he was practicing earlier? Maybe he was, eventually. But when I took off he was pulling z's in bed."

If she'd looked shocked it would've been better, I would've felt less like ripping out my tongue. But instead she just looked away, out at the dark between stations, and sighed loud enough I could even hear it over the noise of the ride.

"Yeah," she said, "well." We both watched her hands, red with cold still, turn over in her lap. Then her eyes came to mine straight on, old as she had looked yesterday but with something else I could hardly stand to look back at there too.

"He's having a hard time right now, Jim," she said. "You'll see when we get to Millis tonight."

I wanted to ask more, like just how bad it was, but finally was able to keep my mouth shut, period. And Sharon kept quiet too, until the ride was over and we were back outside walking across this cobblestone-and-brick open space with people everywhere, like Harvard Square only more commercial and less hip, straight people with money it looked like from their coats, clothes, and the packages they had. There was Faneuil Hall all lit up right ahead, an old stone building where our forefathers once did something or other now restaurants and stores, and out beyond it an inlet with a few boats still docked there in spite of it being November, and on the other side of the water a finger of land lined with an old factory or warehouse spruced up and gone condo for big bucks, you could tell from even this far away. The water out there under the clouds was the color of nails except where the wind was tearing whitecaps off it, the same wind pushing from behind the happy shoppers coming towards us, bending the two of us over as it shoved them on ahead. It was no easier to talk than it'd been on the train, but someone had to say something, and it might as well be me.

"What's going on?" I said. "What's the trouble with Bob?"

"It's not Bob!" she called back, squinting up and over.

"It's not Bob," she said again, once we were out of the wind and stray cold rain, standing in a glass-covered walkway in to Faneuil Hall, glassed-in sit-down restaurants on either side. She pulled off her knit cap, swept her fingers through cropped silver hair, looked around at the folks finishing up their Sunday brunches. "It's the spaces," she said.

I followed her eyes as if that might give me a clue. "Spaces," I said. "You mean the places where he plays?"

"Where he used to," said Sharon, a fresh smoke in her mouth. "That's what I mean. Used to be, when we first got here, he'd play Somerville or Cambridge two nights a week, weekends in the North End, plus maybe a couple more nights around J.P. Now the folky bars and old coffee-houses went under, or else stopped booking acoustic blues. Or else they just stopped having live music at all."

She'd said it out grim, like an announcement to a crowd; but then her face came back to life. "Hey, listen," she said. "I don't know what's the matter with me. We can go someplace nicer than this. You wanna go someplace nicer? I mean, unless you wanna go through, look at the stores—"

"Stores?" I said. "Baby, you got me confused with somebody else."

So she laughed and took my arm and we went back outside, heading away from the water and underneath a freeway overpass. A few blocks more, and not only are we out of the wind, away from the traffic; we're in a whole different town.

I looked around at the little side streets twisting off the one we were on, the paving-stone brick of the roadway and skinny sidewalks and low old brick two- and three-stories crowded in on either side of them, the gabbling pigeons way outnumbering the mostly old folks out toddling around. "I didn't know Boston had anything like this," I said. "This is great."

"Yup," she said. "While it lasts. Come on, in here."

The place she took me into had no name on its steamed-up windows, and only about eight small wooden tables inside, two with card games that stopped the second we came in and a third with dominoes. We headed up to the counter past both kinds of men, the squat old redfaced guys with their black suitcoats and white shirts open at the neck, and the younger guys, still tall and thin, in dark shirts and shiny black coats to match their hair.

"Sharon," I said, feeling their eyes on us, hearing the quiet, "you sure you been in here before? I mean, it's okay like to—"

"Hi!" Sharon said, loud and clear with her brightest smile for the greyfaced woman squint-eyeing us from in between the wood-and-glass display cases and cash register, in her white-on-navy polkadot old-lady dress. "Could we get two cannoli and two expresso for here, please?"

"Sure, sweetheart," said the old lady, face cracking to smile right back. "You two set down, I have it for you right away."

"You know," Sharon said later on at the table with our stuff, "you always were a wussy, Jim DeMott. You remember back in Cleveland, going into Carbone's?"

"Hold on," I said. "You forget I knew Carbone's, I grew up two blocks away. With my mom, my dad both telling me, Hey that's members only, you don't go in there, okay?"

"Which," she said, wagging a finger tipped with powdered sugar, "it turned out was wrong."

"Which it turned out I was wrong," I said, "only because it was you with Bob and me, and those old guys in there thought you were cute."

She tossed her head back and laughed at that, remembering, and before they could catch themselves all the old guys plus a few of the younger ones looked over grinning too, almost like we were back there again. Which actually it seemed to me we were—and not just because the tiled floor the color of old teeth, the raggedy palm tree in the corner, even the guys themselves seemed so much the same.

"Okay," I said. "So I don't go where I'm not wanted. So I am a wuss."

"But you are wanted," she said. "You're wanted right here."

"What, here?" I said and laughed. "I don't think so, Sharon."

"No." She gave my arm on the table a little slap. "Come on. You know what I mean. You could quit your sucky job at the General and come out here and get something better. A couple computer science courses you could pick up here and there, a little training in programming, you could snag something out along Route 9 just like that, at least as good as what you got and probably better."

"Yeah," I said, lifting a forkful of cannoli. I put it in my mouth; I chewed and swallowed it. "I could do that," I said.

"Yeah," she said, streaming out smoke. "You could but you won't, cause you're a wuss."

"Hey," I said, holding my hands up palms out. "Back off, okay?" Knowing, though, she could tell I wasn't actually ticked.

And then anyway we got off onto other stuff. Mostly Sharon telling me about this part of town, what they call the North End, how the younger folks've left and the old ones're getting pushed out by the yups coming in bumping up the price of everything. I told her it was happening all over, even back home, and described a couple neighborhoods she'd remember.

Gradually, as we sat bitching away, the old guys went back to the click-clack of their dominoes and slap of their cards, the young ones to hanging out and giving each other shit. Pretty soon the Italian was as rich and steady as the coffee smell, the steam on the windows sealing us off into the warm gold glow of this no-name place that'd been here it seemed like forever with all of us in it, just this way. I looked at the old lady we'd ordered from, standing up there at the counter leafing through the Sunday paper and shaking her head too over how piss-poor the world was, and said to Sharon, "You know what? This is okay."

"Yeah," she said. "It is, isn't it?" But then something tugged on her lower lip, pulling at her smile.

I put my hand out, touched the wrist of the hand that wasn't stirring the spoon around her expresso cup. "Hey, Sharon," I said. "Hey."

She looked up and past me and off to the side, wet-eyed. "It's nothing," she said, "I'm okay. It's just I didn't think it would turn out like this."

I couldn't tell if everything had really gone quiet, or was it just me. "Like what?" I said—wanting to hear if only for her sake but not wanting either, half knowing and half not.

"Like—" Her face frowned and she twisted away, digging in her purse for another cigarette as the words spilled out. "Like I don't *know*. Like you think things are moving, something's happening, right? You don't like what's here you can look around, wait for something else to open up. But now I'm in the same old nothing job, and Bobby's having a hard time and I'm not seeing any openings. And I don't know whether it's how old we are or 1987 or what, but it's starting to hit me things don't have to get better. Things can get worse just as easy. Or they can even stay the same."

She lit her cigarette, shakyhanded. I looked away, trying to find something to say back, and saw it wasn't just me. The men were either looking over or else really not looking and the old lady up at the counter gazed back with a turtle's blank face. I wondered how much English they knew, how much they'd heard. I looked down at the hands in my lap and imagined them picking up a few things, cups and saucers maybe, tossing them around.

"Which is why"—I heard Sharon say, and looked up to see her swig her cup empty—"which is why I say if you've got some room to move, like here to Boston, for God's sakes take it. Or by the way and speaking of chances, how about you and Jean, what do you think?"

"Jean," I said. "Who's talking about Jean?"

"I am," said Sharon. "Listen, we better start moving." We both stood up, started getting our coats on. "Bob was kidding last night," Sharon was saying, "but it's really true we talked about you this morning—you, I mean, among other things. And she definitely thinks you're nice."

"*Nice?*" I heard my voice swoop up, felt the guys looking over again.

"Thank you," Sharon was saying, waving, smiling to one and all. "Thanks very much, goodbye!"

"She doesn't know me from Adam," I whispered over by the door.

"I'm not saying you gotta marry her, she wants your baby," Sharon said back just as soft. "She's been around, she's got a kid, she's got no intention of getting messed up again. All I'm saying—"

"Whoa," I said, fake-lurching as I opened the door, "hold it right there. I didn't know she had a kid."

"You see?" Sharon said, shooting me her old smart-ass grin as we hit the grey cold outside again. "You don't know everything about her after all, do you? And maybe she does know a few things about you."

On the way out to Millis, Sharon gave me directions and filled me in some more. The kid was something like twelve, thirteen now, Jean'd had her when she was in her teens herself, just barely out of high school before having to get married in her hometown in New Hampshire somewhere, where the boyfriend had a job with the gas company. They'd moved down here around the same time Bob and Sharon came in from Cleveland. Eventually the guy got on as a lineman with New England Telephone, but not before he started drinking, knocking her around, taking off for days at a stretch, til she sued for divorce and he took off for good. For the next few years, Sharon said, she held it together taking in other people's kids with her own and calling it day care, until Deirdre, the kid, got old enough to spend the whole day in school. But then it was '82, nobody was working, so she had to bump along with her so-called day care plus whatever Reagan and his boys had left of benefits, til a few years later, when she locked on to this state program for displaced homemakers, got her real-estate license out of it and landed this job.

So okay, you had to respect that. But even so, and granting she was pretty, I wasn't sure I wanted to give it a shot. For one thing, I wondered what we'd be doing with this rich guy Simon around, and Bob too, regardless of what Sharon said. Plus I wasn't sure I wanted to hook up with anyone on any terms just now, for any length of time.

But Jean wasn't all we talked about on the way out. We talked about a bunch of other things. About a bar in Cleveland called Ed's Place where the three of us used to hang out with all the older smart-but-stupid juicers, white and black, all on the slide, and about how my older brothers and her younger sisters were doing, and our parents and Bob's. About the difference between Ohio and Massachusetts cold in late fall and early winter, and why cigarettes smelled so much better than they tasted, especially in a cold car. And about how Sharon'd changed her work schedule around for tomorrow, working 7 to 3 so she could come back out for the Monday night gig, which she said it'd be better if I didn't come along to, probably.

That surprised me enough I started to look over then thought better of it, what with these winding country roads starting to freeze over, black ice on two-lane, black trees against the sky on either side. Boston to Millis turned out to be some trek. "Say what?" I said.

"Monday night at this place," Sharon said, "is open mike. Anybody can get up there. Nobody gets paid. The owners asked Bob if he'd do it so there'd be at least one decent act. And backed it up by letting him know if he said no tonight would be it."

She'd been talking so low I could hardly hear her over the wind and engine noise, but now we were coming in to a scatter of stray houses and lights. So she went back to directions, which I followed without paying much attention. It was hitting me now just how far out this place was.

"Jesus, Sharon," was all I could say, at a stoplight near the middle of the town of Millis.

"I know," she said between drags. "Take a left here and go half a block. It's the first bar on the right, the Buckaroo."

At 7:30 on a Sunday night, the dirt lot in front of the Buckaroo was mostly full, which I took for a good sign. On the other hand, walking up the plank steps to the porch, the only notice for Bob I saw was two orange pages of regular-sized paper with his name stamped on them in block print, tacked up on either side of the swinging wooden doors. Inside was same as outside, all stained knotty pine, a box of a room half-divided by its mid-beams, two foozballs and a shuffleboard on the left side and the bar at the back, jukebox over on the right trying to push country-western through the noise, tiny thrust-stage on the right side to the rear. Folks sitting and drinking, talking and laughing at every one of the round wooden tables on both sides, dead ringers for the white folks I worked with at the General—for most of my own family, even, far as that goes. I recognized their quilted club jackets, their brushcuts and perms, their stretch slacks, flowered sweaters and western-cut shirts. I knew

the extra pounds on their waists, the flashes of metal
when they showed their teeth, their flushed faces and the
hollering exaggeration in their laughter, like comic-book
characters with bubbles over their heads saying HA!
HA! HA! And one thing I knew for sure about a crowd
like this, sure as the sick in my stomach: they would not
care a shitting thing about the blues.

"There they are," Sharon said next to me, and
waved across to a table on the right, near the stage,
where Bob and Jean sat next to a younger blond guy in
a dress shirt and corduroy sportcoat, looking so miserable you could tell it even from here.

"See?" she called over the noise as we threaded
our way across. "You got nothing to worry about
with Simon."

She was coming on strong but I could brush it aside,
especially with all there was to keep track of. Besides, she
was right about Simon, who looked up close even more
like a whipped cocker spaniel. Once we got to the table,
I reached across, of course, and shook his hand around
Jean's introduction. Then Bob stood up, with a smile but
looking sort of numb, and I put my arm around his
shoulders and slapped his back.

"Thanks for coming," he said, like a sick friend in
the hospital. "I appreciate it, man."

"Hey," I said, zippy as could be, "wouldn't have
missed it, champ. Looks like you got a great turnout."

"Yeah," Bob said, deadpan, "great crowd," and sat
back down.

So then I got to spend the next few minutes worrying which it was, if he thought I was making a crack or

knew I was lying, and harshing myself out either way. But nobody else was talking much either. Sharon sat down beside Bob across from Jean and wrapped his near arm in hers; Jean revolved between smiling at Bob and Sharon, swigging her wine and sucking on her smoke; Simon was finger-drawing on the varnished table with the sweat from his scotch glass; and between the two of them, Sharon and Jean, Bob stared off and across to where the roof met the side wall, like someone adding up numbers in his head.

We went on killing time like that until he finally got up, went back behind the bar, came out with his guitar in one hand and a chair in the other, and got up on the tiny stage. A skinny ferret-faced guy with a trimmed wedge of beard came behind him with a microphone stand, and when it was set up said "Ladies and gentlemen, Bob Krivak" into the mike in the same voice that gives out exact time on the phone. The crowd clapped a second and quieted down, but when Bob started fooling with the mike stand, bending to pick up more guitar, they went back to what they were doing. One guy came over to the jukebox but made the mistake of looking over towards us, and gave up his plan of punching selections when I glared at him hard. Up on the stage, Bob was saying some things, Glad you could make it, hope you like it, so low and off-mike I could hardly make it out. But then he was playing, opening it up a way I've heard a hundred times easy, with a single low note that then slides lower, snarling on its way down like running your hand down barbed wire, tearing meat and going on down without slowing, snagging again and not even bothering to look, running down til it catches again, same place same time absolutely no surprise. He was playing slide, leaning over the guitar, one bootheel thunking the wooden stage every time the notes fell and tried to get up and fell again. The guitar was singing by itself and telling a story, but it wasn't personal, wasn't for you, didn't know or give a shit that you were here. It was so torn up it couldn't care less.

It went on a while longer, over and over, while he waited at the edge, and then walked into it too.

> *I don't know . . .*
>> *why everybody's down on me . . .*
> *I don't know . . .*
>> *why everybody's down on me . . .*

Thanks to Bob I knew who it came from, Mississippi Fred McDowell, but that didn't matter either. It went down past whoever first played it on a record, past whatever record it was on and all the times I'd heard it in whatever place Bob and Sharon were living in or whatever stage Bob was on, making it happen again. Past my staying on in Cleveland, keeping on at the plant, past Cindy and the other ones I thought I was in love with, my folks old and sick now and me getting older, my brother who drinks too much like Dad and the other who sells drafting equipment and says so much crazy shit I can't talk to him any more. He was on another song now, this one about a train that was coming, a woman who was gone, but that was no more important. It was what was underneath it and behind every story, the work that hurts the hurt that works, that same old never-ending no beginning grind . . .

Some people were clapping between songs, but only a few and only for a little while. I had my back turned to them anyhow, and was paying them no more attention than I was to pretty-boy Simon, until after maybe the fourth or fifth number I picked up on Sharon across and down the table, making quick sweeps of the place with nervous eyes.

Then, before turning to look for myself, I was brought up short by something else. By the sight of Jean in between the blond guy and Sharon, Jean with eyes half-shut and her cigarette down to its filter but still holding its ash. By her thin face like a drumhead struck again and again by the blues.

She must have shifted, something must have moved; because a fragrance drifted to me, smoke mixed with her perfume and something else. Her eyes opened and found mine. Pupils large as if in darkness, irises the color of steam. I heard Sharon coming out of Fanueil Hall alongside me, *And maybe she does know something about you* . . .

I turned and looked away to catch hold of my breathing. So it took a few seconds to register what I saw. While I'd been listening with my back turned to the crowd, more than half the bozos at the Buckaroo had moseyed on home. Gotta get up bright and early for work tomorrow morning, make the payment on the house, don't wanna be late. And most of the ones left were doing their best to yak it up as though there were no live music here at all. A couple guys were over at the foozball table spinning and slamming the various rods. And over in front of the bar, the bearded bartender-m.c. stood with his arms folded on his skinny chest, an acid-stomach look on his ferret face.

Given all this, I can't say as I blame Bob for his next move, though for all the good it did he might as well have left it alone. I saw him look up from where he had just finished playing a mean Mance Lipscomb tune, and the sick and tired of his face was enough to make you wince. There was even one awful moment when he'd managed to pull a smile but everything else was just the same.

"Well"—he said through that shit-eating grin, careful now to speak right into the mike—"don't want to get too far down on a cold Sunday night, do we? How bout we try a little change-up, see what all we can shake loose?"

I don't remember what he did from then on in very much detail. There was some Beatles acoustic, and a few folks sang along. He did "Lay Lady Lay" and some other Dylan tunes. He even tried some '30s and '40s songs, riffs skimmed off the Django records he had. This was after a little intro on Django and the Hot Club, stuff he'd played for me years back and now dished out like a talk-show host to whoever was left. It was all fine for music you'd hear in a bar. Only problem was, it wasn't any more than that.

After a while I stopped looking at him altogether. Not him, and not behind me either, no more checking how many were left. I ordered a couple pitchers from Ferret Face, enough for me and anybody else wanted to drink beer with me, and spent the time filling my glass up, watching bubbles rise from the bottom and foam thin out on top, thinking over just when and what size my next swallow after my last one would be. I couldn't stand to look at Sharon either, the way her stiffened face looked out at the other tables and her hands stayed in her lap, like the minister's wife back when my mom took us kids to St. Marks Lutheran. And Jean I also left alone.

Finally 11 o'clock rolled around, and it was over. Bob thanked us all and said goodnight; we clapped and whooped, together with whoever might still have been there. I think there were a few others, that at least a few other chairs besides ours scraped as we got up to leave but I couldn't be sure. My campaign on the pitchers had worked well enough it was all I could do to get my coat on and walk a straight line. I picked up on Ferret Face putting the chairs up, seemed like practically before Bob'd stepped down off the stage. I had my hand around Bob's shoulders, I was slapping his back, telling him what a wonderful goddamn beautiful set it'd been. I took a final gander at Simon the stick holding Jean's coat open for her to get into. He was looking almost happy, and I bet I knew why—cause maybe now he'd been a good boy, put his time in, she'd be nice and they could do something he liked. Seeing him cheerful made me want to smack his face but that'd be stupid. Besides, Sharon was in front of me, asking if I'd be all right driving home alone if she went back with Bob.

So I concentrated on not slurring and said Sure, sure I would, see them back at the ranch, aimed a goodbye smile at them both but mostly at her so I wouldn't have to look at Bob beside her with God only knows what on his face. Then I turned and headed off for the door ahead of the rest of them, just thinking about clearing enough fog out to get home safe, keeping my thoughts to that.

So how Jean ditched her rich Dutch Boy and got there before me I sure couldn't say. But surprise surprise, there she was, swinging open the outside door, smiling like she was laughing at the both of us not just me.

"Goodnight," she said.

"Goodnight," I managed to say back.

"Listen," she said. "You want to get together sometime? You know, just have a drink, talk?"

"Yeah," I said, feeling stupid excited—you know, that high light feeling in your chest—on top of the drunk, and at the same time thinking we either ought to shut the door or I should go out. "Yeah sure," I said, "I'd like that. But we oughtta do it soon, I gotta head back sometime in the next few days."

"Okay," she said. "How about tomorrow night?"

"Tomorrow night?" I said. "Sure, okay."

"I'll call you tomorrow," she said.

"Okay," I said, "goodnight," and took a deep breath and walked out the door.

The whole slow way back to Jamaica Plain I sobered up thinking over Jean and me. About first finding out she had a kid then having that eye contact, flirtation, whatever, at the Buckaroo just now. I tried to figure, had my feelings toward her really changed? Or was it just me wanting to get into it again, more or less regardless? Or lower still, just wanting to get laid? And while I was at it, why'd I told her I was going back so soon, where'd that little ditty come from anyhow?

I didn't come up with anything much but at least the questions kept me going til I was back up the stairs and onto the couch, where good old Sharon, bless her soul, had already spread out the sheets and blankets before going off to bed herself. I could still hear her and Bob moving and murmuring off in the bedroom, but I barely managed to call Goodnight before the walls collapsed. Then, at some point later on, I was lying there half-awake and sweating underneath dreams like a blanket I was too weak to throw off. There was a woman, not Cindy not Jean but not *not* them either, somebody who showed up whenever I was doing the dumbest dullest things then took off before I could turn to her. If she would have stayed just a few seconds longer, I could have shown her my juggling, my gracefulness, the mud already slipping off my boots, and now the boots themselves and now me flying to join her. But it had taken too long and she was gone. I'd had too much to drink and so had to square dance with the others, treading the cement to the point where it would stand up and we could use it to build the ugly house, the pile of stones where I would have to live now I had lost her, only there she was again . . .

For the longest time I tried either to get all the way down or else wake up, until when I finally did Monday morning I felt already wiped. My head held layers of accumulated gunk, my bones and joints felt all banged up. A few more hours sleep would have been perfect but barring them it was okay to lie here a few minutes more without thinking anything, not about Bob and Sharon, much less Cindy, much less Jean and what would happen tonight . . .

So I was lying there, weak but sort of turned on, watching the bright grey sky out the bay windows scatter gusts of swirling pellets, half hearing and half feeling the furnace roll over and wheeze on below, when the phone went off in the next room.

I jumped up, wrapped a blanket around me, caught it by the second ring. What time was it anyhow?

"Hello?" I said. "Bob and Sharon's, Jim speaking."

"Hello," she said in a voice that made me remember her smile. "You just getting up?"

"As a matter of fact," I said. "What time is it?"

"Put it this way," she said. "Deirdre's up and off to school. I made the beds, cleaned up the dishes, got to the office, and have looked over two properties so far."

"I'm impressed," I said. "And a little hung. You telling me like eleven o'clock?"

"A little after noon," she said, and I heard her take a puff off her smoke. "You still interested in our getting together tonight?"

Come on, come on, I was saying to myself, feeling how close I was getting to backing off, to not even liking her again. On my palms and the back of my neck a coating of day-after beersweat had sprung up. "Sure," I told her. "What's the plan?"

Simple: she'd be done with work by 4:30, pick her kid up from the after-school playground program, get her home and fed and spend some time with her before the sitter, a teenage kid from next door, Jean used her all the time, came over at 7. Then how about if we just got together at the Wedgewood again?

It did get me wondering how she must be with this kid Deirdre, being babysat tonight for minimum the third night in a row. But I still just said, Fine, see you then. I would have said it was okay to meet at Harvard Square, the Buckaroo, wherever, just to get off the phone, I felt so much like shit.

Then felt that much worse when I hung up and turned around. Because there was Bob sitting at the kitchen table, looking like I felt. His hands spread flat on his knees, his bearded head bowed, you'dve thought he was asleep with his eyes open or in a coma or something, the way he was staring down at his cereal bowl, red mouth hanging slack.

"Hey Bob," I said. "How's it going, man?"

He looked up at me. "Hey Jimmy," he said.

It must've been chilly wearing nothing but jeans and no shoes and a Robert Johnson t-shirt shot with holes. I could feel the draught myself from the wind rattling the panes.

"Guess I had a little much last night," I said, wrapping my blanket tighter around me, flashing him a wobbly smile. "At the old Buckaroo. I'm pretty cheap drunk nowdays, I guess."

His eyes took on a little focus. "Yeah," he went. "Yeah, well, it's a bar."

"Well I didn't get to tell you how good you were," I said, shifting foot to foot. "You were great, you know that, don't you? You were great."

Slowly one corner of his mouth lifted up. "Yeah," he said. "yeah, you told me. Glad you liked it, man."

I could tell how fast I was starting to talk, how fast I was moving, weaving like a boxer, shuffling to warm my feet, but I couldn't stop. "So," I said, "looks like I'm gonna spend some time with Jean. Meet her at the Wedgewood later on, have a drink, dinner maybe, I don't know, talk about our lives or some shit. What you got planned for today—I mean, you know, before tonight? You wanna go somewhere, do something this afternoon?"

His gaze met mine a second; then moved away. He leaned back and scratched his chest. "I don't know," he said. "Better stay here and practice, I guess."

"Okay," I said, thinking *Okay*. "Guess I'll take a shower and get out of here then. Yeah, and by the way, looks like I'll be taking off tomorrow, man."

Which I know came out with an edge on it; but I couldn't help it, I was pissed. The whole time I was in the shower it was still going. Sure, I was sorry about what was going down with him, but I'd had it with having to protect his poor wounded ass. I had my problems too, shit, plenty of them, but I wasn't gonna dwell on them night and day, much less lay them on everybody else I knew. My blood was singing, the shower-spray was stinging me awake, God*damn,* I was thinking, almost like being ripped all over again, I've *had* it with this shit, I'm going out tonight and have me some *fun* . . .

But when I finished up and came back out of the bathroom, Bob must have been doing some thinking of his own. He was sitting on the couch across from where

I'd piled up my bedding, doodling around on his guitar to a tune off the stereo, first time it'd been going since I'd come, playing John Hurt:

Avalon's my home town—always on my mind . . .
Avalon's my home town—always on my
mind . . .

Real happy sweet music any way you cut it, not to mention how far it went back for us.

And as soon as I got out he was talking, practically doing a talking blues: "Hey man," he said: "why *don't* you think about taking off, anyway? Permanente, man, no more Ohio once and for all. Think about coming out here, find a place, get a job, check it out—"

"Maybe cause it's not that easy," I said, feeling just fine thank-you-very-much for stepping on his lines. Said it while combing my wet hair back, pulling on a clean shirt, fishing in my gym bag for the juggling balls to stuff back in my jacket, getting ready to go. "Maybe cause not all of us have somebody else to cover our ass while we do what we want."

Then I didn't even bother looking around; just said "Check you later, have a good afternoon," opened the door, bounded down the stairs and out.

Outside I strolled on past the Wedgewood where I'd meet Jean tonight, then took a jog off the main drag and started back through the side streets. It was like a maze in there, a piece of cracked ice, the way the space was cut block by block into off-kilter chunks, but after a while you could still see the pattern and get the point.

The part Sharon and Bob lived in, Centre Street near the T-stop, was except for a few places like their house all spiffy, full of yuppies who'd repainted and refurbished and fixed everything up. But the farther you got from that main drag the more the houses had that faded cheap aluminum siding or even that old tarpaper-shingle stuff, the more squat brick duplexes and sagging three-families you saw with broken gutterpipes and peeling paint, the more the few people out and around tended not to be white.

I probably should've been reaming myself for slicing Bob that way, but the anger was still riding me, I wasn't even all that cold. After a while I took out the orange balls and started tossing them around while I kept walking. It was tricky, making microadjustments for the usual differences plus the gusts of freezing wind kicking up, plus all the curbs and cracks and frozen puddles to cross. What few people were out gave me looks like What is this white boy, crazy? But I figured Let them look, let Jean herself drive by on her way to or from one of her so-called properties, I could give a sweet shit.

At a certain point later on, though, my hands were aching, my knuckles were raw. And I wanted to at least see Sharon long enough to say Hey how you doing before she took off for Millis with Bob. Figured it was 1:30 when I went out, I must have been walking a good hour and a half, with the balls back in my coat it'd still take another hour to retrace my steps. On the way back I remembered how Cindy used to say I kept my feelings bottled up but that just made me think Fuck Cindy. I still didn't feel much like patching things up with Bob, or worrying about what would happen with Jean, or thinking over was I really going back and if so why. Whenever I tried to think about any of that stuff the headache over my eyes was back just like that.

I reached the apartment, must have been around 4:30, 5 o'clock. When Sharon came down to let me in she had her coat and hat still on. On the stairs she told me they'd decided to head out early, the gig, if you could call it that, started at 7, they'd catch something to eat out there. I wondered what Bob had said to her about what I'd said, but couldn't imagine him really telling her anything. But I felt a little shitty about it anyhow, whether she knew or not.

Then, when we walked in off the landing, Bob was standing there just inside the door all scarfed and buttoned up, black guitar case dangling from one mittened hand. Until I saw him there like that, I still might've said something about what a jerk I'd been, how I hadn't meant to x or y or z. But now, running into him like this, I didn't know what to do.

"Ready, honey?" she asked him.

He looked at her and nodded, a tight smile on those rosebud lips.

"Give 'em hell tonight, buddy," I said as he brushed past.

"Don't mind him," Sharon turned in the doorway to whisper through his tromping down the stairs. "He's just keyed up, you know, about tonight."

"I know," I said, whispering same as her. "Listen, you back to normal schedule tomorrow?"

"Yeah," she said, "three to eleven. How come?"

"Cause, I don't know," I said. "It might be time to get on back."

Down below us we heard the front door open, creak and close. "You're kidding," Sharon said. "You got a date tonight and you're leaving tomorrow?"

"What?" I said. "You think we're gonna fall in love, start a big romance? How'd you find out anyways, Bob tell you or what?"

Both of us still whispering, with no need. She shook her head, and one last time that tomboy smile got out in front of the sad tired eyes. "Jean called," she said, and plucked at my coat. "Listen, I gotta go. Have a great time, and don't you dare leave tomorrow without checking in with me, okay?"

"Okay," I said; and we gave each other's cheeks a couple awkward kisses and she was gone.

I could watch tv or listen to records. I could practice my juggling. I could call up one of the guys I worked with, Marty or Leon, get the word on when and if we'd be going back. I could make some coffee for myself, have a beer, jerk myself off. Or lie back and calm down, maybe even take a nap.

From the front room windows I watched their old VW pull out, join the traffic on the street and disappear. The streetlights were blinking on and here inside was already dark. I turned on a few lights and sat down in Bob's easy chair for a while. Then I switched them off and lay down on the couch to watch the shapes move behind my eyelids, get some distance on the stuff drifting in. I wasn't going to feel bad about Bob, what was done was done. I wasn't going to hold out for anything from this night with Jean. Wasn't going out to be disappointed. Wasn't going to disappoint myself.

I opened my eyes again and it was 6:30. I turned on the tv and the night's top story was the stock market still, from the big crash or whatever a few weeks back. I left it on while I changed into the best shirt I'd brought, spit-wiped my shoes with toilet paper in the blue fluttery light. Then I spun the channels for a weather report, but nothing doing. Have to see what the roads and sky would look like when I got up.

Finally I'd frogged around long enough it was after 7, so I turned off the tv and left. Outside the traffic had thinned out, the snow had stopped falling, the sky was clear with a half-moon and stars I could see even through the city lights, and anything that might happen from here on was about to start now.

In the Wedgewood the jukebox was playing classical, the place was half-full and smelled like what a couple straight-looking guys in sportshirts and hornrims were serving, pasta with different sauces it looked like as I headed through the blur of warmth and noise. She was sitting in back like the day before yesterday, already set up with a carafe of wine.

"Beethoven," I said, smiling back as I sat down. "Third concerto, movement two."

Across the table she looked partly tickled, partly confused. "You don't really know, do you?"

"Hell no," I said. "It's all *Fantasia* to me. How you doing?"

"All right," she said. "Want some wine, want a drink? Sandy—" she looked up and called.

I ordered a scotch on the rocks, but when the waiter left confessed I shouldn't be having anything. "Last night's two pitchers still running through my system," I said, "I been acting weird all day."

"Oh yeah?" she said. "Like what?"

"Forget it," I said. "Nothing interesting. But hey, listen—" I started, as Sandy came back, bingo, with my drink so I had to dig a five out to cover what it'd be— "listen, I didn't know you had a kid."

Her eyes hardened, slid away. "That's right," she said. "So what?"

"Whoa, take it easy," I said, nervous-laughing, holding both hands up. "I didn't know, is all."

She took a slow drag, exhaled, and her face softened. "I'm sorry," she said. "It's just, you know, she is my kid. And I act a little crazy about her sometimes."

The scotch caromed against the back wall of my skull and cleared it out for the first time today. Inside the space I heard the standard follow-ups, *How old is she?* followed by something like *She must be beautiful if she looks like you.* Where those lines come from, when they first got wired in, I swear to God I'll never know. "How old is she?" I said.

She blushed a little, like a shy cute kid herself. "Twelve," she said. "Twelve and reading everything she can get her hands on about King Arthur, Guenevere, Sir Lancelot. It's this weird Camelot kick, it's what she lives for, practically."

I took another sip. "Is that right," I said.

232

"Yeah," Jean said, and turned back into herself. "Next thing you know it'll be straight romance like every other stupid girl her age. Then she'll want to live them. God, I don't look forward to that."

"What do you look forward to?" I said, wondering where'd *that* come from? right as I said it.

She seemed startled too. Or at least had to wait a sec, moving her eyes away, flicking the ash from her smoke. "To making more money," she said. "Enough so I don't ever have to worry if there's enough."

"I can understand that," I said; though I wasn't sure I liked it all that much.

"I know you can," she said. "I figured that about you right off."

I didn't know what to say to that, so we had a little staring match instead. I looked at her hard thin face, high cheekbones, rich reddish-brown hair touched up just perfect with that shade of red lipstick, that black dress; I looked at the blue-grey eyes looking back, and had to look away. I picked up my glass and tipped my head to pour in the rest of the scotch. It went down cold but sent out heat where it landed; better still, it brought the rest of the place back, the sound of other people and jazz on the juke, and when I looked again she had her smile back on too.

"I told you what I do last time we were here," she said. "How about you? I got from Sharon you work in a plant, but doing what?"

She had her head cocked as she said it, acting serious but flirty. "I'll be more than glad to answer that question," I said, "once we have some fresh drinks.

Sandy?" I called, tossing my head like King Shit as I threw up my hand.

We had him bring us a double scotch and a fresh half-liter; we said we'd let him know about dinner, if and when. Then Jean lit a fresh cigarette, poured her first glass from the new carafe, I took a sip of scotch and started in.

"Okay," I said. "You already know I work in a plant. You probably think a guy like me's gonna be on a belt line, assembly line, right? Wrong," I told her, "I got a higher skill level and more smarts. Plus the guys on the lines're the ones they're letting go. Union pisses and moans, but you start getting rough back they'll move the whole show to Mexico, fuck you all. Which they'll probably do eventually, regardless. Anyway," I told her, "what I do is work the control room on hot end. Mostly sit there with a clipboard taking readings, monitoring the machines. It's a good-paying job," I said, "and boring as shit."

She took a sip herself. "Okay," she said. "So what about when you're not working?"

"What," I said, "you taking a profile or something?" But with a smile, still having a good time. "Okay," I said, "when I'm not working back in Cleveland." I wrinkled my brow to show I was thinking. "Have bad relationships," I said, "and try to keep from being an asshole."

"Really," she said. "How can you tell you're not?"

"How can *you* tell?" I said, flashing back. "I could ask the same of you."

"You could," she said, straightfaced. "That's why I'm asking you first."

So then I felt sort of bad. "Okay," I said, "I'm sorry." Then took another mouthful of scotch, let it sink in, actually did try to think.

"How I can tell," I said. "A variety of ways. I don't hang around with the other guys I work with outside of work. I don't watch sports or a lot of tv, or say shit about Blacks. I never got married and don't have kids and I still blow a little dope now and then, and I don't like fucking Reagan, and don't even want to own a VCR."

"And these live-ins with younger women," Jean said. "Does that count too?"

Thanks to the booze all I could do was shake my head. "Jeez," I said, "who's been feeding you this shit anyway?"

Her face lit up and that pretty hair shifted, caught the light, as she laughed too. "Who do you think?" she said. "Sharon, of course. Besides, I'm hardly blameless where cradle-robbing is concerned."

Which of course brought up Simon, but not just that. The way she was talking now, plus her outfit, I could see how she got away with moving in those circles, going out with guys like that. I thought over what I was going to say next listening to Elvis Costello, "Accidents Will Happen" coming off the juke. "Okay," I said. "What all you get from your young guys?"

Not expecting she'd be pissed, and she didn't seem to be; though she did stop to take a swig and puff.

"The obvious," she said then, with a shrug. "Go places I'd never go otherwise, get money spent on me I don't have. Sexually I'd have to say they're pretty much a disappointment. But at least I get to order them around."

I thought a sec, and took another chance. "Sexually?"

"Every which way," she said, and touched her tongue to her teeth.

So at this point the dumb drunk part of me starts hollering *Hey man she wants to get down!* But I wasn't drunk enough yet to move on it, so I tried something close by instead. "That the only kind of guys you go out with?"

"Now it is." She started running a finger around the edge of her wine glass. "Back after Ray left, when I did the day care, there were a few other guys. Dads mostly, guys I knew from dropping off and picking up their kids. I hated their asses even more than the guys I go with now, but cooped up like I was they were the only ones I had any contact with. Besides, there was a long time in there after Ray when it was hard to like myself much."

The silence hung in the music and voices around us like a draft from outside. Finally, against my better judgement, I stretched out a hand to one of hers.

"Sharon told me some of it," I said. "So we're even, I guess."

"Sharon." She took her hand out from under mine, but smiled back. "Sharon's one great woman, you know that?"

"I know it," I said, and raised my glass.

Jean poured what was left of her carafe into her glass. "Right," she said, "to Sharon," and drank. Then, carefully, with a crooked smile, set her glass down. "Who certainly thinks the world of *you*."

I felt my cheeks go hot, my head go swimming, it took me totally by surprise. "You kidding?" I said. "Jesus, Jean, we're old friends!"

Across the table she cocked her head, raised an eyebrow. "Old friends can't get turned on to each other?"

"Listen," I said. "I don't have anything going on Sharon, Sharon's got nothing on me, that's the God's truth, okay?"

She gave me the same look; then shrugged, let it go, reached into her pack for yet another smoke. "Okay," she said as I reached over for her matches, "don't get excited. I didn't mean to be disrespectful or whatever. As far as Sharon is concerned she is a jewel, not to mention practically my best friend."

We were leaning towards each other by this time, fairly close. I struck the match, she tipped her face into its flame then settled back.

"Okay," I said leaning back too, though I still felt the current up and down my arms, I still wasn't calm. "Well then?" I said, with a wave of my hand.

"Well what?" she said.

But without meaning to, I had summoned up Sandy. "Ready for some dinner?" he asked, up over and beside us somewhere.

We shot each other quick side glances like captured spies agreeing to hold out. Then I looked up at Sandy the waiter.

"Tell you what, pal," I said. "How bout you just bring us back a couple more of what we been having, okay?"

The way he nodded, about-faced and left, we both had to laugh. And then there was another double-scotch rocks and another carafe, she was pouring I was sipping again.

"It's funny," I told her. "I still don't get it."

"Don't get what," she said.

"You said there were those husband types, those assholes," I said. "Then the rich young assholes now. You said Sharon's like your very best friend. Where's your whole thing with Bob come in there, you know what I mean?"

I was pretty much to the point where it was hard enough to get out something that bulky, never mind how the other person might take it. But it didn't seem to bother Jean. She took a drink, rested her elbows on the table and stared past me, smoke purling from the hand that grazed her cheek.

"First time I heard Bob Krivak play was April '82," she said. "Place down on Newberry Street called the Glencove. He was there every Thursday back then. Some guy took me, some administrator type in the job training program I was taking, I don't even remember his name. Anyway," she said, "we walked in and sat down and I saw this guy up there with just a guitar and his voice, and the music coming out of him completely bowled me over. I mean, I know I must've heard blues that good on the radio or off a record *someplace, sometime.* But I never really *heard* it, you know? And it never *occurred* to me someone could make it happen just like that."

She stopped to tap the ash off her cigarette. "Yeah," I said—knowing she didn't need it, saying it at least as much for myself—"yeah, he's pretty amazing, all right."

She stubbed her smoke, looked over to remind herself or make sure I was there, then went right back to where she'd left off. "I felt like I wanted to know, *had* to know whoever could make that happen. So I went up afterwards, introduced myself, asked if he wanted to get together for a drink."

And then she was out of it; she gave me a tight polite smile, and took hold of her glass. "That was how it began."

I'd forgotten how we'd got on this, what I'd asked. It was all I could do to take another drink myself to lubricate my lips so they'd say what I intended.

"God damn," I said, "I'm envious."

"No reason to be," she said. "I *was* crazy about him there at first. But it was really all downhill from there."

I was learning the way to maintain focus was to keep my eyes narrowed on her at all times. It made me realize I was drunk, but I couldn't think about that. "Old Bob," I said, "not much of a lover?"

Jean touched her fingers to her hairline, made a funny little smile. This I saw in precise detail.

"We gave it a shot for a couple months," she said. "He did the best he could. But it was pretty clear pretty fast he wasn't really into sex or romance."

For the moment I had decided to scratch my own head before taking the next drink from my glass. "Yeah?" I said. "So what happened?"

"What happened was, eventually I told him flat out," she said. "Said my guess was he was only doing this cause he thought it came with being a bluesman."

I found my grin and the scotch at my lips at the same exact instant. "What'd he say to that?"

"I'll tell you what he said." She was holding her head in her own hands again, rubbing her forehead but smiling too. "He laughed long and hard and then he said *How'd you like to meet my wife?*"

Jean and I laughed too at this point, though who the hell knows if it was at the same thing. In fact I was starting to lose my handle on a number of things, stuff I could not even name. And part of me cared and another part said *What the hell let it go . . .*

"Guess I'd still have to say he's the love of my life," I heard her say; and then go on for some time. How it was more like the way she loved Deirdre, really, he was an artist in the sense he put his art first and lived for that and didn't give a shit about anything else, and that made him strong in certain ways and weak in others, and it was okay because Sharon understood that too, completely, so much so they were really more like sisters than anything else, more than even best friends . . . And I was keeping up eye contact and nodding, knowing this was important, but it was hard tracking it over the jukebox now playing some really complicated piano piece. I had to keep pulling back to what she was saying. I had to think ahead to what to say when she was done. I understood it should be about my buddy Bob Krivak as the love of her life.

The waiter named Sandy was telling us the kitchen was closing, the music on the juke had changed to rock without me noticing. "I did a shitty thing to Bob today," I had just said to Jean, or words to that effect.

"Oh." She straightened up, put a cigarette in and lit it up, all at the same time. "What was that?"

I checked my glass but it was empty. Even the ice-cubes were melted and gone. "I said some shit about

Sharon and him," I told her. "About her carrying the weight."

Her face, her pretty face, squinched up. I saw some lines I hadn't seen before but still it was pretty. "Ouch," she said. "How'd he take that?"

I looked at her with my eyes wide open as they'd go, and worked on keeping my talking speed up close to normal. "Not so great," I said. "it was a stupid thing to say."

"Why'd you do it then?"

She was holding herself back now, face flat as a mask; and I knew why I'd done it, knew exactly why. But I also knew whatever I said would be held against me. I realized I was feeling miserable, physically and every which way. I checked my glass again, but my drink was still dead, and it was time, past time, to say something back.

"I don't know." Looking away, hating her almost, my face all hot. "It was stupid. It was wrong."

"Yeah," she said, dead as a recording. "Well, I'm sure Bob'll get over it. If nothing else, Sharon'll bring him back around."

She reached for the cigarette pack on the table between us and crumpled it up. I pretty much knew what was coming next.

"You want another drink," she said, "or you want to split this pop stand?"

I felt my body lighten and felt disappointed, all at the same time. Here I'd just got done wishing it were over and now it was, and I felt bad. Which was why, when Jean called Sandy over, I plucked the check out of his hands and paid it all myself, pulled the bills out of my pants and tossed them down on the table plus a good healthy tip.

"You don't have to do that," she was saying as she rose, "I don't expect you to, you know—I expect to pay—"

"Hey," I said, waving her words away at the same time as putting on my coat. "Just forget it, okay?"

The waiter, Sandy, said Thanks a lot, goodnight, Jean smiled and said Goodnight back, the juke struck up some symphony-type thing as we hit the door, and the cold wind blew her smoke-soaked perfume past me in the doorway. All in all, by the time I reached outside I felt a lot more sober. She was standing on the sidewalk, under a streetlight a few steps ahead. "You coming back to my place," she said, "or do we call it a night?"

To put it mildly, not what I'd expected. So I played for time a minute there beside her, looking up past the streetlights as if the night beyond them, frozen blue with those few stars, might give me a clue. I could go back to Ohio tomorrow. It was stupid to act like I knew what she was offering, just go home and leave it at that.

I looked over, shrugged, gave her what I hoped was a grin. "Your place. Why not?"

She looked back tightlipped, hands in her coat-pockets, and then we took off. For a few blocks we walked without talking. The street, the neighborhood, the night around us so frozen quiet you felt you were breaking into them just by the sound of your steps.

Then, right beside me, she said "How'd you learn to juggle anyway?"

"I don't know," I said the same way, without looking. "Just pretty much taught myself, I guess."

"Never wanted to do anything with it?" she said.

Both of us still facing straight ahead, close enough
to see and hear each other's breath. Here was where, on
another night with more or less alcohol, or maybe with
somebody else, I would've told my story about almost
going off to this clown and juggling school. How I'd
gone up to check it out fresh out of high school, driving
solo to Chicago, chasing down the address. About how
eventually I stood across from this decrepit brick building in this disgusting run-down neighborhood and
thought a while, then got back in my beat-up old Chevy
Caravelle and drove away. It had been a pretty good
story all these years—Cindy cried when I told her, and
she wasn't the first—so I couldn't say why I didn't feel
like trotting it out for Jean. Was I afraid she wouldn't
buy it, or just sick of my own shit?

Whichever, whatever, now was no time to figure it
out. "Wanted to?" I said. "Yeah, sure. Have the guts to
go after it? Hell, no."

She didn't say anything to that either; and when I
looked her face might just have been closed against the
cold. Another couple blocks, and she turned into one of
those old driveways that's two lanes of inset sidewalk,
next to a two-story bungalow of stucco and brick. I
thought the whole place might be hers til we stopped at
a door with a second street number above it to the side.

"Gotta be quiet now," Jean whispered, getting out
her key. "Babysitter's gonna be asleep." Inside, we went
up groaning steps toward a doorline of light. Jean gave

a soft knock and opened the door at the top. Behind her I came into a low-ceilinged small kitchen, its dull gleaming counters and small round table barely visible in the thin light from a curtained window over the sink. She motioned me to stay put and moved on ahead. In another minute I heard hers and another voice; then the kitchen light came on and a kid maybe sixteen with tiny zits like freckles all across her forehead walked in looking grumpy-groggy, followed by Jean.

The kid already had her coat on, a parka with a hood, so I couldn't tell much more about her other than the pimples and the pin stuck in her nose. "Thanks again, Lisa," Jean was saying softly, big smile on her face. "Really appreciate it. G'night now—"

"Unh," Lisa said, gazing straight past me, and went out the door.

I turned to Jean; her shoulders slumped, the smile dropped off her face. "Babysitters," she said. "Gotta keep 'em happy, you know. 'Nother drink?"

"Sure," I said. "What the hell."

While she got out the glasses and poured from the half-gallon in the fridge, I tried taking stock, making a few decisions, knowing as soon as I took the next sip I was going to get fucked up all over again. Okay then, quick: you like her okay as a person and she's pretty. But to put it mildly you're not that turned on. As for what she wants, can't tell, the signals're mixed. So what was I, what were we, doing? What was my next move? What was it for?

"What's gonna happen to you and Simon?" I said out of nowhere as she handed me my wine.

"Me and Simon," she smirked. "You mean to-gether?" Her eyes stayed on me as she drained her glass. "Oh," she said when it was lowered, "I expect we'll get married and move to Wellesley Hills. Shall we go in to the parlor and make ourselves comfortable?"

I took a mouthful and followed. The living room was on the other side of a tiny hallway, another small sloped space under the eaves. The wine tasted and felt like nothing at all. "No," I said, "really."

She settled herself on the torn foam cushions of a scuffed Danish modern shoved under the slanted roof as far as it would go. Nearby were a stuffed armchair and a wooden rocker, but I felt more like staying upright now, across from her, alongside the tv on its banged-up gold stand.

"Really then," she said, unwrapping the fresh pack she'd snagged from the carton in the kitchen, tamping them solid and sliding one out. "Okay—we'll fuck around with each other a few months longer. Then I'll shit on him once too often, and he'll take his marbles and go home."

So why do that? I wanted to ask, but couldn't get myself to come out with it. So I nodded like it all made perfect sense, no problem, and swallowed the rest of the wine in one single gulp.

"Have some more," she said, indicating the bottle she'd also brought in, and rising to her feet. "Feel free. I just wanna look in on Deirdre, be right back."

I poured myself another as she brushed past me, and refilled hers while I was at it. Then I took a look around at the rest of the low narrow room. On the other end a mobile of colored fish twisting down beside a bookshelf of pine boards and bricks, a bunch of kid books sharing the space with a bunch of big blue notebooks, possibly real-estate shit. I thought of sitting down right here on the couch, smoking one of her Carltons though I hate fucking cigarettes. But instead I stepped over to the bookshelf, picked up one of the photo-cubes she had setting there as well, and checked it out. A few pictures of her alone, Jean standing frowning in the middle of a snowy field, at the beach with the sun glinting off her hair: otherwise, all of the kid who had to be Deirdre. Baby pictures in Jean's arms, in a bassinette, bunch of pictures taken in this room with other kids, around birthday cakes, class pictures from school, against that grey curtain, the whole shebang. I looked at another cube, it was pretty much the same. I was fantasizing picking up all four, five photo-cubes and getting them going, when I heard her coming back. I put the one I was holding down, lumbered over and picked up my wine, drank it down and filled it again.

She came back in the room, over past where I was standing. Again what passed between us was less like a nice buzz than the jumper cables hooked up wrong and you holding on, the charge running *zap* down through your body into ground.

I stepped back towards the tv; she sat down and crossed her legs. We each took a drink. "Everything okay with the kid?" I said.

"Just fine," she said. "How bout you? Everything all right with you?"

"Yeah," I said, shifting foot to foot. "Yeah, sure, fine."

"Good," she said, and we each took another drink. "So," she said, "What's your scenario?"

Needles prickled my distant hands. "You mean like with Cindy," I said. "Like with my last girlfriend and other girls I've had."

"Yeah," she said. "Like with your girlfriends, that's what I mean."

"Oh," I said. "Well," I said. "What can I tell you? I meet somebody, we get together, everybody thinks everybody else is cooler'n shit. Then we live together til we think each other is an asshole. And then we break up."

All of which was hard to think of, and harder still to say. But then the way she was holding up her glass and beaming back, like in a commercial for the good fucking life, she must've been drunk too.

"What'd you say?" I said, cause I hadn't heard her.

"I said," she said, "we make one hell of a pair."

I decided not to say anything back. It seemed to me silence was best. Even though it was impressive, my ability to come up with answers, continue to stand up against all these shifts of weight.

"Looked at some of your pictures," I said. "Had the day-care pre-school thing right up here, huh?"

"Yeah," she said. "Let's not talk about that." Carefully she picked her cigarette out of her mouth, put her glass down on the floor, leaned toward me. "Listen," she said, "I'm drunk too. We're both drunk."

I propped myself back against the wall, beside the heating element. "No argument there," I said.

247

Across the room her mouth twisted and her face went sour. "I'm not proposing," she said. "Just trying to figure if we're gonna fuck or not. Okay?"

I nodded my head. "Okay," I said.

She put her cigarette back in, settled back against the couch. "And looks like we're not."

I closed my eyes and thought a second about that. "Oh yeah?" I said. "What makes you think so?"

"What makes me think so," she said; and let her head drop the way the people do to say *What are you, kidding?* Then she turned and grabbed the bottle on the endtable, I couldn't believe it, and poured herself another glass.

"I don't know," she was saying, raising her glass as if giving a toast. "Maybe on account of you haven't made a move all night."

I considered this too. It was true, but that didn't have to mean that she was right. Why was she not right?

"I don't do that so much," I said. "That's not my style."

She was still drinking, it was amazing. Her eyes were half-shut but the open parts still looked back at me. She was supposed to ask what my style was, so I could say I liked to get to know the person first, but she wasn't saying anything. So probably instead I had to go over and start touching her, which I didn't want to do and felt too drunk to do, combination of the two. Which meant she was right.

"I looked at some pictures of your kid," I said. "She's cute, you know? Looks like you."

"Right," she said, "thanks. Are we gonna go to bed or not?"

I tried to think. But there was nothing to think about, really. "Sure," I said. "Great, let's go."

She got up and I pitched forward so we bumped together in the middle of the room. I was standing there with her against me, thinner than I would've guessed, and my face in her hair, smelling of smoke and her shampoo. Then I came along behind her down the hallway from the kitchen, past a john and another room, probably her kid's, with the door shut. At the end of the hall was the door to Jean's room, which we would now be going into, though I still had my doubts. Not just a matter of not having any of that nice queasy lightness down there either. Near as I could tell I wasn't feeling much of anything at all.

Then Jean opened the door and went in and I followed, and was punched right away by the cold. It must have been a good fifteen, twenty degrees colder in there than out in the hallway, and dark as a mine. I felt her near me as the door closed, heard her low ragged breath. Then one of us must have reached for the other because we were grappling again. I went for a breast, more or less missed, felt one of her hands reaching down and in to rake the insides of my thighs. Our mouths mashed together, readjusted, made a seal; I touched her tongue, then fell into the ashy sicky-sweet of her mouth.

Then, as quickly, that was over; she broke and I twisted away. A shaded lamp came on at the edge of a vanity table with three-sided mirrors, combs and brushes and cosmetics strewn over the top. She was there, across the room and half-turned away, removing her earrings, untying her scarf, unfastening her dress and letting it drop as if there were no one else around.

I stood where I was for a second. Then, thinking to the best of my ability how much warmer I'd be underneath the covers up against someone else, started undressing too. In another minute she struck a match to a halfmelted candle on her nightstand, and switched off her makeup table lamp. I looked over in time to see her skinny body's white almost incandescent in the shuddering flame she bent over to light herself a fresh cigarette.

"You got no heat in here?" I said.

"You guessed it," she said, slipping quickly into bed. "Hurry up now," she patted the blankets. "Get in."

Which sure as hell didn't work as a turn-on. If anything, being ordered around made me pissed off. I was tired of her laughing at me, calling all the shots. So once I slid myself in and her face was a silhouette beside me, I said "How much longer you figure Bob and Sharon gonna be able to stay where they are?"

The sheets against my skin, front and back, like cold water. When she rolled to the side, the covers rippled like icy waves.

"Hah," she said, turned away from me, scrounging for something on the frozen wooden floor. "Depends what you mean. Where they are on Centre, probably not much longer. But they'll find something else half-decent after that."

There must have been a bottle over there off her side of the bed. Or glass of wine anyway, because that's what she came back up with. She was holding it on the covers over her chest and lifting her head up from the pillow to sip at it, and I could hardly admit she was doing it, the thought of drinking any more made me so sick.

"Scuse me," I said, "but these are like your best friends, aren't they? Doesn't that make you feel even a little bit like shit?"

"Mmm," she said, her head falling back. "You think makes any fucking difference, someone else pricing properties? Give up my job, I feel so bad?"

The hand with the drink slid off and dropped the glass, I heard it dink and roll on the floor.

"Shit," she said, "sure I feel sad. Whyn't you cummere, get this show on the road?"

I rolled over toward her, she hitched herself against me. Again we met and held. I nuzzled in around her hair and got to her neck and started kissing there and behind her ear, and she started breathing heavy and pressing herself more against me. The bra and panties felt sort of scratchy but her skin was soft, and she was at least warmer than I was. Maybe this thing was going to happen and be all right after all.

But no: now, already, things were off. Now in with her shallow panting she was making these high noises, little chirping moans I would have never in a million years associated with her. That and the rhythm, the way she was moving, hands rubbing down my shoulders and arms, moving down to clutch and claw hips and ass as she ground herself against me down there, hard enough I could feel that crosswise bone between her legs, through her underwear and skin, butt and grind against my cock.

"You got safes?" she cooed in that high fakey voice, then dropped down to normal. "Okay if you don't, I got some in the bedside table."

No chance to say anything back. She was curled up under the covers going down me, making more high noises till my numb cock was in her hands and mouth.

So there I was, watching the blankets heave and hearing her do her little muffled moans whenever she took her mouth away. And I had to admit things were off on a number of counts, starting with the alcohol, the late hour, the cold. Plus I also just plain did not believe she was into it either, not for all the sucking and moaning and stuff she was doing. Not really any more than me.

For a minute longer while my cock stayed dead I tried one of two possibilities. Either I was wrong and she was into it; or I was right but shouldn't give a shit. For all I knew it was what she did with Simon and Bob and the other guys she'd been with and they all thought it was all right, so why not me? Besides, I thought, what you gonna do at this point? Stop the woman and tell her she's not making it, you don't want to go on any more?

All this time, of course, she's down there slaving away while I'm looking off across to where the candle's shadow of us lumped together flutters on the wall. I'm thinking *Man, this is one hell of a vacation. Shit, might as well be home as here.* It made me wonder what had happened, not just to me but to all of us, that my visit had come down to this, lying in this fucking icebox with this woman I don't know and maybe don't even like pretending to get off on sucking my cock while I watch the wall and pretend to like it.

252

I got that far, and that was pretty much it. I reached down the hand that wasn't already down there patting her shoulder and rubbing her back. I latched on to both her shoulders and tugged til she came up. When we were eye to eye, I smoothed the hair away from her face, and kissed her on the cheek and kept my face smiling and close in while I spoke.

"Hey," I whispered. "It's really late. How bout we just take it easy, what do you say?"

Figuring one of two, maybe three, possibilities. She could be pissed enough to say something about my performance, or lack thereof; or else be glad to let it go. Or, I realized, freak out, take it as her fault, get back to work that much more frantically.

But actually this last one didn't cross my mind until what happened next. I still had my arms around her, smiling at her, looking into her eyes just an inch or two away. Now, at the same time as her face relaxed, I saw behind the darkness of those eyes something quivering and small. It freaked the shit out of me but I didn't look away. I felt her breath, no longer panting, coming out against the skin of my face. The air outside us, all around us, still so cold both our breaths were making steam.

So when she slid down to rest her head against my shoulder, I thought we'd made it through, it'd be all right. And so it was, for maybe thirty seconds. She was lying against my side, head on my chest, topmost leg over mine. I had my arm around her, one hand stroking the smooth slope from cheekbone to jaw. Finally I actually did feel fond of her, pretty woman in a hard life, doing the best she knew how. And at least the two of us could go to sleep this way and not wake up miserable; we could give each other that, anyhow . . .

The new voice reached me from a distance, I had drifted halfway out. It was soft and high yet throaty, like a kid asking Mommy for something and at the same time the good witch from *The Wizard of Oz*. It was Jean saying something slow, part question and part cry, as she clutched and pressed herself closer to me.

It was my name. She was saying my name.

Jim-meee, she was saying, *Ji-mm-meee* . . .

So now was the opposite of a minute ago; now I wished she were faking it. But it was too spooky for that, and too real. This was a Jean the one I knew, if she hadn't been so wasted, would've never let me see, any more than it would want to see itself. And it could just as well have been Bobby or Sharon calling out some other name, pressing up against some other person's body in the cold dark. Or for that matter it could have been me.

Or that was how it felt right at that moment anyhow, which was why I was even more scared than before. Still, I managed to hold it together, barely. Just kept telling myself the last thing she needed was to have the one she's holding onto, me, start flailing around as well. Get a grip on myself, push that wave back, she'll calm down too.

Which, ultimately, was what I did. Tucked my chin against the top of her head and hugged her closer still, and stroked her back and side and whenever she started in with *Jim-mee Jim-mee* said things like *There now there now it's okay,* whatever shit like that came into my head to say.

Ji-mm-eee . . . Ji-mm-ee . . . Ji-mm-ee. . . .

Shhh now. Easy baby, take it easy. It's all right.

Eventually you do fall asleep. As we did that night, her first then me. Only even then, after all that long weary shit, I still couldn't quite leave it behind. Instead when I went down it was just a little ways, more like lying under a few inches of water than sleeping. I could feel Jean against me, bony, soft-skinned and warm, hear the storm window rattle in the winter wind outside. I could hear and sometimes see the sputtering candle-flame we should've blown out on the bedside stand. But even more I was looking up at all of us, me and Bob and Sharon and Jean, through a distance that showed what I hadn't seen before. For a long time, half-asleep, I watched us move around in these half-dreams, if that was what they were, even while at the same time I kept on trying not to hear or know or see what they were showing me more clearly every time. That Bob would stop playing. That Sharon would leave Bob. That I would not leave the General til it shut down and moved away like everybody said it would, and even then I would just stay there in Cleveland and get something else. That Jean would eventually stop finding rich young guys to date and abuse. And that our hearts—my heart—would continue to close.

I woke, if you could call it that, in pale morning light. The blankets were thrown back where Jean'd been, but beside me it was still warm so she must've just left.

Through the walls I heard first one voice, a little girl's crying, then Jean's voice under hers low and soothing, doing what I'd done with her a few hours ago. Kid must've had a nightmare, I thought, and hitched myself up, and hauled myself out of bed—Jesus, it was cold—and into the clothes I'd dumped on the floor. The idea struck me I could go into her room, introduce myself, grab whatever I could find on her dresser, floor, whatever, do some juggling for the kid til she calmed down. But the better move was to get up and get dressed so when in a few minutes Jean came back, I'd be on my way out. After all, I still had Bob and Sharon to say Goodbye to, plus lots of miles yet to cover, there was no sense wasting time showing some kid I'd never seen how to toss things up and keep them moving through the air.

FREEWAY BYPASS (detail from map)

Circulation is the movement in which general alienation appears as general appropriation and general appropriation as general alienation.

Same billboard's still there acourse, right off the crossway from I-94. That beltway over to 78, you know. Maybe three miles in on the east side. Tween Exit 3 and 4, Black Creek Boulevard and Ardmore Ave. I donno what else to tell you. Though that one ad, the one you're talking about, they took that down a while ago. Got another one up now, couldn't tell you what.

What we know we know from newspaper and police reports, tv coverage having been both spotty and brief given the scant amount of newstime, need for brighter fillings for pre-sports and weather newsholes to maintain or increase income from the ad-slots. Nobody likes it but that's the way it is, what are you gonna do? Anyway, what we know is, the guy was hit coming home from work on a Saturday night, late, Sunday morning technically, and managed to get himself over the highway to the divider there, and managed somehow, incredibly, to hold on there for three days and four nights before somebody noticed him and stopped to call 911.

Owner and leasing agent for the property, the Patrick Media Group Inc., a privately held national firm specializing in outdoor advertising. Net profits, 1990, including all divisions, $250 million.

Though the whole of this movement may well appear as a social process, and though the individual elements of this movement originate from the conscious will and particular purposes of individuals, nevertheless the totality of the process appears as an objective relationship arising spontaneously; a relationship which results from the interaction of conscious individuals, but which is neither part of their consciousness nor as a whole subsumed under them.

The image a familiar, practically generic one, and so hardly struck any startled response from Bill. A giant translucent blonde stretched across a black background raising a glass or holding a cigarette or stroking a cylindrically-shaped hair care product with one hand, the sort of thing you see every day. Only difference was, when the ad appeared out of the corner of his eye, as it did, as they do to us all, made itself slightly known to Bill's mind then disappeared, it registered as something off, something to be fixed. Though if you asked them, any of the four of them what it was like, they would have spoken awkwardly of polluted consciousness, mind control, stilted phrases like that. But between such language and the real rage, the sickness and hope at the base of it all, there was mainly this sense: the ad went by off to his right, at the edge of his vision, like a smokepuff from a small inaudible explosion, as he was driving home from work in the truck; and Bill thought, with an inward sigh of weariness plus something else, Oh yeah, okay, got to take care of that too.

This would be what he remembered later as the last moment when things were right: here atop the embankment, beside the highway, when it was still possible to see the halfmoon white as goat's milk behind the screen of clouds, beyond the throbbing dark orange of the city, its reflected warmth against the night. This serrated bone-joint of moon in its gauze of ice, this sight like a thought. It was late at night, it was after work, he was on his way back from the restaurant where he washed dishes to the room where he slept. The only sound that distant susurrus of traffic on all the roads and streets of all the city stretched around him, an omnipresence he now understood to be, in effect, this country's wind, through which, on each side of the highway in front of his eyes, these two thick smooth streams of asphalt soiled by the yellow streetlight falling down on them, he saw and heard the heightened rush of this or that stray late-night early-morning car in its occasional flight. The vehicle that struck him when he stepped out into the road might have had its headlights off, might well have been driven too fast: however, it was, when he first stepped out it was invisible in this tapestry in which he too had seemed, for all the exile of his long trip to this astonishing moment, to fit. He stepped off the gravel, over the curb, onto the rolled macadam of the northbound lanes, bisected by its perforation lines of gold. Another step, another, and three more, each as simple and accentless as ordinary breath. He turned hearing the sound like the roar of a hand slicing through space held stiff for a slapping just in time to see the car's complex of dull and gleaming, sharp and curved surfaces, a single frame from a film even now still rushing past. Sick needles prickling his hands and legs, a taste or smell of must and hot engine oils flooding his head just before or just as the front fender on the right or passenger side struck his hip and upper leg on the left side flipping his body up in air.

You are familiar with our terms; for a single site with a high daily flow-rate of traffic we would be asking $4000 for a four-week rental, or somewhere thereabouts. But I would assume you would be coming to us with more than one site in mind, in which case we would want to be talking together about site patterns and price packages. And of course all the more so insofar as you come to us carrying a number of clients and/or campaigns. There I think you'd find we could put together a most attractive and effective package, at a surprising—and I do mean surprisingly attractive—rate per board, depending on how many sites and/or signs you have in mind.

The structure as complementarity, set of neutralizing valences, zero-sum game. Either way you look at it, horizontally or vertically, moving across or up anddown. Across, from regions with developed industrial economies and a comparatively low level of state violence, to others with a low level of industrialization, dependent on foreign investment and the export and sale of raw materials for processing in the more developed zones, and consequently with states which, given the misery of the majority of their citizenries, must employ various means of legal and extra-legal violence to maintain the status quo. From Japan or the U.S. to Guatemala and Zaire, say, with any number of slots for other nation-states along the way. And the same as we travel down within the developed "democratic" world as well, from the full world citizenship enjoyed by the wealthiest elites, individual and corporate, to the repression visited, directly or indirectly, upon those situated at or below the level of production itself. At or below: large-scale unionized manufacture, large-scale non-union, small shop, service industries, agricultural workers seasonal and year round, and under- and un-employed.

I donno what to tell you, it just makes me mad is all. Just going along back and forth to work minding your own business and then look up and see out of nowhere they've gone and ruined another of those things. I suppose you can say it's no skin off my nose and that's true as far as it goes, but somebody paid good money for that space. Course the younger ones down at the shop, they think it's pretty funny; but I'll tell you, I ever caught the ones doing it up there at it some day or night I'd write over them, I'll tell you that right now.

Their collisions give rise to an alien social power standing above them.

They were in their late 30s, early 40s, except for Steve, who worked with Bill and was 26. More or less middle-class backgrounds; various anti-war, anti-nuke, anti-intervention, and anti-racist, anti-homophobic, pro-labor, pro-peace, pro-choice, pro-environment actions/groups/experiences under their belts. Jim had resisted the draft and done two years of jail time around it; Bill had been an SDS-er; Nancy, who'd also done some real time for a Trident action, had started out from the Catholic left, her favorite saint even now long since her lapsing Dorothy Day, whereas Steve simply called himself an anarchist. Nancy an RN in a poor women's health clinic about to disappear, Jim ran an off-the-books house-cleaning business, Bill and Steve built cabinets and decks and did light house repair. It started out one night maybe four years ago, drunk and stoned at a party, with a couple cans of spraypaint in the back of Bill's van and a gross Be All That You Can Be army poster down the block. By now the deal was simple: whoever saw one that needed doing and was do-able went by or called the rest of them, until at least three of them had agreed on a color or colors, counterslogan, and a night.

In a striking convergence of these two axes or spectra, moreover, those at the bottom end of the vertical you'll find are often either descendants of emigrants from states at the harsh end of the horizontal, or such emigrants themselves. Put differently, we might say it is in general far easier for a given individual to move from the—impoverished, repressed, violent—losing side of the horizontal line to the downside of the vertical than for anyone to move to the up or winning side of either line. As, for example, the comparative ease with which the aforementioned victim of this story, having fled the country of his birth and reached this one, was able without papers or prior experience to find a dishwasher's job and a shared rented room in which to sleep.

Let us at least not pretend that his name is important to us: let us at least allow the man—the "poor man"?—to keep his name. He was lying on his right side, his right arm underneath, and pulled down too far towards his feet. He was lying on the road, in between the near and middle lanes, two strips of yellow paint. As soon as consciousness returned and he moved, several widespread but specific brushfires began along that side, as if a number of matches had been tossed at a given signal on the edges of baked fields called Shoulder, Shoulderblade, Hip, Thigh. In his mouth a sooty gruel of asphalt stones, dust, chips of teeth he supposed, plus an acridness he knew would signify blood. A cool breeze playing on his face bestowed upon him, absurdly, a moment of ordinary lucidity: the thought that the jacket, shirt, and pants he was wearing were all torn too badly to fix with needle and thread, and would cost money to replace. Already he knew what had happened on his left was certainly more serious than the fires on his right, and that the first thing he must do now is get himself out of the road. When he rolls over onto his stomach and attempts to rise to his hands and knees his left side speaks to him at last, loudly sharply, from the regions of his ribs and pelvis, and forces an answering scream to hurl itself out of his mouth.

I

I AM

Circulation is the movement in which general alienation appears as general appropriation and general appropriation as general alienation.

AVA

AVAIL

Although the main arteries are for the most part state and federal, the city retains jurisdiction over and responsibility for rights of way, embankments, dividers and the like. So it became our problem several years back now when it was discovered that the foliage and ground cover of our most heavily utilized routes had begun to register a rather severe rate of, uh, *attrition* in response to the concentrations of pollutants, especially those of course from auto emissions, to which such plantings were subject. Estimates were, moreover, that over the next ten years, barring the construction of additional parkways and/or superhighways, which no one expects, this problem of the dying plants and trees would only grow that much more noticeable, i.e., worse.

"She's not here," said Andrea. She shook her head, an abrupt shiver, opened the screen door, gave Bill a greeting hug out on the porch. "She had to stay after for a staff meeting. I'm sorry I'm so logey, I just woke up. I was like this all day at work today too, I don't know what it is. How are you anyway, what's up?" It was like that with Andrea: you had to wait an extra minute, but you got your chance. Bill told her about the board, asked her to ask Nancy to call. "Ask her too," he said as he finished up, "if she has any ideas for a new line or if we should just go with the usual." Andrea looked off over his shoulder, squinting at where the sun was descending, orange-swollen, over the backs of the bungalows across the street. "I wish I could help you," she said. "Not with the slogan, I mean. I mean I wish I weren't so scared of heights and chickenshit about cops." "Hey," Bill said, "don't worry about it. You do lots of stuff, you do enough." They gave each other another smile, he turned to go. "I know what she'll say about the slogan," said Andrea. "Why not stay with what works?"

The small-time boys with their two, three homebuilt boards, spiked into the sides of 8-apt. 3-flr. brick shit-holes with plywood boards on their ex-windows, Hotel Junkie, the only one left up in the rubble of what once was a block. Or the ones with their paint cracked and flaking, wooden scaffoldings rotting on some pitted two-lane off in the boonies winding from one dead smalltown to the next. Carros Usados, Kobena's Hair Salon, Hidden Valley Camper Campground, pin money, chump change. Then in your larger towns and smaller cities you have your little home-grown outdoor advertising firms, typically one per such area, so even Budweiser, McDonald's, the big accounts have got to write their contracts with them. Which, of course, they'd rather do with nationals like Patrick or Gannett, themselves often as not a division or subsidiary of some yet larger transnational, Time-Warner, Philip Morris, something like that. But just as the Patricks and Gannetts push against that next nearest surface—to supplant, to deprive of nourishment, to press to death—moving into as many mid-sized areas as is consistent with overall profitability, so the mid-sized locally-owned firms may also be found in every major metropolitan area, pressing back with whatever resources—pricing structure, number and replacement of boards, package deals—they possess. Think of a blastular cell formation in perpetual development, always feeding on itself; think of wheels within wheels in the middle of the air.

I AM NO

It is my personal belief to this day that if the department had simply been somewhat less public about the shift in policy, few people would have noticed and fewer still cared. But just because it was a first, I suppose the feeling was that the story had to be released. Then of course once it reached the papers, radio and tv that the city was taking out its real ground cover and putting in synthetics, the proverbial material hit the fan. By the end of the week the phones at the office are ringing off the hook with outraged citizens. As if they weren't the same people whose cars killed off the natural cover we put down; but that, I suppose, is another story, and, in any case, you can't tell them that.

No way to write of pain without aestheticizing, speak of exploitation without abstraction: each obscenity requiring yet another merely to be expressed. The following morning he comes to or wakes to the sounds, smells, and breezes of a traffic registering as senseless convulsion without origin or end, a chaos of occurrences, intensities, speeds. Turning his head to one side then the other, he discerns through the bushes between which he lies one blur of wheels and colors moving up and past his head, another down and past his feet. The sun is up but has not yet been able to warm the day's air, which takes on an added chill from the contrapuntal buffetings of this traffic, these cars and vans and trucks which struck him down and now imprison him here. He knows there is something wrong with this thought but not what. The traffic is slowing, has slowed almost to a dead stop, but even now when it has become separate machines producing specific noises—brakes clamping, tires rotating, bleat of horn, blare of manic radio—the notion of calling out for help remains distant, depending as it does on the double assumption that there are people within those phantasm machines, and that there is some tie between them and there and him here. So that later, even when his cries begin, it is not with any intent to communicate, really. More familiar altogether are the maroon sinews of the bushes and the green waxy leaves, edged with translucent yellow when the sun is overhead; and through those leaves, the sight he can behold with his head thrown back and turned rightward, of the smiling white woman up over road and traffic and himself, the woman lying on her side as he can almost remember from seeing her on a billboard or poster during the market day back where he came from, a woman holding up her product, something he cannot see for the leaves and branches in his way, and cannot remember thanks to the pain, especially down below now, where his hip is, which was a little like a noise itself when he woke up but now is like nothing else whatsoever in the world.

AVAILA

The formative impulse behind this 'peripheral' urbanization, here and elsewhere, has been the creation of a dense nest of transactional linkages and technologically advanced production and service systems that enable increasingly vertically disintegrated industrial production processes to be flexibly and efficiently re-attached horizontally, in a burgeoning territorial industrial complex.

Far as that goes I don't see it any different than what you see anywheres nowdays. These kids want to write some filth or foolishness on a building or bus or wherever they feel like it, like so many dogs taking a piss. I don't mind telling you that's the way I see them, the way they hang out here on the streets. You can't tell me they even want to work. Just want to get messed up on drugs and beer and cheap wine and make babies and that's about it. Least the ones that get up on them billboards, they at least make something more than a doodleblotch, write *Fuck You* the way some of them did across that siding I put on just two summers back. I bust their ass I catch them, same as these ones here, but they at least give you a whole sentence with some actual fuckin words.

Nevertheless the totality of the process appears as an objective relationship arising spontaneously; a relationship which results from the interaction of conscious individuals, but which is neither part of their consciousness nor as a whole subsumed under them.

Back at the house Bill told Jim about it while washing up at the kitchen sink. Jim's night to cook, and he was making a raita to go with the felafel; the two of them had to move around each other somewhat delicately in the small kitchen space. Bill positioned himself in the kitchen doorway to use the phone, turning away from the sizzling and popping from the frypan on the stove. As Steve's number rang one two three four he let his mind float, looking without looking at the ensemble of Sandy, Jim's partner, folded up on the couch with her headphones on, inside one of her meditation tapes, Tonio the house mutt dozing near her on the floor, square-jawed bespectacled Emma Goldman staring down from the

271

poster above, If I Can't Dance I Don't Want to Be Part of Your Revolution. Bill himself had been married once, too young, back straight out of school. Split up more than eight years ago, for reasons as personal as political and vice versa, a sad useless headache even to try to sort it out. Emma and Gene, 14 and 10, in Albuquerque with their mother during the school year, here with him, with the three of them in spite of the close quarters, over the summers. A certain sense, every now and then, of thinness, resonances disallowed, unacknowledged disappointment of a life correctly lived. No answer at Steve's but Jim had said Yeah sure, anytime, so if Nancy called back willing, then maybe tonight. A jolt of excitement, strictly kid's stuff but what the hell, as he hung up the phone and turned to see Jim smiling back, holding out a platter of cakes draining on a paper towel. "You want to rope Sandy back in from the cosmos, let her know it's time to eat?" "Yeah, okay. What do you want to drink?"

How many of them is it now we see every day—750? 2000? Some staggering, some inconceivable number, but who's counting anyway? What does it mean, for that matter, to "see" an ad? Isn't the degree of conscious perception involved right down there with seeing the people in the cars you drive past on your way to work, as that of hearing the traffic we hear all the time, even indoors? If so, could we say the experience of seeing an ad is roughly what it is like to run one's eyes across a stranger, a fleeting stranger on the street or in a car, as if she or he were her- or himself a thing for sale? What it is or would be like if that sound of traffic were composed of so many cries for attention, calls for help?

Afterwards, he was interviewed only twice at the hospital where the police and ambulance finally took him. Understandable, given that his English was almost nonexistent, the reporters spoke nothing else, and it was just Human Interest anyway. Among the questions they did not ask, though, was one he asked and answered himself. The question had in fact occurred to the state trooper who responded to the billboard call and found him instead: why had the guy not only crawled over to the divider rather than the nearer curbside, but then, at the divider, dragged himself into a thicket from which he could only be seen with difficulty even from a slow-moving or stalled car? But the cop was wrong, had picked the wrong fear. He figured the guy, given how rough the neighborhood was around here, had hid himself away so as not to get discovered, picked over, finished off by the first kid, junkie, gang to come along. But what the man himself realized was that he had without knowing it been following instructions ingrained in him from the country he was from, the people he was of, where if you are away from your village and lying hurt at the side of the road no one would dare touch or help you because the Army might be there, and if the Army is there and sees you they kill you. That was his mistake, his silly mistake, mixing up the two places; it seemed funny when he looked back on it now. So that even with the other worries on his mind, even though that mistake

could have killed him, he found himself wishing someone had asked him that question in one of the two inter-
views, either that one from the paper or the other
dressed-up one from the tv, so he could have shared the
joke with them.

The Burkean theory of the sublime, the apprehension
through a given aesthetic object of what in its awesome
magnitude shrinks, threatens, diminishes, rebukes individual human life.

So whatever your outdoor display needs, you'll find our
thoroughly skilled and professional staff, from consult-
ing agents to our display staff itself, ready to serve you
and your clients here at Patrick, known coast-to-coast
for quality and reliability for over 45 years.

Then on top of that you got these other ones coming in
and overrunning the place. See them everywhere now, all
over, wanting to live here too. Just go down where I
work, any direction from the shop, poke your head in
first door you find open in one of them old warehouses
and plants, tell me what you see. Bunch of people in
there working don't even speak English. At their machines when you get there in the morning, still at it when
you go back home at night. Probably sleep down there
too, all I know. Plus your people from Central America,
Mexico, down there, coming over in waves and waves
and waves. Like that fella they found, night I was coming home off swing shift and saw that crew up there on
that billboard writing away bold as you please. One the

state boys found out there later, after I called them up and got them on it when those other jokers got away. Had it in the paper there, day or so later on. They ever find out where he was from, what the hell he was doing lying out there like that in the weeds?

A relationship which results from the interaction of conscious individuals, but which is neither part of their consciousness nor as a whole subsumed by them.

AVAILABLE SP

Always a rush, the scramble from the road up through the lupine or what have you to the hollow-steel post on which the board is mounted, one carrying the ladder, the other one if only out of nervousness still jiggling the spraycan. Then with one of them holding, the other one quick up that ladder to the short set of steps on the post, swing-step around the scaffolding, go to work. Nancy stiff-arming the can before her face as though aiming from the nozzle, going over the letters a second time to make sure they stand out from the sprawled body they are written on. Not that it makes any difference to speak of, but who knows? Doing something at least means you have said to yourself that this shit does not go down. Plus to be honest, it is really a kick. And if lots more people started doing it, saying no? Jim's voice urgent from the van down below at the edge of the road. "Somebody slowing up ahead, guys—time to get down!" Bill hisses a call up to Nancy but she is already on her way. "Watch your step, watch your step," he is saying as above him she descends; muttering it to himself, adrenaline dancing through head/chest/arms/hands. Running back down the embankment, folded ladder wobbling under one arm, hearing the ragged saw of Nancy's breath behind, reviewing agreed-upon procedures for what to do, how to hang together if the bust comes down. Then, just as he throws the ladder in the side Jim has opened up and reaches out to grab Nancy in after himself, Bill looks down the road and sees this old guy walking fast down the burm from his truck, maybe a hundred yards ahead. Nancy is in, gasping, Jim pulling the van out with a yelp from the tires and the old motor whining, revving hard. "That's not a cop!" Bill says. "I never said he was!" says Jim. "Look at him, man, he's running back to his truck! He's coming after us!" The three of them look in the mirrors and out the back window: sure enough. By now they are all laughing uncontrollably, practically laughing themselves sick. "Well," Nancy says in a rush, throwing herself back against the seat with a flourish, "we got it anyway."

People have their own lives to live, after all, for the most part, aside from the few zealous citizens we have always with us. So the following week it seemed the furor was dying down—as it generally does in such cases, truth be told. Then, I don't know, a few weeks later, sometime around the beginning of June, the first reports came in from state and local authorities to the effect that some of the synthetic coverings and plantings we had installed along and on routes with the highest utilization rates had been—well—had been firebombed, in effect. Specifically, it appeared that some person or persons unknown had applied something in the nature of a flamethrower to our installations in the area of, I believe it was the Crosstown, near the exit for Ardmore Ave. That first incident stayed out of the papers thanks to the cooperation of the police, our shared hope being that it would turn out to be an isolated incident. By the end of the week, though, there had been three more such occurrences, and the police felt they could no longer hold the story back. So once again, there we were in the media for replacing living foliage with so-called plastic trees on our city's most polluted highways; only now the story had guerrillas with flamethrowers as well. The following week the story was national and the copycat effect was in full swing; there were something like a dozen incidents in just three days. The City Manager had our department head in for a dressing-down; the City Council passed a special resolution requiring us to return immediately to natural cover. Which of course we have done ever since, even though it represents a considerable expense to the city, since replanting and recovering needs to take place now on the average of—what's it down to?—something like every six months or less. But as we say in public service, Give the people what they want.

It remained itself but blended with other things as well. It stained the fleeting, fragmentary narratives of his mother and father and sisters and brothers, his grandparents, his own wife and children, and the others in the village, and still others met on the way here, so that as they flickered and unreeled across the screen unfurled behind his eyes each became haunted by yellow hues of shame and despair. It entered his breath, shit and rust to the taste on top of the sour metal of car exhaust. Or blotted everything else out, even though when it rose up and made him scream and shout he often as not still cried out words. Help me. Mother. Jesus. In his own language of course, and who knows how often or loud? The leaves over his head glowed yellow, faded black; the light on the white woman overhead came off and on. His respiration merged with the sound of the cars and when the pain woke him again when he was done screaming it would strike him that the cars were gone. But it was important not to count. Not the number of steps to the wire fence along the border then beyond it, not the number of days or weeks or months or miles away are those loved and remembered, betrayed and disappointed, in those same soiled dreams. Counting equals assessment, assessment presumes the luxury of hope. There is a thirst loose and buzzing inside him, whispering the lie that if only it were fed the pain would cease. When he shakes with laughter at smelling like a bowl of old garbage, old piss-soaked garbage version of himself in another restaurant like the one he works in used to work in here, something heavy breaks loose in his chest and belly like a new sadness, a pain like a sentence that cannot be unsaid. So he lets it be. He goes away, lets the little pieces fly off home to all who have known him, all the places where the body with his name has ever lived, even the small dirty room on the other side of this large road, the three others like himself, too tired and too frightened and too sad to talk. There is now only the body inside this body, a waiting, a dark huddled warmth. Which was where he was when he was discovered, quite by chance, by the Highway Patrol and brought via ambulance to the county hospital. To be tossed back in the stagnant water with the thrashing, gasping others of his kind, of course, upon his recovery, but minus (of course) his dishwashing job, a fact or fate which like many of these others attracted no media attention at all.

AVAILABLE SPACE

It was not enough, of course. More and better than nothing, but not nearly enough. Ideally they would have a message, a short burst of words true and witty and accessible to all, good for any billboard, not just the obviously offensive ones. Language breaking the link once and for all between pleasure, need, and desire on the one hand, things for sale on the other, exposing the link between production and purchase, who makes it and who buys it and who profits from it all. All this in a short burst of words. What would they be?

AVAILABLE SPACE
CALL 957–4653

We have offices in more than 1000 cities. We offer a full range of services. This 800 number is good anywhere, anytime, night or day. You may find us in more than 45 countries, on four continents. We would like nothing more than to welcome you into our ever-growing family of preferred clients. We look forward to hearing from you.

Their collisions give rise to an *alien* social power standing above them.

I AM NOT FOR SALE

[Note: This story makes use of several lines quoted without attribution in the text from other writers' works: specifically, and in order of their appearance, from the Grundrisse of Karl Marx, Postmodern Geographies by Edward Soja, and "Pleasure: A Political Issue," by Fredric Jameson.